THE DEVIL'S BONES

Also by Jefferson Bass

FICTION

Carved in Bone

Flesh and Bone

NON-FICTION

Death's Acre

Beyond the Body Farm

THE DEVIL'S BONES

BONES

JEFFERSON

BASS

Quercus

To our families

First published in Great Britain in 2009 by

Quercus
21 Bloomsbury Square
London
WC1A 2NS

The moral right of Jefferson Bass to be
i identified as the author of this work has been n
asserted in accordance with the Copyright,
Design and Patents Act, 1988.

A All rights reserved. No part of this publication n
r may be reproduced or transmitted in any form m
or by any means, electronic or mechanical,
including photocopy, recording, or any
information storage and retrieval system,
w without permission in writing from the publisher. er.

A CIP catalogue reference for this book is available
from the British Library

ISBN (HB) 978 1 84724 806 0
ISBN (TPB) 978 1 84724 813 8

10 9 8 7 6 5 4 3 2 1

Printed and bound in Great Britain
by Clays Ltd, St Ives Plc.

CHAPTER 1

THE LAST DROP OF DAYLIGHT WAS FADING FROM THE western sky—a draining that seemed more a suffocation than a sunset, a final faint gasp as the day died of heatstroke. To the east, a dull copper moon, just on the downhill side of full, struggled above the crest of the Great Smoky Mountains. From where I stood, in a ridgetop pasture above the confluence of the Holston and French Broad rivers—above the headwaters of the Tennessee—I had a ringside view of the demise of the day and the wavering birth of the night.

Just below the ridge, across the river on Dickinson Island, the lights of the Island Home Airport winked on, etching the runway's perimeter in white and the taxiway in cobalt blue. The main landmarks of downtown Knoxville shimmered a few miles farther downstream—two tall office towers, a wedge-shaped Mayan-looking Marriott, the high bridges spanning the river, and the looming waterfront complex of Baptist Hospital. A mile beyond those, as the fish swims, lay the University of Tennessee campus and Neyland Stadium, where the UT Volunteers packed in a hundred thousand football fans every game. Football season would kick off with a night game in three weeks, and the stadium's lights were ablaze tonight, in some sort of preseason scrimmage against the darkness. The lights loomed high above the field; a series of additions to the stadium—an upper deck and skyboxes—had taken the structure higher and higher into the sky; another expansion or two and Neyland Stadium would be the city's tallest skyscraper. The lights themselves were almost blinding, even at this distance, but the water softened their reflection to quicksilver, turning the Tennessee into a dazzling, incandescent version of Moon River. It was stunning, and I couldn't help thinking that even on an off-season night Neyland Stadium was still the tail that wagged Knoxville.

Tucked beneath the stadium, along a curving corridor that echoed its ellipse, was UT's Anthropology Department, which I'd spent twenty-five years building from a small undergraduate major to one of the world's leading Ph.D. programs. A quarter mile long and one room wide, Anthropology occupied the outer side of the stadium's dim, windowless second-floor hallway. Mercifully, the classrooms and labs and graduate-student offices did possess windows, though the view was a bizarre and grimy one, consisting mainly of girders and cross braces—the framework supporting those hundred thousand foot-stomping football fans in the bleachers, keeping them from crashing down amid the countless human bones shelved beneath them.

Many of the bones catalogued in the bowels of Neyland Stadium had arrived by way of the Anthropology Research Facility—

the Body Farm—a three-acre patch of wooded hillside behind UT Medical Center. At any given moment, a hundred human corpses were progressing from fresh body to bare bones there, helped along by legions of bacteria and bugs, plus the occasional marauding raccoon or possum or skunk. By studying the events and the timing as bodies decomposed under a multitude of experimental conditions—nude bodies, clothed bodies, buried bodies, submerged bodies, fat bodies, thin bodies, bodies in cars and in sheds and in rolls of scrap carpeting—my graduate students and colleagues and I had bootstrapped the Body Farm into the world's leading source of experimental data on both what happens to bodies after death and when it happens. Our body of research, so to speak, allowed us to pinpoint time since death with increasing precision. As a result, any time police—police anywhere—asked for help solving a real-world murder, we could check the weather data, assess the degree of decomposition, and give an accurate estimate of when the person had been killed.

Tonight would yield a bit more data to the scientific literature and a few hundred more bones to the collection. We were conducting this experiment miles from the Body Farm, but I had brought the Farm with me—two of its inhabitants anyhow—to this isolated pasture. I couldn't conduct tonight's research so close to downtown, the UT campus, and the hospital. I needed distance, darkness, and privacy for what I was about to do.

I turned my gaze from the city's glow and studied the two cars nestled in the high grass nearby. In the faint light, it was hard to tell they were rusted-out hulks. It was also difficult to discern that the two figures behind the steering wheels were corpses: wrecked bodies driving wrecked cars, on what was about to become a road trip to hell.

.   .   .

THE TOW-TRUCK driver who had brought the vehicles out to the UT Ag farm a few hours before—minus their cadaverous drivers—clearly thought I was crazy. "Most times," he'd said, "I'm hauling cars like this *to* the junkyard, not *from* the junkyard."

I smiled. "It's an agricultural experiment," I'd said. "We're transplanting wrecks to see if a new junkyard takes root."

"Oh, it'll take root all right," he said. "I guaran-damn-tee you. Word gets out there's a new dump here, you'll have you a bumper crop of cars and trucks and warshin' machines before you know it." He spit a ropy stream of tobacco juice, which rolled across the dirt at his feet and then quivered dustily for a moment. "Shit, I know all *kinds* of folks be glad to help with *that* experiment."

I laughed. "Thanks anyhow," I said. "Actually, I lied. We are doing an experiment, but it's not agricultural, it's forensic. We're going to cremate a couple of bodies in these cars and study the burned bones."

He eyed me suspiciously, as if I might be about to enlist him forcibly as one of the research subjects, but then his face broke into a leathery grin. "Aw, hell, you're that bone-detective guy, ain't you? Dr. Bodkin?"

"Brockton"— I smiled again—"but that's close enough."

"I knew you looked familiar. My wife's a big fan of all them forensic shows on TV. She talks about donating her body to you'uns. But I don't think I could hardly handle that."

"Well, no pressure," I said. "We can use all the bodies we can get, but we're getting plenty. Nearly a hundred and fifty a year now. We'll put her to good use if she winds up with us, but we'll be fine if she doesn't."

He eyed the bed of my pickup truck, which was covered by a fiberglass cover. "You got them bodies yonder in the back of your truck?"

I shook my head. "If I did," I said, "you'd see a huge swarm of flies around it. Hot as it is, you'd be smelling something, too. We'll wait till the last minute to bring them out here. And we'll use a UT truck, not mine."

He nodded approvingly—I might be crazy, I could see him thinking, but at least I wasn't dumb enough to stink up my own truck. After unloading the cars from the bed of the wrecker, he'd given me a big wave and a couple of toots of the horn as he drove away. If he told the tale well to his forensic-fan wife over dinner, I suspected, he might be able to persuade her to donate her body to *him* tonight.

"I'M STILL shocked we're replicating something that happened at the Latham farm." Miranda Lovelady, my research assistant of the past four years, edged up beside me in the twilight. "I've been in that barn a dozen times and been in the house two or three. I always liked Mary Latham. Hard to believe she died in a car fire."

"Apparently the D.A. has a hard time believing it, too," I said, "since he personally called both me and Art to look into it. You never told me how you knew the Lathams."

"It was during my brief career as a veterinary student," she said. "Mary was friends with some of the vet-school faculty, and she liked to throw parties out at the farm. I got on her guest list somehow. Or her husband's." Her voice took on a slight edge when she mentioned the husband—now the widower.

"You don't sound too fond of him," I said, hoping she'd elaborate. She did.

"I had to fight him off in a horse stall once," she said.

"Jesus," I said, "he tried to rape you?"

"No, nowhere near that bad," she said. "He made a pass at me, and he didn't want to take no for an answer." She fell silent, and I had the feeling there was more to the story than she was telling. "He was a jerk, but he wasn't dangerous. At least, I didn't think so. But maybe I was wrong."

"I might wish I hadn't asked," I said, "but what were you doing in a horse stall with him?"

Another pause. "It was a vet-school party," she said. "The animals were part of the guest list. And *no*," she said sharply, "I don't mean it *that* way. The beer keg was always in the barn. There'd be bowls of apple slices to feed the horses." Despite the darkness, I glimpsed a smile. "I still half-expect to smell hay and hear horses nickering whenever I smell beer." The smile faded. "It was a lot of fun. Until it wasn't." She shook her head, as if shaking off a bug or a bad memory.

"When's the last time you saw the Lathams?"

"Her, right after I switched to anthro; him, about a year later. I quit going to their parties, and he showed up at the bone lab one day. Said he wanted to make sure I knew I was always welcome at the farm. Anytime, he said." She nodded toward the cars. "We all set here?"

"I think so," I said. "Let me check with Art." I looked around and finally spotted Art Bohanan's dark form half hidden by the lone tree in the pasture. "Art!" I yelled. "Mind your manners— there's a lady present."

"Oh, sorry," he called back, stepping away from the tree and tugging up his zipper. "I thought it was just you and Miranda." He pointed at the tree. "I was just making sure this fine botanical specimen won't catch fire."

"Very eco-friendly of you, pig," said Miranda.

"That's 'Officer Pig' to you," said Art pleasantly. Like me, he'd long since learned to enjoy Miranda's sarcasm, since it was tempered by forensic smarts, a tireless work ethic, and a big heart. Besides, Art had an equally sizable streak of smart-ass himself. His East Tennessee roots had infused him with a down-home sense of fun. His three decades of crime-scene and crime-lab experience—he was the Knoxville Police Department's senior criminalist—had added a dark, gallows topspin to the hillbilly humor. Working with Art practically guaranteed a Leno-like monologue of deadpan jokes about murders, suicides, and extreme fingerprinting techniques. ("Give me a hand, Bill," he'd once said at a crime scene; he was asking me to amputate a murder victim's right hand so he could rush it to the lab for fingerprinting.) To someone unaccustomed to daily doses of death and brutality, our humor might have sounded shocking, but Art—like Miranda, and like me—took his work seriously. It was only himself and his colleagues he took lightly. It made the bleakness bearable.

"Okay," I said, "we've got both bodies in position, we've got an amputated leg in each backseat, we've poured two gallons of gasoline into both passenger compartments, we've hosed down the area till it's the only patch of mud within a hundred miles, and we've got the water truck standing by with another five hundred gallons just in case. Anything I've forgotten?"

"You've forgotten to explain why it is we had to wait till my bedtime to get started," said Art. "It's not like the night's all nice and cool for us. It's still ninety, easy, and if that moon burns off some of this haze, it could get back up to ninety-five here pretty soon."

"It's not the heat," I said to Miranda, "it's the stupidity. You want to explain it to Sherlock here?"

"Sure, boss," she said. "I live to serve." She turned to Art. "Our primary objective, of course, is to incinerate all the soft tissue, so we end up with nothing but burned bones—comparable to the ones in the case you're working."

"I understand that," said Art, "and I do appreciate it. No, really. But don't dem bones burn just as good in the daytime as they do in the dark? Or is there something you osteologist types know that we mere mortals are not privy to?"

"Many things, grasshopper," said Miranda. "The bodies and bones *burn* just as well in the daytime, but they don't *photograph* near as well, and we want to document the process in detail." She pointed to the four tripods and digital video cameras we'd set up beside the vehicles. One camera was aimed through each vehicle's windshield, another through each driver's window. "If we did this during the day, the video would show nothing but smoke. Lit from the outside, by the sun, the smoke steals the show. Lit from within, by the flame, the tissue shows up clear as a bell while it burns away."

"I knew that," said Art.

"I know you knew," said Miranda. "You were just checking to make sure *I* did. Right?"

"Right." Despite the slight grumbling about the late start, I knew that Art was glad to be out here, rather than bent over a computer screen swapping chat messages with pedophiles. Six months earlier he'd been given the unenviable assignment of creating the Internet Crimes Against Children Task Force, dedicated to ferreting out sexual predators who trolled the Web for young victims. Since then he'd spent countless hours posing as "Tiffany," a fourteen-year-old girl who loved to chat online. Although Art took pride in catching and arresting the sort of men who preyed on the Tiffanys of this world, he found the work sad, stressful, and dispiriting. So getting permission to work even one old-fashioned murder case—something he found wholesome by comparison to pedophilia—was a welcome break for him.

"Okay, you two," I said, "a little less conversation, a little more incineration."

Miranda fished around in a pocket of her jumpsuit. "Rock and roll," she said. She flicked a disposable lighter, and a jet of flame appeared at the tip. She swayed like a drunk or a stoner, waving the lighter, and sang, "SMOKE on the WA-ter, a FIE-uhr IN the sky-y."

I laughed. "Aren't you a little young to know that song, missy? That's from back in my heyday."

"My grandpa used to play it on the Victrola," she said, "whenever he grilled up a woolly mammoth he'd clubbed." She grinned, and her teeth shone golden in the glow of the flame.

"Very funny," I said. "Remind me to laugh on the way back to the old folks' home."

"Ouch," she said, but she wasn't smarting from my snappy retort. She took her thumb off the trigger, and the flame died.

"Serves you right," I said. "Okay, let's get some data." I walked toward one of the cars, and Miranda headed to the other. Fishing a book of paper matches from one pocket, I lit one—it took three tries to get enough friction from the tiny strip at the base of the book—then used that match to set off the rest. The matchbook erupted in a fusillade of flame, flaring bigger than I'd expected, and I reflexively flung it through the open window of the car. The gas-soaked upholstery ignited with a flash and a whoosh, and I wondered if I'd been too liberal with the accelerant. I also wondered, as I felt the heat searing my face, if I had any eyebrows left.

Through the rush and crackle of the growing fire, I caught the drone of an airplane overhead. A small plane, just off the runway from the nearby airport, banked in our direction. As it circled, the flash of its wingtip strobes illuminated the smoke from the burning cars in bursts, like flash grenades, minus the boom. I tried to wave them off, but if they could even see me, they ignored my frantic gestures.

Backing away from my vehicle, I glanced over at the other car, also engulfed in flames. Despite the intensity of the inferno, Miranda stood barely ten feet from the car, one arm shielding her face, a look of utter fascination in her eyes. I forced my way through the blast of heat and took her by the arm. "You're too close," I shouted over the hiss and roar of the fire.

"But look!" she shouted back, never moving her eyes, pointing into the vehicle at the figure slumped in the driver's seat. I looked just in time to see the skin of the forehead peel slowly backward, almost like an old-fashioned bathing cap. As it continued to peel backward, I realized that what I was seeing was a scalping. A scalping done by fire, not by knife.

"Very interesting!" I yelled. "But you're still too close. That's what we've got the video cameras for. This is dangerous."

As if to underscore my point, a thunderous boom shook the air. Miranda yelped, and I instinctively wrapped both arms around her and tucked my head. I saw a puff of smoke from one of the tires—the heat had increased the pressure and weakened the rubber to the bursting point. Miranda and I scurried to join Art in the shelter of the water truck. "I hope you took off the gas tanks," Art shouted, "or filled them up with water!"

"Why?"

"In case there's any gas left. You don't want any vapors," he said.

"Since they came from the junkyard—" I began, but I didn't get to finish the sentence. Just then the gas tank of the car Miranda had been standing beside exploded, and pellets of hot glass rained down on us like some infernal version of hailstones. The car's spare tire—launched from the trunk by the blast—arced toward the water truck, slammed into the hood, and smashed through the windshield. *It's going to be a long, hot summer, Bill Brockton,* I said to myself, *and you've got some serious 'splainin' to do.*

The circling airplane beat a hasty retreat into the safety of darkness, and a moment later I heard sirens.

CHAPTER 2

MY PHONE RANG FOR WHAT SEEMED THE EIGHTY-SEVENTH time of the morning, and I was hardening my heart to the plea of the ringer—resisting the reflex to answer—when I noticed that the caller was my secretary, Peggy.

It wasn't as if Peggy could just roll back from her desk and lean her head through my doorway. My office—my working office, as opposed to my administrative, ceremonial office—was a couple hundred yards from hers, clear on the other side of the stadium. Years ago I had laid claim to the last office at the end of the long, curving hallway that ran beneath the grandstands. I was as far off the beaten track as it was possible to get, at least within the shabby quarters inhabited by the Anthropology Department. The isolation allowed me to get five times as much work done as I would if my desk were situated along the daily path of every undergraduate, grad student, and faculty member in the department. But the deal I'd made with Peggy, when I latched on to this distant sanctuary, was that any time she called, I'd answer. I could ignore the rest of the world, but not her.

"Hey," I said. "What's up?"

"Incoming," was all she said.

I was just about to ask for clarification when I heard a sharp rap on my doorframe. "Gee, thanks for the warning," I said. I hung up just as Amanda Whiting strode in, all pinstripes and power pumps.

"Do you have any idea how many local, state, and federal ordinances you violated last night with your little bonfire of the vanities?"

Amanda was UT's general counsel, and she took both her job and herself quite seriously.

"From the way you phrase the question," I said, "I suspect that 'zero' is not the answer you're looking for."

"It's the answer I wish I had," she said, "but it's not the answer I've got."

"Okay, I give up," I said. "How many?"

"I don't even know yet," she said. "For one, you didn't have a burn permit—hell, Bill, there's been a moratorium on open burning for the past month because everything's dry as tinder. For another, you destroyed state property."

"What state property—the circle of grass we burned?"

"The Ag farm's water truck."

Ooh. I had hoped she didn't know about the truck. "Come on, Amanda," I said. "I've seen university presidents throw out thousands of dollars' worth of perfectly good carpeting just because the office hadn't been redecorated lately. You're busting my chops about breaking the windshield and denting the hood of a twenty-year-old farm truck?"

She glared. "And the Federal Aviation Administration says you're a menace to air traffic."

I couldn't help it; I laughed. "That's like saying the candle is a menace to the moth," I said. "That plane went out of its way to come down and circle those burning cars. If anybody's a menace, it's that idiot of a pilot. Miranda and I could have been killed. Hacked to bits by the propeller. Aren't pilots supposed to keep at least five feet away from innocent bystanders and enormous fires?"

"You think this is all a joke," she said, "but it's not. What if the truck had caught fire? What if the house on the adjoining property had burned down? What if the plane had crashed or your graduate student had been hit by that wheel? Any of those things could have happened if something had gone just a little more wrong. And then the university would be held accountable. And I'd be the one who had to clean up behind you."

"But none of them did happen, Amanda," I said gently, trying to soothe her now.

"But they could have."

I was tempted to reply, *But they didn't,* only I didn't see much to be gained by it. Amanda and I could contradict each other all day long, like two bickering dogs, but we wouldn't have anything to show for it except sore throats and ragged nerves. "Can I show you something, Amanda?" She eyed me suspiciously, as if I were about to unfasten my pants and flash her, then acquiesced with a shrug. Twisting around to the table behind my desk, I picked up a left femur—a thighbone, burned to a grayish white—and held it under the lamp on my desk. "This is from one of the bodies we burned last night," I said. "You see these fractures? This rectangular, rectilinear pattern?" I pointed with the tip of a pencil, and she leaned in, curiosity gradually outweighing her indignation. "This body was partially skeletonized when we put it in the car, and the bone was already drying. Now look at this one." I took another femur from a second tray of bones and held it alongside the first. "This was green bone," I said, "from a fresh body. Lots of moisture still in the bones—just like green wood with lots of sap in it. See the difference in the fractures?" She gave it a perfunctory glance, but then her gaze sharpened and took hold of something, and her eyes darted from one bone to the other.

"The fractures in the green bone aren't as regular," she said. "They're more random." She peered closer. "They kind of spiral or corkscrew around the shaft, don't they? Almost like the bone is splintering apart instead of just cracking."

"Very good," I said. I debated whether to play her the video clip showing the scalp peeling off the skull but decided that might be too graphic. "You'd have made a good forensic anthropologist."

Her guard went back up—she guessed I was herding her somewhere that she didn't want to go. "So why are you showing me this? What's your point?"

"This difference in the fracture pattern of dry bone and green bone could be important in a murder case," I said. "Actually, not 'could be'—*is* important in a murder case. That's why I needed to do the experiment. The difference tells us whether the victim was burned alive or whether she'd been dead awhile." She frowned. "The police and the district attorney are trying to decide, right now, whether to charge someone with murder in this case." I was pushing my luck, but I decided to press a point. "Tell me the truth, Amanda," I said. "If I'd come to you and described this experiment—setting fire to two cars at night, with bodies and amputated limbs in them—how long would it have taken to get the approvals you'd need? Weeks? Months? Forever?"

She shrugged and held out her hands, palms up, unable or unwilling to guess.

"Let me ask you something else," I said. "You've been here, what, five or six years now?"

"Seven," she said.

"The Body Farm was already a fixture here when you came. If it hadn't been—if I came to you today and said, 'Listen, I think we need to set aside a piece of land where we put dead bodies and study what happens to them as they decay,' what would you say?"

"Frankly, I'd say you were nuts," she snapped. And then something shifted in her expression, and she laughed. "And I'm pretty sure I'd be right."

I laughed, too. "Maybe so," I said. "But the police and the FBI and the TBI don't think so. Or maybe they do, but they also appreciate the research we do. It helps them solve crimes. Isn't that worth a broken windshield or an FAA reprimand every now and then?"

She gave me a stern look, but it seemed at least partly for show. "Are you asking me for permission to break the rules? I can't give you that."

"No," I said. "Not permission. A little understanding. And maybe occasional forgiveness."

She took a deep breath and puffed it out between pursed lips. "I'm going to the beach next week for vacation," she said. "Would you promise to try—really, really hard—not to stir up any more trouble the rest of this week?"

I held up the first three fingers of my right hand, my pinkie folded down and tucked beneath the tip of my thumb. "Scout's honor," I said.

"Fair enough," she said, then hesitated. "There's one other thing," she said awkwardly.

"I've done something else wrong?"

"No," she said, "you haven't. Actually, I have. When Dr. Carter was killed . . ." I froze, and she faltered, possibly because of what she saw in my face when she mentioned Jess's murder. "I was too quick. . . . I didn't give you the benefit of the doubt," she said.

"You mean when you exiled me? Told me I wasn't allowed on campus?" I hadn't meant to sound bitter, but I did. Jess was a smart and capable medical examiner; she was also a lovely and spirited woman, and I was just beginning to fall in love with her when she was killed. Her death had devastated me, being suspected of her murder had stunned me, and being treated as a pariah by the university had just about knocked the last prop out from under me.

She reddened. "Yes," she said. "That's what I mean. We should have stood by you. *I* should have stood by you. I was wrong, and I apologize. It might be too little, too late, but it's all I can do at this point. Even attorneys sometimes need—what was it you said?—understanding and occasional forgiveness. But I was harsh when you were on the ropes, I know, and forgiveness might be too much to ask." She glanced down at her sleek black pumps, then turned to go.

"Amanda?" She stopped in the doorway and looked back at me. "I understand why you suspended me. I didn't like it—still don't—but I do understand it. Now I'll try to work on the for-giveness part. " I stepped toward her and held out my hand.

She shook it and said, "Thank you." And then she was gone, leaving only the brisk echo of her heels in the hallway. That and the ghost of Jess Carter in my office.

CHAPTER 3

THREE HOURS AFTER MY EXCHANGE WITH UT'S TOP
legal eagle, a hawkish young prosecutor—Constance Creed was
her name—looked up from a yellow notepad, adjusted her glasses,
and took a step toward the witness box where I sat. "Isn't it true,
Dr. Brockton, that there had been conflict between yourself and
Dr. Hamilton for quite some time?"

"I'm not sure I would characterize it as conflict," I said.

"How would you characterize it, then?"

"I disagreed with the conclusions of one of his autopsy reports," I said. She waited, seeming to expect me to say something
more, so I did. "And I expressed those disagreements."

She closed the distance between us and leaned forward, her face
no more than two feet from mine. I shifted in the straight-backed
chair and wished I could not smell the onions she'd eaten at lunch.
She wore Coke-bottle glasses, the lenses round and a quarter inch
thick at the edges; instead of magnifying her eyes, the concave

lenses made them appear small and beady. "You 'expressed' those disagreements?" She removed the glasses and glared at me. As nearsighted as she must be, I knew that the gesture was purely for effect, and I wondered how blurry my features appeared to her. I briefly considered making a face at her, to see if she'd even notice, but decided that the outcome of the experiment could get unpleasant if she did notice. Creed's eyes were an icy blue, and even without the distortion of the lenses her pupils were barely the size of buckshot. "Wouldn't it be more accurate, sir, to say you destroyed Dr. Hamilton's reputation as a medical examiner?"

"No, I don't think—"

"Did you or did you not testify against Dr. Hamilton in the case of Billy Ray Ledbetter?"

"No, I didn't testify against Dr. Hamilton."

"No? I have a copy of the hearing transcript, and it quotes you at length. Was that another forensic anthropologist named Dr. William Brockton?"

"No, that was me testifying," I said, resisting the urge to mirror her sarcasm. "But I wasn't testifying against Dr. Hamilton; I was describing an experiment. I tried to reproduce what Dr. Hamilton had described as a stab wound that killed Billy Ray Ledbetter. It wasn't possible to reproduce it—a rigid knife blade couldn't make the wound he described." As I spoke, I used one hand to demonstrate the zigs and zags that Hamilton's theory would have required. "My testimony disproved Dr. Hamilton's theory, but I wasn't attacking him. I was just reporting my research results."

"Just 'reporting your research results,'" she said sarcastically. "And were you also just 'reporting your research results' when you told the state board of medical examiners that Dr. Hamilton's conclusions 'violated the laws of physics and metallurgy'? Would you call that objective, scientific reporting?"

"I probably wouldn't use that phrase in a peer-reviewed journal article, but the fact remains—"

"The fact I'm interested in," she interrupted, "is who initiated the contact between you and the board of medical examiners—the board or you?"

I felt myself redden. "I think maybe I did."

"You think? *Maybe?* Do you consider it a trivial matter to call a physician's competence into question? A matter not even worth remembering?"

"No, I—"

"I'll ask you once more, then. Who initiated the contact, the board or you?"

"I did."

"So you could 'report your research results' to them, too? Are all anthropologists so eager to report their research results?"

Something in me snapped then. "Damn it," I said, "Dr. Hamilton nearly sent a man to prison for a murder the guy didn't commit. A murder no one committed, because it wasn't a murder. That—*that*—is not a trivial matter, Ms. Creed. And I am not the one on trial for killing Jess Carter."

She leveled a finger at me, almost as if she were aiming a gun. "But you nearly were, weren't you, Doctor?"

"Okay, stop right there," I said.

"You were the prime suspect, weren't you, Doctor? In fact, initially *you* were charged with killing her, weren't you?"

"I said stop!"

"How did it feel, Doctor, to get off the hook for the murder and be able to point the finger at Dr. Hamilton?"

"Enough!" I shouted, leaping to my feet. "I loved Jess Carter, and I will not . . . How dare you . . ." My voice failed me, and I put a hand over my eyes.

I felt a hand on my shoulder, warm and steady. "I'm sorry, Dr. Brockton," I heard her say, suddenly sounding human and pained. "I hate to put you through the wringer. But believe me, this is gentle compared to what Hamilton's attorney will do next week during the trial. When he gets up to cross-examine you, he will go for your throat like an attack dog. You're our key witness, so the defense will do everything they can to undermine you, throw you off balance, make you mad."

I looked up, and she met my gaze steadily, compassionately. Her eyes didn't look beady now; they just looked tired, from years spent straining to see the world through a wall of glass and the darkness of crime. "God, this is hard," I said. I fished out my handkerchief, wiped my face, and blew my nose.

"I know," she said, "and I wish I could tell you it'll get easier. But it won't."

Great, I thought, *nothing like an encouraging word*.

"Think of this as a scrimmage, or maybe war games, so you're mentally prepared for the real thing. You were doing great till right there at the end. It's okay to get sad on the stand. Just don't get mad. If you get mad, you're playing their game. They'll make you look vindictive, and they'll make him look like a victim."

"But there's a recording of him admitting he killed Jess. A recording of him *bragging* about killing Jess."

"They'll try to suppress that. Or undermine it any way they can. Besides, it's a recording, and a pretty scratchy one to boot. Your testimony will carry a lot more weight with the jurors than that. So roll with the punches and hang on to your temper, for God's sake. For Dr. Carter's sake."

We sparred a few more rounds, the prosecutor and I. Finally, after two hours of rolling with the punches of her mock cross-examination, I was allowed to step down from the witness stand she'd set up in the practice courtroom. I left the City-County Building and headed along Neyland Drive feeling jangled and unsettled. It wasn't until I found myself taking the Cherokee Trail exit off Alcoa Highway that I realized I wasn't heading back to my office but to the Body Farm. Even after I realized that, it took a moment longer to grasp *why* I was headed there.

There were no other cars in the distant corner of the hospital employees' parking lot that bordered the research facility. The chain-link gate was locked, as was the high wooden gate within. Even so, after letting myself in, I called out to make sure I had the place to myself. When I was certain of that, I locked the gate behind me and walked up the hill into the woods.

It was the first time I'd had the nerve to visit the spot in the three months since I'd dug the recess in the rocky dirt and laid the slab at the base of the big pine. The black granite was dull with dust, so I knelt down and took a handkerchief to it. The grime proved more stubborn than I expected, so I wiped my face and neck with the cloth to moisten it—one pass got it plenty damp—then set to work on the marker again. "Sorry about the sweat, Jess," I said. "You never were the squeamish sort, so I'm thinking you wouldn't mind."

The moisture loosened the dirt, and after I'd turned and folded the handkerchief several times to expose clean fabric to scrub with, the black granite gleamed again, silver flecks of

mica shimmering within its depths. Closing my eyes, I ran my
fingers across the surface. The chiseled edges of the inscription
tugged at my fingertips and clutched at my heart. In Memory
of Dr. Jess Carter, Who Worked for Justice, the words read.
Work is love made visible. I laid my palm on the warm stone,
flat and steady, the same way Constance Creed had laid hers on
my shoulder not long before. I thought back to the period when
Jess and I had been mere colleagues—she a rising star among the
state's medical examiners, me an odd-duck anthropologist who
conferred with corpses as they turned to goo or bare bones. It
seemed several lifetimes ago, though in fact we had collaborated
platonically scarcely six months before. Then I flashed ahead to
the night everything had changed.

"God, Jess, I miss you," I said. We had spent just one night
together, but that night seemed to encapsulate years' worth of
meaning. And it had cost Jess her life. Garland Hamilton had
followed me to Jess's house, had lurked outside, listening, as we
made love, and then—just days later—had abducted Jess from a
restaurant parking lot, taken her to his basement, and shot her.
In a final, perverse twist, he'd staged her body in a gruesome
tableau here at the Body Farm—here at this very tree—and had
nearly succeeded in framing me for the murder.

It haunted me to realize that, given a chance, Jess and I might
have built a remarkable life together, a rare partnership of like
minds and kindred spirits. "I guess we'll never know," I said
aloud, but even as I spoke the words, I knew they were false: I did
know, all the way down to my core. Only three things in my life
had ever rung true enough to redefine everything else. The first
was the life I'd built with Kathleen, my late wife, and our son,

Jeff. The second was the bizarre career path I had half followed, half created. The third, I was realizing only in hindsight, was the love I'd begun to feel for Jess.

Kathleen and I had shared a solid, steady love, and it carried us through three decades of partnership and parenthood, until cancer claimed her three years earlier. I'd spent two years grieving for Kathleen. Then, to my surprise, I was ready for love again; ready for Jess.

Back when I was in college, I'd taken a class in Greek mythology, and we'd read Homer's *Odyssey*. Since Jess, an image from Homer kept coming back to me: the marriage bed of Ulysses and Penelope. Ulysses had carved their bed from a mammoth tree trunk, still rooted in the earth, and then built their home around it. It was a secret known only to them—the secret by which she would recognize him when he returned from his years of warfare and wandering. The love Jess and I were starting to discover could have been like that, I sometimes thought—something rooted in earth and bedrock, a mystery understood only by us—if we'd had the chance to build around it. If Garland Hamilton hadn't uprooted it, driven by jealousy of Jess and hatred of me.

Hamilton had been enraged to learn that Jess was about to become the state's chief M.E. But he had murdered her not just out of a misplaced sense of rivalry. He'd done it mainly to hurt me—to break my heart before killing me as well. The second part of his plan had failed, and Hamilton was now facing a possible death sentence for killing Jess. But Jess's death was a wound I'd carry far longer than if he'd killed me. Yet I'd also be carrying the memory of Jess, and though I'd always mourn the loss, I'd never regret the love.

"I miss you, Jess," I said. "And I'm so sorry."

The only answer was the dull thud of helicopter rotors as a LifeStar air ambulance skimmed low above the Body Farm, inbound to UT Hospital with a patient hanging between life and death.

CHAPTER 4

AFTER MY VISIT TO JESS'S MARKER, I WASN'T READY
to face my empty house. I called Jeff, my son, and asked if I could
swing by for a visit.

"Sure," he said. "We're just about to grill some burgers. Come
on out—I'll throw one on for you."

"Hmm, charbroiled meat," I said, picturing my recent nighttime experiment. "I'm not sure I'm all that hungry."

"Have you seen a doctor yet? You must be ill. I've never known
you to turn down anything cooked on the grill."

"Long story," I said. I realized that my need for company outweighed my aversion to the smell of searing flesh. "I'll tell you
over dinner."

Jeff's house was about fifteen miles west of downtown Knoxville, in the bedroom community of Farragut. Compared to
Knoxville's other bedroom communities, Farragut tended toward
bedsheets with a higher thread count. Named for a Civil War

hero born nearby, Admiral David ("Damn the torpedoes") Farragut, the town was a sprawling collection of upscale shopping centers, golf courses, and subdivisions with names like Andover Place and Berkeley Park. There was no downtown; the "town center" consisted of a municipal building that housed a library branch and a county clerk's office. Across the parking lot was a post office, a bank branch, and a couple of restaurants. Farragut wasn't my idea of a town, but it seemed to suit a lot of people, because it was the fastest-growing part of Knox County.

Jeff and his wife, Jenny, and their two boys, Tyler and Walker, lived at the end of a quiet cul-de-sac, the sort of place where parents still let their kids roller-skate and ride bikes in the street. Maybe that was the appeal. Maybe in some ways Farragut was a town, or pieces of a town, the way towns used to be, back before the streets became places of peril.

I saw a wisp of smoke curling up from behind their house, so I let myself in the wooden gate to the backyard and circled around to the patio. Jeff was just spreading out a glowing mound of charcoal briquettes. His hands were smudged with soot, and his face glistened with sweat.

"Glad to see you haven't gone over to the dark side and switched to gas," I said.

"Never happen," he said. "You taught me well, and I've eaten too many tasteless burgers at my neighbors' houses."

"You know, of course, it's the carcinogens that give the good smoky flavor," I said.

"Actually," he said, "not necessarily. Apparently some researchers at Johns Hopkins did a study on this very thing. The carcinogens form when you let the fire flare up—for some reason that particular temperature causes a chemical reaction that creates the carcinogens. So you don't want to cook the meat over open flame—just hot coals. Close the lid, hold in the smoke, keep the fire low, and everything's okay."

"I'll sleep better knowing this, son."

Jenny came out the back door with a platter of burgers. "Hey, Bill," she said. I liked it that she called me "Bill" rather than "Dad" or some other in-law title; it allowed us to relate as equals. "Good to see you."

"Good to see you, too," I said. I noticed their boys peering out the glass of the storm door. Tyler was seven, and Walker was five. Both were wearing the baseball uniforms they seemed to live in all summer long.

Jenny followed my gaze. "Guys, come on out and see Grandpa Bill," she called, a little too cheerily.

They did as they were told, but they hesitated, and that hesitation nearly broke my heart. It had scared and confused them when I was charged with Jess Carter's murder. Their friends had said cruel things to them, as children will do, about Grandpa the killer. A parent can do a lot of explaining, but it might still take years to restore the openness and easy trust my grandsons had once felt with me. By then, of course, they wouldn't be five and seven anymore.

Jenny set the burgers down on the patio table and came up to give me a hug and a kiss on the cheek. The warm greeting was partly for my sake, but partly for the boys as well—a message to them that yes, I was still their grandfather, and yes, I was some-one safe to love.

Jenny looked searchingly into my eyes, and this part, I knew, was just for the grown-ups. "How are you?" she said.

"I'm okay," I said. "Mostly."

"I think about you all the time," she said. "I'd give anything if I could undo all the things that went wrong last spring."

"Me, too," I said. "Sometimes I feel lonelier than I did before Jess—or maybe I just notice the loneliness more now. The trial starts next week, and I figure that'll be hard. But maybe once it's done, I'll feel some closure. I want to hear sentence pronounced on him. And I want it to be a harsh one."

"Would you like us to be there when you testify?"

I didn't trust my voice to answer the question, so I just nodded.

"Then we will," she said. "You tell us when, and we'll be there. And if there's anything else you need, you call Jeff or you call me."

I nodded again.

"Promise?"

"Promise."

CHAPTER 5

"Dr. Brockton? This is Lynette Wilkins, at the Regional Forensic Center."

Lynette didn't need to tell me who she was or where she worked; I'd heard her voice a thousand times or more—every time I dialed the morgue or popped in for a visit. The Regional Forensic Center and the Knox County Medical Examiner's Office shared space in the morgue of UT Medical Center, located across the river and downstream from the stadium. There was also a custom-designed processing room—complete with steam-jacketed kettles and industrial-grade garbage disposals—where my graduate students and I could remove the last traces of tissue from skeletons after they'd been picked relatively clean by the bugs at the Body Farm. From fresh, warm gunshot victims to sun-bleached bones, the basement complex in the hospital dealt with them all.

"Good morning, Lynette," I said. "And how are you?"

"Fine, thank you."

"Glad to hear it," I said, although she didn't actually *sound* fine. She sounded extremely nervous and formal—an odd combination, I thought, in a woman who had once, at a Christmas party, planted a memorable kiss on my mouth. Spiked punch could be blamed for most of that lapse in office decorum; still, our frequent conversations—in person and by phone—had been marked by the ease and casualness of comrades-in-arms, fellow soldiers in the trenches of gruesome accidents and grisly murders.

"Dr. Garcia, the medical examiner, would like to speak with you," she said, and as I pictured an unfamiliar M.E. sitting a few feet away from her, I understood why she didn't sound like her usual self. "Could you hold on for just a moment?"

"Sure, Lynette," I said. "Have a nice day."

The line clicked, and I waited. Nothing. I waited some more. Still nothing. Then I heard a man's voice say, "Ms. Wilkins, are you sure he's there?" A pause followed, then, "I don't think so."

"Hello," I said.

Another pause.

"Mr. Brockton?"

Now it was my turn to pause. "This is Bill Brockton," I said. "Dr. Bill Brockton. How can I help you?"

"This is *Dr.* Edelberto Garcia," said a cool voice, whose careful emphasis was meant to let me know that not all doctors are created equal. His first name sounded elegant and aristocratic the way he pronounced it—"ay-del-BARE-toe"—but then I remembered a bit about Spanish pronunciations, and I realized that the English version of his name would be "Ethelbert," and I nearly laughed. "I've been appointed by the commissioner of health to serve as director of the Regional Forensic Center."

"Sure," I said, resisting the urge to add "Ethelbert" to my answer. "I had lunch with Jerry last week. He told me he'd hired you. Welcome to Knoxville."

"Thank you," he said. If he noticed my first-name reference to Gerald Freeman, the health commissioner, he didn't let on. I considered adding that six weeks earlier Jerry had shown me the files on the three finalists for the job, and had asked for my opinion. Garcia had been my second choice—and Jerry's, too—but the strongest of the finalists had taken a job at a far higher salary in the M.E.'s office in New York City.

"We're currently investigating the death of a Knoxville woman whose burned body was found last week in her car," he said. Again I nearly laughed out loud.

"Why, yes," I said, "I believe I heard something about that. Can I be of some assistance?"

"I'm told by a police investigator, a Sergeant Evers, that you've done some—shall we say *research*?—that might be relevant."

"Ah, Sergeant Evers," I said. "Good man, Evers. Dogged investigator. Fearsome interrogator." I didn't add that Evers had fearsomely interrogated *me* only a few months before and had arrested me on suspicion of homicide, in the death of Jess Carter, who had served a brief stint as acting M.E. here in Knoxville. Maybe Garcia already knew that; if he didn't, he was the only person in a hundred-mile radius who didn't. "If Sergeant Evers thinks my research might be relevant, far be it from me to disagree." I could hear him weighing my words and my tone for the sarcasm I'd added to them, and I suspected he was about to respond by turning even more stuffy and condescending. No point getting into a pissing match with the new M.E., I decided. "Actually, Dr. Garcia, that research *is* pretty interesting. What we've done is compare fire-induced fractures in green bone—fleshed bone—with fractures in dry bone. We burned two cars containing cadavers and limbs from the immediate postmortem interval, as well as from one week and two weeks postmortem. No point going past two weeks in the summer—by then you're down to bare, dry bone already."

He mulled this over briefly. "And have you documented your research results? Do you have something you could messenger over?"

"Nothing in writing," I said. "Got some burned bones I could messenger over."

"Thank you, but without some methodological context, I'm not sure—"

"Hell, I'll be the messenger, and I'll give you the context," I said. "I'm coming over that direction anyhow. I'll bring a few of the bones and show you what it is I'll be writing up, soon as I get around to it. You can ask questions, and I can try to answer them. If any of it's relevant, great. If it's not, neither one of us has lost more than a few minutes. You want to take a look?"

"Very well," he said.

Very well? I thought. *Who says "Very well" anymore? And why does this guy have such a big broomstick up his ass?* "Swell," I said, then thought, *Who the hell says "Swell" anymore, Brockton?* Then I thought, *Apparently I do.* "I'll be over there in about ten minutes. Looking forward to meeting you."

"I'll see you then," was all he said before hanging up.

I selected half a dozen bones from the fiery nighttime experiment, then wrapped them in bubble wrap and laid them in one of the long boxes we used to store the specimens in the skeletal collection. As I headed down the hall that traced the curve

of the stadium's end zone, I passed the open door of Jorge Ji-
menez, a Ph.D. candidate in cultural anthropology from Buenos
Aires. Jorge's name sounded anything *but* aristocratic, I realized,
since the first syllable was pronounced like "whore." I tapped on
Jorge's door with one knuckle. "Come in," he said, not looking
up from his computer screen. The screen showed a young couple
doing what appeared to be the tango, but suddenly they spun
apart and began break-dancing.

"That's an interesting dance," I said. "I don't believe I know
that one."

"Ah, Dr. Brockton," he said, looking up. "Sorry to be rude.
This is actually research. Did you know that in Buenos Aires,
where this dance video was shot, one out of every twenty teenagers has posted a video on YouTube?"

"I didn't," I said. "What's U-2?" It didn't sound like he was
talking about a Cold War spy plane or a rock band.

"Not U-2. YouTube." He scrawled it on a piece of paper for
me. "An Internet site where people post videos they've made.
Very popular with young people. Like MySpace."

"Your space? You have a Web site that's popular with kids?"

He laughed, then typed an address into his computer's browser
and called up a page filled with flashing ads and thumbnail pictures of faces and pets. "Not *my* space," he said. "MySpace
.com."

After a few seconds, he clicked it back to the tango break
dancing. "At first all the videos on YouTube were very clumsy
and silly," he said, "but a lot of them these days look like something straight out of Hollywood." He studied my expression
again. "But I think you didn't stop to talk about cinema or the
Internet."

"No, I stopped for advice," I said. "Do you have any tips on dealing with a Latino physician who seems to have a chip on his shoulder?"

"You mean Eddie Garcia?"

Eddie? I smiled. It was better than Ethelbert. Or Ethel. "How'd you know?"

"Lucky guess." He smiled back. "What you need to remember is that he's not just Hispanic, Dr. B., he's Mexican, so you might need to cut him some slack."

"What does *that* mean?" I asked. "If you weren't Hispanic yourself, I'd think that was more than a little patronizing."

"If I were a gringo, it *would* be patronizing. But I'm Latino, so it's not." Confusion was written all over my face, and he speed-read it and smiled. "All Latinos may be created equal," he said, "but we're not all treated equally, even by one another. East Tennessee has Latinos from just about every country in Central and South America, and some of them look down on the Mexicans as harshly as any Tennessee redneck or Georgia cracker ever did."

"How come?"

"Part of it's just snobbery—there are so many Mexicans in the States that they're not exotic, the way Venezuelans or Chileans are. It's like a lawn or a garden—if one strange plant bursts into bloom, it's a wildflower; if a bunch of them spring up, they're considered weeds."

"Not by the other plants," I pointed out.

"True," he conceded, "so the analogy's not perfect. But you get the point?"

I nodded.

"Then there's the pecking order of the workplace. Mexicans often take the shit jobs. They mow yards and lay brick and wash dishes and change linens—anything to get their foot in the door—while people like me get visas to study engineering or anthropology or medicine. So the white-collar Latinos look down on the blue-collar Latinos, and the Mexicans are mostly blue-collar."

"But Garcia's not," I pointed out. "He's a board-certified M.D., a forensic pathologist."

"But that's recent. He's been Mexican all his life. And his parents were working class, so he knows what it's like to be looked down on. He comes by that chip on his shoulder honestly."

"I wouldn't have thought of that," I said. "So you know Garcia?"

"A little. Eddie's okay. Yeah, he's a little touchy. But cut him some slack, talk some shop, and things should be fine. He's a forensic guy, you're a forensic guy. Bond over the bones, Dr. B."

"Jorge" I said over my shoulder, "you could have had a brilliant career in psychology. You're pretty damn smart, for a Latino."

He laughed. *"Bastardo!"* he called after me. I decided that was Spanish for "Amen, brother!"

GARCIA STOOD and nodded slightly when I entered his office at the Forensic Center, but he didn't offer a hand, so I simply returned the nod. "Please, have a seat," he said.

"It might be a little easier if we laid these bones out on a lab table," I said.

"Very well," he said again. *Swell*, I thought. *Mr. Personality.* I followed him down the hallway to the main lab and set my box on a countertop. The counter was covered with a large, absorbent blue pad, which helped cushion the fragile bones. I had brought three femora—femurs; thighbones—which I laid side by side. Garcia leaned down toward the closest, which was from the body that had been fully fleshed when it burned. The bone exhibited a range of colors, from ashy white at the distal end, near the knee, to a deep reddish brown at the proximal end, where it had joined the hip.

I chose my words carefully, as I didn't want to appear to be lecturing him, even though I was. "We used two gallons of gasoline in each car, so it was a very hot fire," I said. "It peaked at around two thousand degrees Fahrenheit—about eleven hundred Celsius. It burned away all the soft tissue, except for some on the central region of the torso." I pointed to the femur from the fresh cadaver. "Down here at the distal end, the bone is obviously completely calcined, since the lower legs and knees get more oxygen and burn away before the thighs and torso do. Up here, where the thicker muscle tissue provided some protection for a while, the bone started to char, but it's not calcined."

He studied the bone closely.

"There's still some organic material in there," I went on. "You could probably get DNA—at least mitochondrial DNA, if not nuclear DNA—from a cross section of the bone up in this region."

He nodded.

"What's really interesting to me," I went on, "is the fracture pattern here. It's very irregular. Notice how the fractures seem to corkscrew around the bone in a sort of helical pattern. There's also some fracturing between layers of the bone."

"Yes, very interesting," he said, sounding more animated. He reached up and swung a magnifying lamp into position, switching on the light that encircled the back side of the round lens. "It's almost as if the bone is peeling apart. From the moisture inside turning to steam?"

"Probably," I said. "Now compare that to the dry, defleshed bone. It's completely calcined, not surprisingly, since there was no muscle to shield it. Notice how regular and rectangular the fracture pattern is, almost like cross-hatching."

He repositioned the magnifying glass over the uniformly burned femur.

"This reminds me of a big log," I said, "that's been burned very slowly in a bonfire."

"Or a dead tree lying in the desert," he said. "After years in the sun, they get that same burned look."

"Here's another one for you," I said. "I was over in Memphis a few summers ago, when they had the worst drought in a century. The Mississippi River dropped fifteen or twenty feet. It exposed huge sandbars, a half mile wide and miles long. Walking on them was like walking along the beach at the ocean. And the river shrank from a mile wide to a narrow channel, a few hundred yards across—I could have skipped a rock to the other side."

His mouth twitched, but I wasn't sure if he was suppressing a smile or stifling a yawn. Either way, I was caught up in the memory.

"It was the most remarkable thing," I said. "The sand was golden and clean—not what I'd expected, since the river is as murky as day-old coffee. Right beside the channel, the sand sloped down like this." I angled my hand at forty-five degrees. "If you took a running jump, you'd go flying over the edge, drop ten feet or so, then sink halfway to your knees near the bottom of the embankment." I had leapt off that slope of sand a dozen times that day, and a hundred more since, in my memory. "There was a beautiful woman sunbathing, topless, in the middle of this vast expanse of sand," I said. "But what really caught my eye were the tree trunks, four or five feet in diameter"—I made an arc with my arms, wide as I could stretch them—"down on a narrow shelf, right at the edge of the river channel. They had that same charred look, and it fascinated me, how being underwater for a hundred years made those trees look burned."

He laughed, a soft, musical laugh from deep in his chest, and it was the first sound I'd heard him make that wasn't tightly reined in. "Are you always doing research, even when a beautiful woman is stretched out on the sand?"

"Pretty much," I said sheepishly. But I could see the absurdity of it, and I laughed along with him.

Garcia's face got serious again, but his gaze and his voice stayed open. "Would you like to see this burn case?" he asked. "No, wait, that's not exactly what I want to ask you. Would you please take a look at this burn case, Dr. Brockton? I would be very interested in your opinion."

"Very well," I said with a smile and a slight bow. "I would be honored, Dr. Garcia."

He motioned me into the main autopsy suite, then disappeared into the morgue's cooler and emerged a moment later wheeling a stainless-steel autopsy table. As he folded back the drape, I felt my adrenaline spiking, the way it always did when I confronted a forensic puzzle. Garcia began talking, almost as if he were dictating notes. "The subject is a deceased white female, positively identified from dental records as Mary Louise Latham, age forty-seven." According to what I'd learned from Art and Miranda and the newspaper stories, Latham had lived in Knoxville all her life.

She and her husband, Stuart, lived on a farm along Middlebrook Pike, in northwest Knoxville. I was fairly sure I knew the property. Middlebrook Pike had been transformed in recent decades into a corridor of warehouses, petroleum tanks, and trucking depots; there was only one farm, as far as I knew, along Middlebrook, and the prettiness of it was underscored by its uniqueness. The land was a mix of rolling pastures and wooded ridges, with a graceful old farmhouse and a well-kept white barn. It wasn't really a working farm these days, more like a hobby farm, with a couple of milk cows, a handful of chickens, and a half-acre vegetable garden. The Lathams had no children, but Mrs. Latham often invited elementary-school groups to visit and learn about farming.

In less than an hour, a burning car had reduced her to charred remnants. Some of the small bones of the hands and feet were missing—probably fragmented and embedded in a layer of ash and debris in the car's floor pan. The blackened bones of the arms and the lower legs were devoid of soft tissue, even burned soft tissue; they were calcined at their distal ends but not at the proximal ends, where they'd joined the torso and had gotten less oxygen. The pelvis and torso still had tissue on them—if you could call the scorched, crusty material clinging to the bones "tissue." What had once been the cranial vault had been reduced to shards of bone, resembling small, burned bits of shell, none of them more than a couple inches across.

Garcia switched on the surgical light above the autopsy station and trained it on the bones. Then he offered me a pair of purple nitrile gloves, which I tugged on, as he did likewise with another pair. He touched a purple finger to the right leg, just below the knee. "This is interesting," he said. "Up here near the proximal end of the tibia, the fractures look like the ones you just showed me in green bone." Leaning in, I saw the spiraling, splintered pattern left behind after flesh has burned away, and I nodded in agreement. "But down here at the distal end"—he pointed—"the fractures are more regular." Sure enough, just above the ankle, the bone was neatly crosshatched with cracks.

"Huh," I said. "Looks almost like two different cases—one involving green bone, the other involving defleshed bone—rolled into one tibia." Studying the rest of the body, I noticed a similar trend in the other limbs.

"What do you make of that?"

I didn't answer. I wasn't ignoring him; I was just distracted. Something lodged in the skull—deep within a shattered eye orbit—had caught my attention. Reaching to the counter along the wall, I selected a pair of long tweezers and eased their tips down into the recess, trying to tease out the tiny object. "Do you know," I asked, "whether the car's windows were up or down?"

"Three of them were up, but the driver's window was down a few inches," he said. "There were several cigarette butts on the ground underneath it. Why do you ask?"

"I was wondering what sort of access the blowflies might have had to the body."

"All the car windows shattered in the fire. So the flies had plenty of access but not much time. When I arrived, the car was still too hot to touch. I don't remember seeing any flies."

"I don't mean after the fire. I mean before."

Garcia looked puzzled.

"Unless her brain was infested while she was still alive," I said, extricating the tweezers from the eye orbit, "the bugs had been working on her for days before that car burned." I held the tweezers over my left hand and deposited my prize in the palm. There on the drum-tight purple surface was an immature maggot, about the size and shape of a Rice Krispie. A Rice Krispie that had been thoroughly charred.

She hadn't been burned alive; she'd been burned dead. Dead and already decomposing.

CHAPTER 6

I STARED AT THE CONTENTS OF THE PACKAGE AGAIN, then stared at the note once more. *"Dr. Brockton, please call me when you get this. Thanks. Burt."*

I dialed Burt DeVriess. I didn't have to refer to the number embossed on the fancy letterhead; I remembered it from the brief, memorable, and ruinously expensive period when DeVriess—better known as "Grease" throughout Knoxville's legal (and illegal) circles—had served as my criminal defense attorney. Grease had charged me an arm and a leg, but he had also saved my neck, so it was hard to begrudge him that fifty-thousand-dollar retainer. His secretary, Chloe, seemed to think that our association had saved some part of Grease as well, the part that passed for the attorney's shriveled soul. Judging by the years he'd spent ruthlessly representing Knoxville's seamiest criminals—his client list read like a who's who of killers, drug peddlers, and pedophiles—salvation seemed too much to hope for. Still, the fact was,

DeVriess had taken to turning down the notorious clientele that had made him rich and infamous. He'd not yet traded his Bentley for a Prius, as far as I knew, or started doing pro bono work for the homeless. But even if he hadn't attained sainthood yet, he at least seemed to qualify for some sort of "Most Improved Karma" award.

Chloe answered on the second ring. "Mr. DeVriess's office, may I help you?"

"Hi, Chloe, it's Bill Brockton."

"Hi there," she chirped. "How are you?"

"Hanging in there, Chloe. And you?"

"Pretty good, but we do miss you. You need to get yourself arrested again, so we'll see you more often."

"I can't afford it," I said, laughing. "If I had to hire Burt again, I'd go bankrupt."

"Perfect," she said. "Then he could represent you in bankruptcy court."

"For free, no doubt," I said. "So speaking of the master of legal larceny, what's the story on this package he sent me?"

"Oh, *that,*" she said. "I think I'd better let him tell you about that. Hang on. And come see us?"

I smiled. Chloe had treated me exactly this way—as a friend—when I first walked in through her boss's art deco doorway with a murder charge hanging over my head, so desperate that I'd stooped to hire the aggressive defense lawyer I despised above all others.

While I held the line for DeVriess, I took another look at the contents of the package he'd sent me. It was a small wooden box, almost a cube, about eight inches square. It was ornately carved, with an engraved brass latch and a hinged top. The box was beautiful, but what really caught my eye was the grainy, powdery mixture I saw when I opened the lid.

"Hello, Doc," said a voice that managed to sound both butter smooth and granite hard at the same time. It sounded like money and power, and I knew that Knoxville's winningest defense attorney had plenty of both. "How's life down on the Farm these days?"

"People are dying to get in, Burt," I joked. "How's life down in the sewer?"

"Stagnating a little," he said cheerily. "There's a vicious rumor making the rounds that I've gone soft, maybe even developed a conscience. It's killing my practice, but it's great for my golf game."

"There's always a silver lining," I said. "As they say, if you can't have what you want, then want what you have. So this little present you sent me—is this what it looks like?" I stirred the upper layer of the mixture with the sharpened end of a pencil, and a tiny plume of dust rose from the box. Uppermost in the mixture was a layer of fine, grayish white powder; beneath that was a layer of grainy tan particles, along with what I quickly recognized as shards of incinerated bone. "I got excited when I opened the lid," I joked. "Thought for a minute maybe these were your ashes."

If he thought that was funny, he hid it well.

"So who is this, Burt?"

"That, Doc, is the sixty-four-million-dollar question," he said. "Supposed to be my Aunt Jean. But my Uncle Edgar? He says not."

"How come?"

"You looked at it yet?"

"Only a little."

"Notice anything funny?"

I stirred around a bit more, creating another miniature dust storm. Down near the bottom of the box, I glimpsed what appeared to be small, rounded pebbles. "Well, there's some rocks in here," I said, "As least they sure look like rocks."

"Damn right they look like rocks," he said. "Doesn't take a Ph.D. in anthropology to tell the difference between bone and pea gravel. Another thing? You wouldn't have any way of knowing this, of course, but Aunt Jean's knees aren't in there."

"Her knees? How do you know?"

"Because Aunt Jean's knees were made of titanium. She had both of 'em replaced about five years ago."

"Crematoriums don't usually send things like that back to the family, Burt."

"Uncle Edgar specifically asked for them."

"Ah. Then that would seem to be a significant omission."

"They couldn't have melted and dripped down somewhere in the oven or something, could they?"

"I don't think so," I said. "Those orthopedic devices are made of pretty tough stuff. But let me do a little research on titanium and cremation and get back to you."

"Could you do more than that, Doc?"

"What do you mean?"

"Something's not right here, Doc," he said. "What'd they do with her knees? What's that gravel doing in there? And how come those chunks of bone are so big? I scattered my mother's ashes up in the Smokies after she died, and there weren't any pieces bigger than rock salt in Mom's urn."

"So you want me to do a forensic analysis on this set of cremains?"

"Cremains?" He snorted. "Who the hell came up with 'cremains'?"

"Not me," I said. "Some funeral director, probably. Easier to say than 'cremated human remains,' I reckon."

"Cornier, too," he said. "Listen, I'll pay your hourly expert-witness rate, for however many hours you need to spend on this." My rate was two hundred dollars an hour; that meant I'd need to poke around in the cremains for 250 hours to recoup the fifty thousand dollars I'd forked over to Grease a few months earlier. I didn't want to spend 250 hours breathing the dust of Aunt Jean, but I was intrigued by the case—and impressed that the lawyer had zeroed in on the puzzling things in the mixture.

"I'll find out everything I can," I said.

"Thanks, Doc," he said. "I owe you."

"Not yet," I said, "but you will."

He laughed. "I guess I'd better sell one of the Bentleys," he said, but we both knew that my bill wouldn't amount to a fraction of what I'd paid Burt to defend me. He gave me a few more details—his aunt's date of death, the name of the funeral home and the crematorium, and the phone number of his Uncle Edgar, who lived in Polk County—then signed off, saying "'Preciate you, Doc."

I dialed the extension for the bone lab, tucked beneath the other end of the stadium, a five-minute walk through curving hallways along the base of the enormous ellipse. "Osteology lab, this is Miranda. Can I help you?"

"I sure hope so," I said.

"Oh, it's just you."

"Try to contain your enthusiasm," I said.

"Oh, ex-*cuse* me," she gushed. "Dr. *Brockton*, how may I be of assistance?"

"That's more like it," I said. "Soon as you finish genuflecting, could I trouble you to dig up the melting point of titanium?"

"I live to serve," she said. "Elemental or alloy?"

"I'm not sure."

I heard the rapid clatter of keystrokes. "Well, if you're talking pure titanium metal," she said, "the melting point is a toasty nineteen hundred and thirty-three. That's on the Kelvin scale, which is"—*clatterclatterCLATTERclatter*—"three thousand and change, Fahrenheit."

"How'd you find that so fast?"

"The wonders of Google," she said. "Google also lives to serve."

"Damn," I said. "Google, YouTube, MySpace—I feel like a dinosaur, Miranda."

"Well, admitting you have a problem is the first step toward change," she said. "So is that it? You just got curious about the properties of titanium?"

"No, actually, what I'm wondering about is the melting point of artificial knees."

I heard another flurry of keystrokes. "Looks like most orthopedic implants are made of titanium alloy, cobalt chromium steel, or stainless steel. Also oxidized zirconium—sort of a cross between a metal and ceramic—which is harder than metal but tougher than ceramic." More keystrokes. "The most common material seems to be titanium-662, though, an alloy of titanium, aluminum, and vanadium, plus a pinch of this and a dash of that."

"Vanadium? Is that really an element, or are you just making that up?"

"Making it up? *Moi?* You cut me to the quick. That would be a violation of the Research Slave Code of Ethics. Besides, if I were going to make up an element, don't you think I could come up with something better than 'vanadium'? I think 'mirandium' has a nice ring, don't you? And 'loveladium' rolls trippingly off the tongue, too."

"What was I thinking? You're right," I said. "The periodic table really should revolve around you."

"I'll let the implication that I'm egocentric pass for the moment, because I'm so delighted to be doing your grunt work. Let's see, titanium-662. . . . Melting point is . . . *durn* it . . . a closely guarded military secret, it would appear. Not really, but I'm not getting any Google hits that look like the answer. You want me to call some equally downtrodden peon in Engineering?"

"Nah, hold off for now," I said. "I wouldn't think the alloy's melting point would be a whole lot lower."

"You know what I think?"

"More often than I'd like," I said.

"Ha, ha. I think if you're running a high enough fever to melt your knees, you're long since toasted."

"Toasted is right," I said. "The question is, could a cremation furnace melt a pair of knee implants?"

"I'd say it depends how hot the furnace gets."

"Really? Amazing. Do the folks who give out the MacArthur genius grants know about you?"

"Don't get smart with me, boss."

"Or else?"

"Or else I'll hang up."

"*Ooh,*" I said, "now you're *really* scaring me."

I laughed when the line went dead. I was pretty sure she was laughing, too.

My next call was to Norman Witherspoon, a Knoxville funeral

director who'd sent me a half dozen or so corpses during the past decade—people who'd wanted their bodies donated to science but who hadn't made the arrangements before dying. "Norm, what do you do when somebody asks to be cremated?"

"I say, 'Sorry, I have to wait until you're dead.'"

"Everybody's a comedian," I said. "Let me rephrase the question. Norm, where do you send bodies to be cremated?"

"East Tennessee Cremation Services," he said. "Out near the airport. In the Rockford industrial park, off Alcoa Highway."

"I've got a case involving cremated remains. You reckon East Tennessee Cremation would let me come look at their equipment and ask a few questions?"

"Long as the case doesn't involve them. Does it?"

"No," I said. "A place down in the northwest part of Georgia—Trinity Crematorium."

"Oh, *that* place."

"Why do you say 'that place'?"

"Well, that's where funeral homes send cremations if they want to save a few bucks or a little time."

"How many bucks is 'a few'?"

"Not too many—about a hundred per cremation. We handle about sixty cremation requests a year, so we'd save about six thousand dollars if we switched. But if you factor in Trinity's pickup and drop-off, the savings would be bigger."

"How so?"

"We have to take the bodies out to East Tennessee Cremation, and then we have to go pick them up, either at the end of the day or sometime the next day. So that's a hundred and twenty round-trips. We're only about fifteen miles from there, so it's not a huge problem, but it can get complicated, especially if we have several burials going on at the same time, too. Trinity picks up the bodies and then returns the cremains, and that can save a lot of time. They courted us pretty hard, and we thought about switching, but in the end we decided to stick with East Tennessee Cremation."

"Because?"

"I've known the folks there for twenty years. They do a good job, they keep their facility spotless, and they're extremely professional."

"Unlike the folks at that Georgia place?"

He laughed. "You sound like some fast-talking courtroom lawyer now. You've been spending way too much time being cross-examined. Look, I don't know anything bad about them. But I don't know anything great about them either. What it comes down to is, I don't want to stop doing business with people I know and like, just for the sake of a hundred bucks here and there."

"Fair enough," I said. "No further questions at this time. Oh, except the name and number of the person I should call at the place over in Alcoa?"

"EAST TENNESSEE CREMATION." The woman who answered sounded slightly out of breath, as if she'd had to dash for the phone.

"Is this Helen Taylor?"

"Yes. Can I help you?"

I introduced myself and began a convoluted explanation of why I was calling.

"Norm Witherspoon told me you'd probably be calling," she said, as soon as I gave her an opening. "I heard you lecture a few years ago at the Tennessee Association of Funeral Directors. You were showing pictures of how a body decays if the embalming job's not good. You're welcome to come out anytime."

I wasn't sure if she was extending the welcome in spite of my criticisms or because of them. Either way, I was quick to accept the invitation. "When would be a good time to visit?"

"Up to you. I'm here Monday through Friday, eight a.m. to five p.m. We've got three cremations scheduled today, so pretty much anytime you come, I'll be putting somebody in, taking 'em out, or running them through the processor."

"Sounds like they're getting their money's worth from you," I said. "No wonder you sounded winded when you answered the phone."

"There's not a lot of downtime, that's for sure," she said. "I'm just finishing one now, and I thought I'd start the next one right after lunch."

I checked my watch; I'd just eaten a sandwich at my desk, but I tended to eat early. It was not quite eleven-thirty.

"All right if I come on over in about an hour?"

"I'll be looking for you." She gave me directions, and after I'd gone through the morning's mail, I headed out. The mail gave me an idea, so on the way I made a quick stop by Peggy's. She wasn't in, luckily, because I was pretty sure she wouldn't have let me borrow her postage scale if she'd known what I planned to use it for.

CHAPTER 7

FROM THE STADIUM I HEADED DOWNSTREAM ALONG Neyland Drive, past the veterinary school and under the Alcoa Highway bridge. The bridge pilings were marked with horizontal lines at one-foot intervals, showing towboat pilots how much clearance they had between the waterline and the bottom of the bridge. *Why are they called towboats*, I wondered, *when they move the barges by pushing, not pulling?* Between the heat and the drought, the river was down as low as I'd ever seen it in summer. That meant there was plenty of clearance overhead—fifty-seven feet, according to the markings, which was two feet more than usual. But two feet more clearance overhead also meant two feet less water underneath. That wasn't a worry here, where the river was narrow and the channel deep, but a few miles downstream the river spread into broad shallows, where even a fishing boat risked a mangled prop if it strayed from the center of the navigation channel. *We need rain*, I thought, *and a hell of a cold front.*

At the intersection of Neyland and Kingston Pike, I turned right, then also took the next right, onto the ramp for Alcoa Highway southbound. Crossing the high concrete bridge that I'd passed beneath only a moment before, I looked downriver, where the mansions of Sequoyah Hills lined the right-hand bank. I lived in Sequoyah, but my house—tucked into an incongruously modest little block of bungalows and ranchers—was probably worth one-tenth the price of these riverfront villas. I'd had the chance, when I first started teaching at UT, to buy one of the big houses, but the price—fifty-five thousand dollars—seemed astronomical at the time, at least on a professor's salary. Twenty years later that house was worth at least a million, maybe more. The ones lining the waterfront were even more expensive. "Yeah, but I don't have to worry about barge traffic washing away my yard," I said out loud, then laughed at myself. "Okay, Brockton, not only are you talking to yourself, but what you're saying is a total crock."

UT Hospital and the hills behind the Body Farm reared up on my left. On my right a UT cattle farm—green pastures dotted with black-and-white Holsteins—nestled in the big bend of the river. It was the place where the Tennessee first curved southward, starting its serpentine slide toward the Gulf of Mexico, sixteen hundred meandering miles away.

Acting on a sudden impulse, I veered off at the Cherokee Trail exit—the exit for the medical center—and threaded under the highway and around to the back corner of the hospital employees' parking lot. We'd received a donated body several weeks before, and I remembered a note in the chart indicating that the donor—a man in his seventies—had undergone double knee replacement within the past two years. That made his knees newer than any I'd dug out of the boxes in the skeletal collection, and I had a sudden hankering to see them.

I found him just off the main trail curving up into the woods and toward the river. He lay on his back near a fallen tree trunk, his skull detached and slightly downhill from his postcranial skeleton. A camera tripod stood nearby, with a black plastic mailbox fastened incongruously to the top. The mailbox was an improvised housing for a night-vision camera; the camera, sheltered by the weatherproof plastic, was connected to a motion sensor, so that when nocturnal carnivores—raccoons and opossums, mainly—came foraging, we could capture their feeding habits. The project was a Ph.D. candidate's dissertation research, and I'd marveled over some of the photos, which showed cuddly raccoons reaching deep into body cavities to pluck out special delicacies. In the cold, clear light of dawn—actually the scorching, hazy light of high noon—I could see gnaw marks on the cheekbones, the hands, and the feet. But I was more interested at the moment in the hingelike hardware installed where the knees had once been.

I'd had the opportunity during my teaching career to witness two orthopedic surgeries—a hip replacement and a cervical-spine fusion—and I'd come away from both procedures marveling at the combination of precise control and bloody brute force. The neck surgery in particular was an astonishingly choreographed performance by a neurosurgeon and an orthopedist. First they yanked and gouged out three crumbling disks from the patient's neck, at times reaming within a millimeter of the spinal cord; next they tapped pegs of precisely machined cadaver bone into place between the sagging vertebrae; finally they screwed an arched titanium bracket onto the front of the neck, to buttress the spine while the bones knitted together. As the pair of surgeons drilled and tapped and bolted, I couldn't help comparing them to cabinetmakers. The hip replacement by comparison was heavy carpentry—sawing off the proximal end of the femur, drilling a hole down into the shaft, and then pounding the stem of the metal prosthesis into the opening.

The body on the hillside—body 67–07, the sixty-seventh donated body of the year 2007—was almost entirely skeletonized after three weeks of decomposition. The metallic knees gleamed dully; faint saw marks were still visible where the arthritic joints had been cut away and removed from his legs. *Remarkable*, I thought, *that people can walk again after having their knees chopped out.* "Chopped" was probably not how this man's surgeon had described the procedure, but as I studied the trauma that had been dealt to the bones, the drastic verb seemed to fit.

My reverie was interrupted by the sound of a helicopter buzzing low over the treetops. The air ambulances of LifeStar often passed directly over the Body Farm on their way to and from the hospital's helipad, but this chopper, I realized, wasn't flying a typical approach. The pitch of the rotor blades seemed steep and urgent, and the aircraft wheeled and banked abruptly, repeatedly. A siren—then two, then more—screamed toward the hospital, and a second helicopter joined the cacophony.

Over the rising din I suddenly heard my name. "Dr. Brockton! Dr. B., where are you?" It was Miranda, and as she called me, I heard something I'd never expected to hear from Miranda Lovelady: I heard fear.

"Bill!" shouted a man's voice, and I saw Art Bohanan running toward me, Miranda two steps behind. Art's face was flushed, his eyes were as focused as lasers, and his weapon was drawn.

"What on earth?!"

Art said only a few words, but when I heard the fourth one, I felt my knees go weak.

"Garland Hamilton just escaped," he said.

CHAPTER 8

ART GRABBED ONE OF MY ARMS AND MIRANDA
grabbed the other, and they practically dragged me down the hill,
through the clearing, and out the gate of the Body Farm. Miranda paused just long enough to close the gates and snap the
padlocks shut, while Art led me to my truck, peering inside and
even underneath before allowing me to get in.

Once Miranda was in her car, Art hustled into his unmarked
sedan, hit the siren, and switched on the blue lights hidden inside the grille. With Miranda's Jetta in the rear, Art led us out of
the hospital complex in a haze of smoking tires. As we careened
onto Cherokee Trail, headed for Alcoa Highway, half a dozen police vehicles—KPD, Knox County Sheriff's Office, and Tennessee
Highway Patrol—screamed past in the opposite direction.

Five minutes later Art, Miranda, and I surveyed one another
glumly across my desk beneath Neyland Stadium. "How did this

happen?" I said. "Where? When? With his trial coming up, I'd have thought Hamilton would be watched like a hawk."

Art sighed. "You and me both."

"Was he in the Knox County Detention Center? Hell, they've got cameras by the hundreds out there—I don't see how a prisoner could pick his nose without three cameras recording the boogers for posterity."

He shook his head. "The reason we hustled you away from the Farm so fast is that he was only a stone's throw away when he escaped." I stared at Art uncomprehendingly. "He was in the ER at UT Hospital. They'd rushed him there after he went into convulsions," Art said. "Or *appeared* to go into convulsions. As they were wheeling him into the ER, he jumped off the gurney and ran into a stairwell."

"Damn it," I said, "that's the worst possible place for him to get loose. He knows every nook and cranny of that hospital. If they didn't have it locked down in sixty seconds, he could have taken a hundred ways out."

"They didn't have it locked down in sixty seconds," Art said.

I didn't need him to tell me that. The chorus of helicopter rotors and police sirens told me Hamilton had gotten away. What I didn't know was where he'd go and what he'd do: lie low, slip away, or try again to kill me?

TWENTY-FOUR HOURS later, I was still in shock. I'd spent a bad night, followed by a dismal day and an even more wretched night. Every sudden noise made me jump, and the only thing worse than the sound of the phone ringing was the sound of it *not* ringing—the sound of Hamilton slipping silently away.

A security camera showed that Hamilton had ducked out through the back door of the Forensic Center only minutes after leaping off the gurney. In fact, he was already outside before the first KPD units were dispatched toward the hospital. Somewhere between the ER and the Forensic Center's exit, he'd tugged on a pair of scrubs and a surgical mask. One of the pathology residents later told police that he thought he'd glimpsed Hamilton in the hallway, but he'd dismissed the notion, since he knew—or *thought* he knew—that Hamilton was in custody.

Once beyond the loading-dock camera's field of view, Hamilton had vanished completely. It was possible he'd stowed away in the back of a linen truck or one of the dozens of other service vehicles entering and exiting the hospital complex daily. It was also possible he'd simply walked across a parking lot and slipped into the woods that bordered the grounds on the south and the east. Two days of searching—by tracking dogs, by helicopters, and by dozens of KPD officers, Knox County deputies, and TBI agents—had failed to turn up any leads.

Hamilton's escape was the lead story in the *Knoxville News Sentinel* and on every local TV station. His picture and Jess's and mine were prominently featured, and my house was once more besieged with reporters clamoring for sound bites describing how it felt to know that the man who'd killed Jess and tried to kill me was on the loose. The only consolation to the media frenzy was that if Hamilton showed up within a mile of my house, he'd be captured instantly, at least on videotape, by several news crews. The two days after his escape were among my life's lowest points—surpassed only by Kathleen's death, Jess's murder, and my arrest.

The third day I rose from the dead, or at least from the deadly paralysis of spirit that had gripped me. The only way to get my mind off Hamilton, I realized that day, was to get it on some-thing else. One such something, I decided, could be unraveling Burt DeVriess's questions about his Aunt Jean's cremation.

I called Helen Taylor at East Tennessee Cremation and apolo-gized for standing her up two days before. "If you're still willing to show me around, I'd appreciate it, but if you don't want to bother at this point, I understand."

She assured me she'd not taken offense—she'd seen me on the news after Hamilton escaped—and invited me to come out as soon as I could.

"Is thirty minutes too soon?" I asked.

"Thirty minutes is fine," she said.

I resumed the journey I'd begun two days before.

East Tennessee Cremation occupied a low, modest building on a grassy corner at the Rockford industrial park's entrance. Facing it, across the street, was a prefab metal warehouse identified as S and S Services. The crematorium was no bigger than a two-car garage and not much fancier, the owners apparently seeing no need to indulge in the frilly sentiment or veneered stateliness of funeral homes. I liked the unpretentious plainness—it was fit-ting, I decided, for a place that took in dead bodies, laid them in an incinerator of sorts, and burned them down to inorganic minerals. The building had a low L on one side, which housed an office with a glass door and double-hung windows. The busi-ness part of the building—the part in the higher, cinder-block portion—had a big roll-up garage door on the front end and two steel exhaust stacks on the other. The building had no sign of any kind; it was the stacks—their tops a swirl of bluish black that be-spoke extreme heat—that told me I'd found the crematorium.

I knocked on the glass storm door, but I didn't get an answer, so I peered inside. The office looked vacant. The door was un-locked, so I stuck my head in and called, "Hello? Ms. Taylor?"

From around a corner, in the garage-looking part of the build-ing, I heard a muffled female voice say, "I'll be right there."

A pleasant, fiftyish woman emerged. Dressed in a gray pant-suit and black pumps, she would have looked at home in a bank or real-estate office, except for the work gloves she wore—the leather-and-canvas kind favored by carpenters and farmers. She took off one glove and held out a hand.

"You must be Dr. Brockton," she said. "I'm Helen Taylor. Sorry to keep you waiting."

"I kept you waiting for two days," I said, "so you've still got a ways to go before you need to apologize. Thanks for agreeing to give me a look around." I shook her hand. She had a firm grip and an open, direct gaze that I liked. For some reason, maybe because so many funeral directors tended to look deferentially downward, I hadn't expected someone so forthright.

Helen had started out more than twenty years earlier working as a secretary in the office of a company that made metal cem-etery vaults. Several years later, when the owner of the vault com-pany branched out and opened a crematorium, he trained Helen to run it. After serving a two-year apprenticeship, she took the examination to become a licensed funeral director. Although she passed the exam with flying colors, the licensing board turned her down—they'd never licensed a female funeral director, nor anyone who'd apprenticed at an independent crematorium. After two years of training, Helen wasn't willing to take rejection lying down. She hired an attorney, who threatened to sue the licensing board for discrimination. A few weeks later, she received a letter containing her funeral director's license.

In its first year of operation, the crematorium had burned only four bodies, leaving her plenty of time for secretarial work. This year, she said, the number would top four hundred. Business was so good, in fact, that the crematorium was beginning an enormous expansion. She raised the blinds behind her desk and pointed out the window at a fresh excavation and enormous concrete slab. Within a year, she told me, they'd be moving to a new building five times this size. It would be equipped with a chapel for services, a viewing window, and a remote-control ignition switch, so a family member could push a button to start the cremation. The old building would remain a crematorium, but it would shift from cremating humans to cremating pets, a business that was growing by leaps and bounds. She pulled out a binder filled with architectural drawings and floor plans of the new building. I noticed it would have three furnaces rather than just two; I also noticed a large room labeled cooler, which I asked about. The cooler would be able to hold up to sixteen bodies, she told me proudly.

"Sixteen? That's a lot of bodies," I said. "Nearly as many as the Regional Forensic Center can hold. You're not planning to start killing people off, are you?"

She laughed. "I don't have to. I've had as many as six or seven bodies come through here in a day," she said. "Not often, but when it happens, I need someplace to put them. Can you imagine four or five bodies stacked up in here on a day like today?" She had a point there. The small building was air-conditioned, but between the blistering sun outside and the ovens inside, the temperature was probably close to ninety. She did need a cooler, and if business was growing like she said it was, it might not be long before she'd have that cooler filled. I was impressed with the operation, and when I said so, she beamed.

"If you'd told me twenty years ago this is what I'd be doing, I wouldn't have believed you," she said. "But here I am, and I love what I do."

"I'm sometimes surprised where I ended up, too," I said, "but I wouldn't change it. I'm never bored, I'm sometimes able to do a good deed for victims or families, and I get to meet interesting people like you."

"Let's go take a look," she said. She led me through a connecting door into the crematorium's work space, which was every bit as spartan and utilitarian as the outside had hinted it would be. This garage was a two-furnace garage, the ovens parked side by side, their stainless-steel fronts bristling with dials and knobs and lights. She pushed a button on the furnace on the left, and a thick door slid up, revealing an arched interior about eight feet long, two feet high, and three feet wide. The interior walls of the furnace were brick—a pale, soot-stained brick, similar to what I'd seen pottery kilns made of.

I edged up for a closer look. "You mind if I stick my head in?"

"Not at all," she said. "Just let me fasten this safety latch first—I'd hate for that door to fall and decapitate you." The door was six inches thick, its steel cladding insulated with a layer of firebrick; it probably weighed at least a hundred pounds. She fitted a stout, L-shaped cotter pin into a slot beneath the lower edge of the door, the guillotine's equivalent of the safety on a gun.

The firebrick—refractory brick, she called it—was tan and fine-grained, with several paler spots where small chips had flaked off. I reached up and rubbed a finger over one. A few grains, somewhere between sand and ceramic in texture, flaked off in my hands. "Does this just naturally flake away over time?"

She nodded. "They have to be relined about every two years."

The floor and the roof of the combustion chamber were made of concrete; a spiderweb of cracks zigzagged through the roof. "Are these cracks a problem? Can you just patch them, or do you have to chip out the whole top when you reline it?"

"Actually, those are normal," she said. "The very first time you fire up a brand-new cremation furnace, you get that cracking—the heat's so intense."

As I leaned in farther, an image from Hansel and Gretel popped into my head. "You're not going to shove me in," I said, "and turn me into gingerbread?"

"Not hardly. " She laughed. "If I turn this burner on, you won't come out looking anything like a gingerbread man. Here, let me show you the 'before' version, and then I'll show you 'after.' It's quite a contrast." A metal gurney was parked along one wall of the building. It held a cardboard box the size and shape of a coffin. She tugged at the lid and raised it enough to give me a look.

An ancient man—not a day less than ninety, I guessed—lay within, slightly to one side of the centerline. He was thin and shriveled and had clearly been shriveling for years. There was room enough in the container for him and two more bodies his size. The man's face was collapsing into his mouth, and I knew without pulling down a lip that the jaws were toothless. The root sockets were probably long gone, smoothed out over the past ten or twenty years, as the bone resorbed and filled them in.

"Looks like he had a long life," I said.

"His *son* had a long life," she replied.

I stepped away, and Helen wiggled the lid back into place, then wheeled the gurney to the gaping maw of the furnace. "Here," I said, "let me give you a hand with that."

"Oh, that's all right," she said. "I do this five or six times a day.

It's not that hard. The gurney has rollers built into the top." She gave a shove to the end of the box, and it slid easily until it was halfway off the gurney and tipped down onto the floor of the furnace. She shoved a little harder, and I heard the bottom of the box scraping along the concrete.

Once the box was all the way in, she removed the cotter pin and pressed the button that lowered the furnace door. She pushed a glowing red button labeled Afterburner, and I heard a low whoosh, like a gas fireplace lighting up. "I knew fighter planes had afterburners," I said. "I didn't know cremation furnaces had 'em, too. Is it faster than the speed of sound?"

She rolled her eyes at the joke.

"Seriously, though, why do you turn on the afterburner first?"

"This is a secondary burner, just before the exhaust flue," she explained. "Makes sure everything's burned before the gases go out the stack. If TVA's power plants burned coal this cleanly, you wouldn't see all that haze between downtown Knoxville and the mountains."

She tapped her finger on a small glass disk set into the door, no bigger than the security peephole in the front door of my house. "You can watch through there if you want," she said, "but you won't be able to see much. Mostly just flame." She reached for a glowing green button labeled Pre-Ignition, and I put one eye to the little window. A jet of yellow flame, roughly the size of the Olympic torch, blossomed from the hole in the roof of the furnace and flickered downward, flaring outward when it hit the lid of the box. Within moments the cardboard began to burn and the flame spread. "Okay," I heard Helen say, "now I'm going to switch on the combustion burner." The bloom of yellow flame suddenly turned blue and filled the entire upper portion of the chamber. I watched, mesmerized, as the cardboard collapsed, revealing the contours of the frail body. And then, for a brief moment before flame and smoke obscured my view altogether, I saw the withered flesh catch fire, and somehow it struck me as a cleansing, even a holy thing. "Ashes to ashes, dust to dust," I heard myself whisper. It was an impromptu benediction from an unlikely source—me, a doubt-filled scientist who dealt daily in death—given to a total stranger, a man I had never seen before, and whom no one would ever see again.

After a moment I stepped back and turned to Helen. She was watching me closely, I noticed, and she seemed slightly embarrassed when I caught her looking. It was as if she knew she'd intruded on some private exchange. "Funny thing," I said. "I see bodies all the time—I actually burned a couple of corpses last week as a research experiment—but this was different. This was a person." She nodded. I could see that she understood what I meant and that I'd eased her embarrassment by what I'd said.

"Do you want to see the 'after' version now?" She pointed at the other furnace, and I stepped four feet to the right. She opened the door, and I felt a blast of heat as the door slid down. A human skeleton was laid out in perfect anatomical order on the concrete floor. The bones were grayish white and brittle-looking, completely calcined. Except for the skull, which had rolled to one side and cracked into several large pieces, and the rib cage, which had caved in like the timbers of a shipwreck, the bones remained intact and in their original positions. "I couldn't have laid it out better myself," I said.

She smiled. "Most people think that when a body's cremated, it comes out of the furnace as cremains," she said. "They have no idea that it's still a recognizable skeleton." She reached in with a gloved hand, pulled out a humerus from the upper arm, and gestured with it. "I always find it fascinating to look at the skeletons," she said. "Every one is different. This one, for example, was a very large woman. About three hundred pounds. I had to really watch the oven temperature on her."

I thought for a moment. "Because of the fat?"

"Right. I learned my lesson on that a long time ago. About six months after I started working here, I had a huge guy come through—he weighed five hundred pounds at least and barely fit in the furnace. This was late one afternoon in December, a few days before Christmas, and it was getting dark around five o'clock. Well, about thirty minutes after I got him going, one of the guys from the place across the street came knocking on the door, asked me if I knew my exhaust stack was red hot. I went out to look, and it was glowing cherry red."

"A five-hundred-pound body's going to have two or three hundred pounds of fat on it," I said. "That's gonna make one heck of a grease fire once it melts and ignites."

"You can say that again," she said. "I came running back in and checked the temperature gauge. Normally these furnaces run at sixteen to eighteen hundred degrees. That guy pushed it up to nearly three thousand. I'm just lucky the roof didn't catch fire. I sure learned my lesson from that."

"So how do you keep that from happening again?"

"The really obese ones, I get 'em going, then throttle the gas back. Once the fat's burning, that pretty much keeps them going for a while. Then, after about forty-five minutes—once I see the temperature drop below sixteen hundred—I relight the combustion burner for another fifteen or twenty minutes. That's enough to bring 'em on home."

"Speaking of obese bodies burning," I said, "you'll be interested in this." There weren't many people I could say something like that to in all seriousness. "We had a master's student a few years ago who did a thesis on spontaneous combustion."

She guffawed. "What did she read for research," she hooted, "the *Weekly World News*?"

"Actually, it was a really good thesis," I said. "One of the best I've ever read. It's not just supermarket tabloid readers who believe in spontaneous combustion. I've talked to several police officers and firefighters who swear they've seen cases of spontaneous combustion—bodies that were thoroughly incinerated but with very little damage to the surrounding structure, or even the furniture." Helen nodded brightly, and I could tell she was intrigued. "Anyhow, Angi—the graduate student—found that in all these cases where someone appeared to have burst into flame, the individuals were overweight, and what had occurred was a low-temperature fire. The bodies smoldered for a day or two, without ever burning hot enough to cause the fire to spread."

"So what caused them to burn?"

"Many of them were smokers, so they probably dropped a lit cigarette onto their clothes," I said. "One woman got her sleeve too close to the burner of a gas stove. The combustion wasn't spontaneous; there had to be an ignition source. Alcohol was another common factor—some of them were drunk, others were asleep, so they didn't notice or react fast enough when their clothes or their bed caught fire. They probably died of smoke inhalation pretty quickly, but the fire kept going. As their fat melted, the clothing soaked up the grease, just like the wick of a candle or a lamp."

"You're right," she said, "that *is* interesting."

"But I'm getting you sidetracked," I said. "Show me what you do next."

"It's pretty simple," she said. She lifted a long-handled tool from a pair of brackets attached to the side of the furnace. It was like a cross between a rake and a hoe: welded onto the handle was a wide metal flange, maybe ten inches wide by two inches tall. She maneuvered it through the mouth of the furnace, stretched it all the way to the back—down beyond the woman's feet—and began raking the bones forward. When they reached the front of the furnace, they tumbled down into a wide hopper, which I hadn't noticed until now. She made several passes with the rake-like tool, then switched to a shop broom, with a broad head and stiff bristles. Once she was satisfied she'd swept everything into the hopper, she bent down and removed a square metal bucket from beneath the hopper.

She carried the bucket to a workbench along one wall of the building and tipped out the contents onto a workbench there. Next she grasped a U-shaped handle, which was attached to a block of metal a few inches square. With it she began crushing the bones, almost as if she were making mashed potatoes. After reducing the bones to pieces no more than an inch or two at the biggest, she dragged the block back and forth through the bone fragments. Soon its sides and bottom bristled with industrial-strength metal staples, and I realized it was a magnet.

"Where'd all those staples come from?"

"The bottom of the shipping container," she said. "The sides and top are cardboard, but the bottom is plywood, stapled to the cardboard."

"Makes sense to use plywood," I said. "You don't want the bottom getting soggy and letting the body fall out."

"Exactly," she said. "Most people wouldn't think about that, but you understand because you've seen what happens when bodies start to decompose."

"Doesn't take more than a day or two for fluids to start leaching out," I agreed. "You fish out the staples so they don't go back to the family?"

"That," she said, "and so they don't dull the blades of the processor. I'll show you that in a minute." She stirred around a bit more, snagging a zipper and a few buttons. "Here you go, a Cracker Jack prize," she said. She fished out a short metal bracket drilled with four holes, a scorched screw threaded through each hole. "She must have had a plate in her arm or leg," she said.

"Do you get a lot of orthopedic hardware?"

"More and more, seems like."

"As the Baby Boomers start to die off," I said, "I bet you'll see even more. All those joggers and tennis players and downhill skiers going in for new parts. What do you do with stuff like that?"

"We bury it," she said, "unless the family asks for it."

"So if somebody had a pair of artificial knees and the family wanted them, you'd send 'em back?"

"Absolutely," she said. She took a hand broom and swept the crushed bones into a small mound, then unhooked a large metal dustpan from a peg above the workbench. Bracing the bone fragments with the broom, she slid the dustpan underneath, scooping nearly everything into it with one quick, efficient push. Then she slid it backward about a foot and carefully swept the remaining dust into it.

At the left-hand end of the workbench was a large metal pot, the size and shape of a restaurant kitchen's stockpot. "This is the processor," she said. "You see the blades there in the bottom?" I looked into the vessel and saw a thin, flat bar attached to a bolt at the center. The pot was roughly fifteen inches in diameter; the bar reached about halfway to the sides of the pot. Both ends of the bar had shorter bars attached to what appeared to be bearings or pivots. "If you flip that switch, you'll see how it works." She nodded toward a toggle on the wall just above the container. I flipped it up, and the blades jolted into motion. I caught a brief glimpse of the shorter bars flipping outward toward the rim, and then the whole whirling assembly disappeared, the way an airplane propeller disappears at full throttle. I flipped the switch off, and the blades spun down, the centrifugal force keeping the shorter bars extended until the assembly coasted to a stop.

"That blade assembly looks like what I feel when I jam my hand down into my garbage disposal to untangle the dishrag," I said, giving an involuntary shudder. "You could sure lose a hand in there fast." She nodded again, then tipped the dustpan into the pot. She started an exhaust fan above the processor, then switched on the blades. A plume of dust eddied upward as the blades chewed through the chunks of bone, sending a swirl of powder and small bits of bone up the sides of the vessel. After a half minute or so, she switched off the motor, and the pulverized material settled, the blades sending smaller and smaller waves spinning through the powder as they slowed. She grasped the two handles of the pot, gave a twist to release it from the central shaft that came up from the motor underneath, and hoisted the pot up to the workbench. Then she tipped it into another hopper, this one emptying into a bag of clear, heavy plastic that was cinched to its spout. She tapped the side of the hopper to coax the last bit of powder to fall, then unhooked the bag, dropped in a small metal identification tag, and sealed the bag with a twist tie.

"Where does the tag come from?"

"I make those here," she said. "Each body gets an ID number, which goes in the file and on this tag."

"Just like at the Body Farm," I said. "You've got a good system here."

"Well, I've had twenty years to work out the kinks," she replied, laughing.

The bag was already inside a black plastic container, measuring about six inches by eight inches wide and eight or ten inches tall. She folded down the box's plastic lid and snapped it shut.

"Could I ask one more favor?"

"Sure," she said. "What?"

"Would you mind if I took the bag out and weighed it?"

"Of course not," she said.

Before leaving the Anthropology Department, I'd borrowed the postage scale from Peggy's supply closet. I was curious to see how the cremains I'd received from Burt DeVriess compared in weight to those from the crematorium. Burt's Aunt Jean had weighed barely three pounds. These cremains tipped the scales at nearly twice that. I commented on the difference to Helen. "Well, this gal was pretty good-sized," she said. "Big-boned, as large people like to say."

"It's true," I said. "The heavier you get, the stronger your bones have to be just to carry your body weight. Bones are like muscles—the more you challenge 'em, the stronger they grow."

She smiled. "I like that analogy. Like muscles."

"A little bit longer-lasting, though," I said. "Especially when there's fire involved."

I thanked Helen for the help and headed back to UT. When I got back to the office, I looked again at the cremains Burt

DeVriess had sent me. With the comparison fresh in my mind, I was struck more than ever by how wrong they looked. The bone fragments were too big and splintered. The granular part was too grainy. The powder was too fine. And those pebbles—they were just plain wrong. I'd known it from the moment I saw them; now, somehow, I took them as a personal affront. With the tip of a pencil, I stirred the mixture, frowning, thinking about various tests I could use to determine what precisely was in this urn besides, or instead of, Burt's Aunt Jean.

The phone rang. "Dr. B.?"

"Yes, Peggy?"

"You haven't seen my postage scale, have you?"

Damn—it was on the corner of my desk, where I'd set it and promptly forgotten it upon walking into my office.

"I need to mail Kate Spradley's bound copy of her dissertation to her down in Pensacola, and I can't find the scale to weigh it."

"I'll look around and see if I spy it anywhere," I said.

"Would you like me to pick up one for you next time I'm at Office Depot, Dr. B.?"

"Whatever would I need with a postage scale, Peggy?"

"Heaven only knows," she said. "And I'm pretty sure I don't want to."

When I hung up, I made a mental note to stop by the men's room on my way to her office. If I was lucky, the electric hand dryer would have enough oomph to blow away the coating of human dust from the crematorium.

I wished it could also dispel the layers of dread and fear that had settled over my heart since Garland Hamilton's escape.

CHAPTER 9

THE PHONE RANG AND I GRABBED FOR IT, HOPING IT
was Art—or a reporter, or anyone–calling to tell me Hamilton
had been captured.

The caller was Robert Roper, the Knox County district attorney general, but he was calling to ask about Mary Latham.
"You're sure she was already dead when the car burned?" Robert was a longtime colleague and friend; I'd testified for him in a
dozen or more murder trials over the past decade, and I respected
his thoroughness and professionalism. I also appreciated the fact
that Robert had recused his entire staff when the police initially
charged me with Jess Carter's murder.

"No way she could have been alive," I said. "Not unless she
was walking around like somebody out of *Night of the Living Dead*, with hunks of flesh falling off and flies and maggots
swarming all over."

"Thanks for sharing," he said. "I was just about to eat lunch. Maybe I'll catch up on my depositions instead."

"If memory serves, you could stand to skip a lunch or two," I parried. "Last time I saw you, you'd put on about twenty pounds."

"You should write a book," he said. "*Dr. Brockton's Gross-Out Weight-Loss Plan*. It could be the next South Beach Diet. You might wind up on *Oprah*."

"I'll be sure to tell Oprah it was you who inspired me."

"Great. Now back to Mary Latham. Can you tell if she decomposed in the car or someplace else?"

"I doubt it," I said. "Normally there's a big, greasy stain where the decomposition occurred, but the car's interior is probably too badly burned to tell. You might want the crime-scene guys to go back and check the house and the yard—anyplace she might have lain for a couple of days before her husband—or whoever—put her in the car."

"How about the freezer in the basement?"

"Not likely, though it might've been a good idea—if he'd frozen her, she wouldn't have decomposed." I thought for a moment. "Thing is, it would have been messy to get her into the car once she started to decompose. Parts fall off, stuff drips out. It's not easy, and it's sure not pleasant. Of course, if you've resorted to murdering your wife, pleasantness might not be high on your list of priorities at the moment. Still, my guess is she was already in the car. I'd be willing to bet he put her in the passenger seat right after he killed her, drove the car out to that field, and wiggled her over to the driver's seat while she was still fresh. Although he'd be taking a chance on somebody finding her."

"Not much of a chance," said Robert. "That spot's pretty isolated."

"Are you sure it's the husband?"

"Pretty damn sure," he said. "During the three-day period before the car burned, nobody besides the husband seems to have seen her or talked to her."

"Makes sense," I said, "since she was dead."

"There's a big problem with the case against him, though," Roper said.

"What's that?"

"His alibi," he said. "Stuart Latham was in Las Vegas when the car burned. The investigating officer got hold of him on his cell phone, and Latham called back from a landline in the Bellagio Hotel."

"But was he already in Vegas when she was killed? If she'd been dead for days, why does it matter where he was when the car actually caught fire?"

"Because," he said, "a good defense attorney will use that to plant doubt in the minds of the jurors. Make them think somebody else killed her."

"Like who?" I said. "A burglar? Somebody after a stereo or a VCR? Why on earth would some stranger kill her, wait a couple of days, then drive her down to the south forty to burn the evidence? Doesn't create much doubt in my mind."

"You're not a juror," he said, "you're a scientist."

"And anyhow," I persisted, "didn't the husband tell the police she was alive and well when he got on the plane that morning? The decay and the bugs prove he's lying through his teeth."

"You know that, and I know that, but we have to convince twelve other people of that," he said.

"Besides the burned bones, what else was found in the car?"

"Not much," he said. "A few cigarette butts on the ground underneath the driver's window, like maybe she sat there and smoked awhile before the grass caught fire. Husband says she liked to do that. Says he warned her a bunch of times about dropping cigarette butts in the grass. People driving on I-640 saw the smoke and called it in, probably within ten minutes of when it caught fire, according to the arson investigator."

"Any sign of a timer?" I asked. "An ignition device, something he could have set to go off once he was out in Vegas?"

"Not that the evidence techs can find," he said. "One of them's just back from Iraq, and he doesn't see any evidence of an IED."

"What's an IED?"

"Improvised explosive device. Iraqi insurgents use 'em as roadside bombs. They're triggered by a cell phone, sometimes. Thing is, you gotta have some skill with electronics or some training as a terrorist to rig one of those, and Stuart Latham runs an Avis rental-car franchise."

"Well, either he killed her or he didn't," I said in exasperation. "If he did, either he had an accomplice or he didn't. And if he didn't have an accomplice, there ought to be something, either in the car or out at the scene, indicating how he set off the fire from the Bellagio."

"Are you willing to take a look? In the car and out at the property?"

"I'm not an evidence technician," I reminded him.

"But you're great with taphonomy," Roper said. I was impressed the D.A. remembered the term. In archaeology, taphonomy referred to the process or circumstances of fossilization, but forensic anthropologists tended to use it more broadly, to describe the arrangement and relation of bodies, bones, and any other environmental or human-produced evidence that could shed light on a murder or its timing. Postmarked letters, a week-old newspaper open to the sports page, milk or meat tagged with a sell-by date, even a year-old sapling or a seasonal wasp nest within a rib cage or an eye socket—all these could be considered taphonomic evidence of when a murder occurred.

"I'll be glad to take a look at the taphonomy," I said. "Be good for me to get out of the office."

"The car's at the KPD impound lot," he said. "When do you want to see it?"

"How about early in the morning," I said, "while it's a mere ninety degrees?"

"I'll have my investigator, Darren Cash, meet you at the impound lot. Just so you know, we're getting ready to ask a grand jury to indict Stuart Latham for first-degree murder, based on the insect evidence you found in the skull. First, though, we'll get a search warrant to go back for another look at the property. If you find anything else in the car, that could help with the warrant."

"I'll see what I can do," I said, "but don't hold your breath. What time should I meet Cash?"

"How does nine o'clock sound?"

"Sounds late and hot," I said. "What about eight instead?"

"I'll have Darren meet you at eight."

"You mind if Art Bohanan comes along? He wasn't available when the KPD forensics team went over the car."

"I'm always glad to have Art take a look."

AT 7:55 THE NEXT MORNING, Art and I turned onto the lane leading to the KPD impound lot. The lot was on a dead-end street in East Knoxville, directly across I-40 from the zoo. Something about the juxtaposition struck me as funny—hundreds of captive animals on the south side of the interstate, I realized, hundreds of captive vehicles on the north side. As we entered the dead end, I imagined a mass escape from the zoo: animals tunneling under the freeway, then speeding off in stolen cars and trucks—chimpanzees and gorillas driving the getaway vehicles, hippos and elephants hunkering in the back of the biggest trucks. I pointed out a car to Art, a red BMW convertible with the top down. "You think a giraffe could fit into the back of that Beemer?"

Art glanced at me, then at the car, then stared at me as if I were some sort of zoological specimen myself. He raised his eyebrows slowly, then shook his head, an expression of deep pity on his face. "We have *got* to get you some professional help," he said.

"Come on," I said, "it's not that far-fetched. Primates have opposable thumbs—they could hot-wire the ignitions."

"Professional help," he said again. "A mind is a terrible thing to lose."

The impound lot was a quarter mile long—four narrow lots, actually—sandwiched between the interstate on one side and a set of railroad tracks on the other. The first lot, an unfenced pad of gravel about fifty yards square, contained vehicles that would be auctioned off on September 1, a sign announced. These were unclaimed or forfeited cars and trucks, along with several horse trailers, which particularly intrigued me. *Surely I could find a use for a cheap horse trailer at the Body Farm*, I thought.

The second lot was a fenced expanse of asphalt measuring the same fifty yards deep—the depth being dictated by the train tracks bordering the back—but stretching a hundred yards long.

This lot held vehicles that had been towed for a multitude of reasons: Fire hydrants had been blocked, parking meters had gone unfed for weeks on end, junkers had been abandoned alongside the interstate, unpaid traffic tickets had mounted to thousands of dollars. Many of the vehicles had open windows, and several, like the red BMW, were convertibles open to the elements. "Good thing for those convertibles we're in the middle of a drought," I said.

Art shrugged, unconcerned. "If the top's down or the windows are open when we tow it, nothing we can do. We don't have the keys."

I noticed a video camera mounted on a pole at one corner of the lot. "Have you had break-ins, right here in the impound lot?"

"You wouldn't believe what a problem it is," he said. "We had one guy sneak in with wire cutters one night, cut a big hole in the fence, and drive away."

"He hot-wired one of the cars?"

"He had the keys. It was his car."

"He stole his own car from the police?" I couldn't help laughing. "Did y'all catch him?"

Art shook his head. "We got the car back—he ditched it over in North Carolina—but we never got the guy."

"That took some nerve," I said with a touch of admiration.

Next came a lot whose fence was screened by blue tarps. I pointed. "What's in that one?"

"Cars seized from drug dealers, mostly," he said.

"Why the tarps?"

"To keep people from gawking," he said. "Your average drug dealer tends to drive a better class of car—we've got Acuras, Cadillacs, Mercedeses—and we had a problem with looky-loos hanging around window-shopping."

"Seems like the tarps would attract more people," I said. "Make 'em wonder what's in there that you don't want anybody to see."

"There's a troublemaker inside you just waiting to get out," he said.

Art pulled into the fourth lot, which was tucked at the farthest corner of the compound, back behind a security building outfitted with rooftop surveillance cameras at every corner. This lot contained hard-core specimens: cars flattened by high-speed rollovers or accordioned in head-on collisions. Many of them were missing doors and roofs, the metal chewed away by the Jaws of Life or slashed loose with a Sawzall. Several vehicles were covered with tarps—cars in which shootings had occurred, Art said. Off by itself, along the westernmost side of the fence, was the burned-out shell of a car. The windows were gone and the paint had blistered off, but I could tell by the lines that it had been a fairly new and expensive car just a couple of weeks before.

A clean-cut young man in his early thirties was peering into the vehicle's interior. When he heard the crunch of the tires on the gravel, he straightened and turned toward us. He was wearing a short-sleeved blue shirt with a yellow tie. The shirt stretched tight around his neck and shoulders, which looked like they'd been borrowed from an NFL linebacker. His crew cut and military posture suggested he'd been either a soldier or a cop before he became a D.A.'s investigator. As the three of us shook hands all around, I said, "I hear good things about you from your boss."

"You've been talking to my wife?"

I laughed. "No, the district attorney."

"Oh, my day-job boss." He grinned. "I've been lucky so far."

"Lucky my foot," said Art. "Darren was the one who broke the Watkins case last year."

I hadn't been involved in it, but I remembered reading about it and being shocked. "Watkins—that was the guy who took out the two-hundred-thousand-dollar insurance policy on the little girl, then drowned her in the backyard pool?"

Cash nodded. "His granddaughter," he said. "The policy had a two-year waiting period on the death benefit. The really sick thing about that case—"

Art broke in. "You mean besides the fact that a man would drown his own granddaughter?"

"Yeah," said Cash, "even sicker than that. He took out the policy, put in the swimming pool, and then waited exactly twenty-five months. That little girl had a rattlesnake coiled around her feet for two years."

"That is sick," I said. "How on earth could somebody do that to his own granddaughter—for any price, let alone a couple hundred thousand bucks?"

"Some people are just plain evil," Art said. "No other explanation for it, I don't care what the forensic psychologists say."

"I'm inclined to agree with you," I said. "I'm not sure about God anymore, but I'm starting to believe in the devil. Not some red-suited guy with a pitchfork and horns, but regular-looking folks. A guy who drowns his granddaughter in the backyard. A woman who feeds her husband arsenic every night."

"A pedophile who trolls the Internet for gullible kids," said Art.

"A husband who kills his wife," said Cash, "and lets her rot for days before burning her body."

I took that as the investigator's hint that we should get down to business. I nodded toward the burned-out car, a short, sleek

SUV. "This looks like it used to be a pretty nice car," I said. "What is it?"

"Lexus RX, 2006," he said. "Probably around forty thousand new."

"That's a lot," I said. "Would have been cheaper to take her on a hike in the Smokies and push her off a bluff—say she tripped and fell."

"Bill loses more hiking buddies that way," Art said. "Never, ever go to the mountains with him."

Cash laughed. "Thanks for the warning." He nodded at the vehicle. "Book value on the vehicle's more like twenty-five thousand now," he said. "But the bank owns most of that. Deductible on the insurance policy's five hundred. Five hundred is dirt cheap if it works to cover your tracks and give you an alibi."

"Well, it didn't quite do the job," I said, "thanks to the bugs. Let's see if there's anything else to find."

Art and I had brought a few things in the back of my truck. We both unfolded white Tyvek jumpsuits and wriggled into them, looking like overgrown toddlers in baggy sleeper pajamas. I opened the tackle box that held an assortment of tools and took out two sharp-pointed trowels and two pairs of tweezers. I handed one of each to Art, then slid a wire screen out from beneath the tackle box. Each opening in the mesh was four millimeters square—about the size of the end of a set of wooden chopsticks from a Chinese take-out place.

Cash showed me how the body had been found in the car. The woman's legs had been down in the driver's well, her left arm hanging down by her side. Her right arm stretched over near the passenger door. Her torso and head were flopped over to the right also.

"As I understand it," I said, "there were no traces of accelerant found in the interior. Is that right?"

"That's right," Cash said. "Arson dog didn't smell anything, and I'm told that dog has a great nose."

"Sure is thoroughly burned for no accelerant," I said, peering into the burned-out shell of the vehicle. The upholstery was completely gone. The seats had been reduced to charred, rusted springs and support rails. The underside of the roof was fully exposed, the same reddish gray as the vehicle's exterior. The windshields and windows were gone. All that remained of the steering wheel was the steel skeleton, including the empty hub where the airbag had been before it fired.

"Used to be cars had a lot of metal inside," said Art. "Now everything's plastic, and once the car catches fire, that plastic keeps feeding it. It's like pornography."

I stared at him, baffled by the comparison. "Pornography? How so?"

"Hot and nasty," he said. "Temperatures in the passenger compartment can go over two thousand degrees. And all that burning plastic releases all kinds of toxic chemicals. Smoke inhalation can kill you long before the heat does."

I recalled the smoke roiling out of the cars we'd recently burned at the Ag farm—dense black billows seething out the windows and windshields once the glass gave way—and nodded. "Any way to tell where the fire started?"

Cash shook his head. "Not for sure," he said. "The ignition was on, though, so the engine was probably idling. We think either the catalytic converter or the muffler set the grass underneath on fire. Most of these luxury SUVs never get off the pavement, but out in that pasture it'd be easy for the exhaust system to set the grass on fire, especially as hot and dry as it's been. Catalytic converter can get up to nearly a thousand degrees, if the car's fairly new and the converter's still working."

"I bet one of you guys knows the ignition temperature of grass," I said.

"Six hundred degrees," they chorused.

"So if that converter was in contact with the vegetation," I said, "it shouldn't have taken more than a few minutes to start a grass fire."

"Right," said Cash.

"Which begs the question," I said, "if the husband did it, how'd he get fifteen hundred miles away before it started burning?"

None of us had an answer, so Art and I squatted down beside the vehicle—me beside the driver's door, him beside the right rear door—and began sifting through the debris in the floor pan. I didn't find much: A layer of ash. A few bolts, screws, and coins. A couple of phalanges, the smallest bones of the fingers and toes. "Hey," I razzed Art, "how come KPD missed these?"

"Simple," he said. "The car burned late afternoon, right after 'Tiffany' got out of school and got on the Web. I was too busy reading love notes from middle-aged perverts to go out to the Latham farm and look for bones. They had to send the B-team instead."

"We gotta get you off that pedophile assignment," I said.

"I'm training a replacement," he said. "I hope to be back to healthier stuff—gunshots and stabbings and bludgeonings—within a month or so."

Art wasn't finding much more in the back than I'd found in the front: springs, seat-belt buckles, and a few coins down where the rear bench seat once met the seat back—that place where every car accumulates loose change and candy wrappers and stray peanuts. I was about to suggest we call it a morning when I heard Art say, "Hmm. *Hmm.*" From one corner of the backseat, he plucked a tiny scrap of partially burned material. He held it up for Cash and me to inspect. It was charred on the edges, but enough remained for it to be recognizable as a shred of crumpled newspaper, not much bigger than a postage stamp. A few words were still legible: "foreign policy" and "Ira," they read. I mentally supplied the missing *q* on the end of "Iraq."

"Darren," I asked, "any other newspaper found in the vehicle?"

"No."

"This little scrap seems odd, the way it's wedged way down in the corner of the backseat. You expect that with pennies and pens, but not so much with newspaper." I knelt down beside the other corner of the backseat and sifted through the debris. The tip of my trowel teased out another bit, smaller and with no type, from a corner of the page. I recognized the distinctive saw-tooth fringe at the edge of the paper, where the roll of newsprint had been cut with a serrated edge. I craned my neck around to look at Darren. "Was the house searched?"

He nodded.

"I don't suppose you remember whether there was a stack of newspapers?"

"You're right," he said, "I don't remember. Why would newspapers be significant?"

"I'm just thinking out loud," I said. "I remember a case in which a woman had stabbed her husband and decided to burn his body in the house. There were no traces of accelerant, but down behind some of the furniture the arson investigator found wads of newspaper, which she'd used as fuel. A couple more minutes and that paper would have gone up in flames. Luckily, the fire department got the fire out before it reached flashover, so some evidence remained."

"So you're thinking maybe Stuart Latham did the same thing?"

"It's possible," I said. "If there's a stack of papers back at the house with a week's worth missing, that might be a clue that he used newspaper to help goose the fire along."

"We'll see," he said. "We can add that to the search warrant, along with what you and Dr. Garcia told us about the bones and the bugs."

"Maggots never lie," I said. "Unlike husbands."

Art and I bagged the phalanges I'd found in the front floorboard, as well as the two bits of newspaper from the backseat. Art folded and taped the bags shut, then wrote the date and time, along with a brief description of the bones and shreds of paper. Then we pulled off the baggy jumpsuits, which by now were plastered to us with sweat, peeled the gloves off our dripping hands, and stuffed the disposable garb into a red biohazard bag, for burning in the morgue's medical-waste incinerator. We gave Cash a sweaty good-bye handshake, then drove back out the way we'd come in—past the drug dealers' cars, past the security building, past the main impound lot and the auction lot.

I pointed at the red convertible again. "That's a pretty small backseat," I said. "The giraffe would probably have to be a baby."

"Not necessarily," said Art. "Not if it was sitting sideways."

CHAPTER 10

EARLY THE NEXT MORNING, AS THE SUN STRUGGLED to burn through a layer of steamy haze, I threaded my way out of Sequoyah Hills and along Kingston Pike. Instead of taking the right onto Neyland and along the river to the stadium, I turned left onto Concord. I bumped across the railroad crossing, then took a right onto Sutherland Avenue, over another set of tracks and past the dusty silos of a pair of concrete plants, Sequatchie Concrete and Southern Precast, their gravel parking lots filled with powdered cement trucks, highway culverts, and staircases. Next, through the pillars of the Alcoa Highway viaduct, I glimpsed the white storage tanks of the Rohm and Haas plastics factory. One of the tanks carried a cartoonish painting of a bespectacled scientist in a white lab coat, captioned That's Good Chemistry. As I wrinkled my nose against the acrid fumes of superglue, or one of its chemical cousins, I thought, *More like* "That's Stinky Chemistry." Then I laughed out loud at the irony of me, the founder of the Body Farm, complaining about any other establishment's unpleasant smell.

I well knew superglue's affinity for human fingers and fingerprints—I'd glued my fingers together on more than one occasion, and Art had actually patented a superglue-fuming device, "the Bohanan Apparatus," used by crime labs nationwide to pick up latent prints on guns, knives, paper, even victims' skin. As I sniffed my way past Rohm and Haas, I imagined every square inch of the factory and its workers to be covered with handprints—layer upon layer of loops and whorls, captured forever in superglue fumes and drifting concrete dust.

Middlebrook Pike was the next intersection after I passed Rohm and Haas. I turned left on Middlebrook, heading west, away from downtown. The road burrowed beneath I-40 and then, an industrialized mile later, crossed over the I-640 bypass. Just beyond 640 the cityscape gave way to farmland, and I knew I'd reached the Latham property. The entire Middlebrook frontage, perhaps half a mile, was lined with white board fence. Huge oaks and tulip poplars dotted rolling meadows, and a small stream—Third Creek, if I remembered Knoxville's prosaic creek-naming scheme correctly—meandered out of the property beside an entry road.

The driveway led to a two-story white clapboard farmhouse, easily a century old, shaded by more of the towering oaks. The house was simple but graceful, with a wide, airy porch and generous windows of wavy antique glass. A handful of law-enforcement vehicles, including a crime-lab van, lined a semicircular drive that approached the front porch. Off to the side of the house was a yellow Nissan Pathfinder, which I guessed to be Stuart Latham's.

Beyond the house, after the asphalt drive gave way to gravel, stood a large whitewashed barn, complete with weather vane and lightning rods atop the metal roof. I'd passed this property many times, but I'd never realized how big it was, or how beautiful. Beyond the barn a dirt track led farther out, winding into the pasture, where a pond glistened in a low hollow. The dirt track looped down past the pond, then angled up a hillside beyond. The only jarring notes in the whole pastoral, picturesque scene, a mere two miles from the heart of downtown Knoxville, were the black circle of grass and the blue strobes of the unmarked car belonging to Darren Cash, who'd told me where to meet him.

Cranking down my window—the morning was already hot but not yet unbearable—I caught the sweet, dusty fragrance of hay, a welcome change from the chemical fumes that had forced their way into my truck only a few minutes before. I idled past the barn, around the pond, and up the rise toward Cash, taking my time so I could enjoy the view. Cash was half sitting, half leaning on the trunk of his car, his arms folded, his biceps stretching the limits of a navy polo shirt. As I pulled alongside and parked, just outside the scorched circle, Cash used one foot to shove off from the rear wheel, then extended his hand through my open window for me to shake. Now that my engine was off, I could hear the steady whoosh of traffic somewhere through the woods to the north—not loud but surprising, considering I could see no signs of the bypass from here.

"Morning, Doc," Cash said. "Nice place, huh?"

"Very nice," I agreed, clambering out. "I wouldn't mind having a place like this myself."

"Well, it could be coming on the market soon," he said. "If we're smart or lucky."

"How long you been here?"

"About an hour. We were waiting for Latham at the gate down at the bottom of the driveway when he headed for work. He wasn't too happy to see our little caravan."

"Did he go on to work?"

"No way," said Cash. "He's in the house, acting all indignant, watching the evidence techs like a hawk. Trying to figure out what they're looking for."

I studied the burned circle, which measured maybe twenty yards across, then turned and looked back toward the house, which was barely visible. "For a place that's as close to downtown as my house, this is mighty isolated," I said. "I can see why nobody would have just happened by and seen a body in the car."

He nodded. "Latham says she liked to park up here when she wanted to think. Sit and smoke and look at the view."

I gazed out over the farmland. From the rise where we stood, the pasture had lovely views to both the east and the west. "Actually, I'll buy that part of the story," I said. "I'd probably do the same if I owned this chunk of land. Except for the smoking."

"Which Latham mentioned three times in his statement. He actually said, 'It was probably a cigarette butt that caught the grass on fire.' When I read his statement the other day, I could almost feel his elbow nudging me in the ribs every time he mentioned the smoking."

"That's because he thinks cops are dumb," I said. "Wanted to make sure they got it."

"Another interesting thing about this location," said Cash. "Once the car was burning, hundreds of people would have seen the smoke from 640—it's only a quarter mile through those trees. Half a dozen people called 911 to report a fire—which I'm sure he wanted."

"To establish the time of the fire," I said.

"Exactly. The first call came at three fifty-three p.m.—while he was playing the slots in the Bellagio."

Cash led me into the burned circle, pointing out four evidence flags, which indicated where the corners of the vehicle had been. A fifth flag marked the spot where five cigarette butts—almost but not quite consumed by the blaze—had been found below the driver's door. I knelt and inspected that area, seeing nothing but the charred stubble of grass and the thin wire of the evidence flag jammed into the ground.

I pointed back toward where the rear of the vehicle would have been. "Do you remember which side the exhaust pipe was on?"

"The right," he said.

Staying well clear of the imaginary vehicle's boundaries, I walked back to what would have been the vehicle's right rear corner and knelt again. The grass there looked exactly like the grass everywhere else within the circle of burned vegetation. "Any idea where the catalytic converter on a Lexus RX is?"

He shrugged. "Um . . . somewhere between the engine and the end of the tailpipe?"

"No wonder your boss thinks so highly of you," I said. "Every answer at your fingertips. Just like on *CSI*." I dropped to my hands and knees and crawled forward, toward what would have been the center of the vehicle, scanning from side to side as I crept. I wasn't sure what I was looking for, and I wasn't sure what it was when I found it. But it was something.

Cash came to the edge of the rectangle and squatted down, but he couldn't see anything from there.

"I've got a big pair of tweezers in the tackle box in my truck," I said. "You mind going and getting it?"

He didn't answer; he just headed to the truck. He might not know a lot about vehicle exhaust systems, but he was easygoing and he didn't seem overly impressed with his own importance. When he handed me the tweezers, I maneuvered the tips down through the burned stalks of grass, squeezed gently, and plucked out the small black shape that had caught my eye. It was hard, oval—more or less—and pinched in the center. Looking closely, I saw that the pinch in the center was caused by a bit of heavy wire, clamped tight.

I held it out for Cash's inspection. "Any idea what that is?"

"None," he said.

"You think it could be something off the underside of the car? A hose clamp or fuel-line fitting or some such?"

He shrugged once more. "You're asking the guy who had no idea where the catalytic converter would be?"

"You're right." I laughed. "What was I thinking?"

"We could check with the mechanics at the Lexus dealership," he said. "Maybe one of those guys would recognize it."

"See, you come up with a good idea every now and then," I said.

He grinned. "Even a blind squirrel finds some nuts."

Something about the shape was familiar to me. Not the blackened blob but the heavy wire. I couldn't place it, though, and when Cash held out an evidence bag, I deposited my find inside. Cash sealed and dated it, but then his pen hesitated.

"Problem?"

"We have to list everything we confiscate when we return the warrant to the judge," he said. "I've got no idea what to call this."

"Call it 'blackened blob,'" I suggested helpfully.

He shot me an unamused look.

"Or 'unidentified burned object recovered from beneath area of burned car.'"

"That sounds better," he said. "I can see why they think highly of you at UT."

Cash and I both went over the rest of the area beneath and surrounding the car, but neither of us found anything else, so he headed back to the house and I headed for UT. As I'd done on my way in, I drove slowly to savor the view. Just as I was nearing the barn, my peripheral vision snagged on something. I stopped the truck and backed up. About ten feet to the left of the dirt track was a small, neat oval, about one foot by two feet, sketched by scorched earth and burned grass. I got out and knelt, using the tip of a pen to sift through the charred stalks. I found nothing. All the same, I retrieved two evidence flags from the back of my truck. I stuck one right beside the circle and the other ten feet away, at the nearest edge of the dirt track.

As I turned from the driveway onto Middlebrook Pike toward downtown, I phoned Cash on his cell, describing what I'd seen and where to find the markers. "Maybe it's nothing," I said.

"Maybe," he said. "But maybe not."

"Maybe a blind squirrel just found a nut," I said.

CHAPTER 11

I BOUNDED INTO THE BONE LAB JUST BEFORE LUNCH-
time, eager to tell Miranda about my finds at the Latham farm.
She wasn't there.

Normally, unless she was out helping me recover a body or
bones from a death scene or dashing to the Body Farm to deliver
a corpse or retrieve a skeleton, Miranda practically lived in the
osteology lab. I could count on walking in to find her bent over
a lab table, measuring bones and keying the dimensions into the
Forensic Data Bank. Every skeleton we got—and this year we'd
get nearly 150, arriving at the Farm as fully fleshed cadavers and
departing bare-boned—had to be measured, their dozens of dimensions added to the data bank. The work was tedious and
time-consuming, and most of it was done by Miranda. Perhaps
I should have been happy she was getting a brief break, but instead I felt slightly annoyed that she wasn't here to listen.

I glanced at Miranda's computer screen—the scene of so much

Googling—and noticed a map filling the display. It was a street map of Knoxville's North Hills neighborhood, which happened to be Miranda's neighborhood. It struck me as odd that Miranda would need a map of her own neighborhood.

I picked up the phone on the desk and dialed Peggy, one floor up. "Have you seen Miranda this morning?"

"She left about fifteen minutes ago," said Peggy. "Said she was going over to the morgue to use the dissecting microscope there."

"The dissecting 'scope? What for?"

"I didn't ask and she didn't tell," said Peggy. "Just like the military's policy on gays."

"Great," I said, "because hasn't *that* approach worked well."

Peggy's mention of the morgue made me want to tell Garcia about my visit to the Latham farm, too, so instead of dialing the morgue and asking for Miranda or him, I hopped into my truck and dashed across the river to the rear of the hospital. Parking in the no-parking zone by the morgue's loading dock, I punched the code to open the door, crossed the garagelike intake area, and threaded my way down the hall to the microscopy lab. The anthropology department had one dissecting 'scope—a stereoscopic microscope, with a micrometer-adjustable stage—but there was sometimes heavy competition for it, so I could understand why Miranda might have come over to use one of the three here at the morgue. She wasn't in the lab, although I did see her backpack, sitting on a table beside one of the 'scopes. A small, U-shaped bone rested on the stage—a hyoid bone, from a throat—and I guessed Miranda was inspecting it for fractures, possible evidence of strangulation. I flipped on the microscope's lamp and took a quick look myself. The arc of bone was smooth and unbroken, except by the tiny numerals "49-06," inked on the bone in Miranda's neat hand, signifying that the hyoid was from the forty-ninth body back in 2006. Number 49-06 had clearly not been strangled, which was both unsurprising and also somewhat reassuring, since this particular man's body had been donated, if memory served, by his widow.

Figuring maybe Miranda had gone to the restroom, I went down the hall to Edelberto Garcia's office to tell him the latest from the Latham case. His door was half open, so I knocked and leaned my head in.

Garcia was standing behind his desk, Miranda leaning over from the other side. On the desk between them, in a circle of light cast by a lamp, was a piece of paper. Miranda's index finger was tracing a zigzag on the page, which I recognized as a map—the same map I'd seen on her computer monitor. When I walked in, she straightened and removed her hand from the map. She looked embarrassed, and for some reason that made me feel embarrassed, too.

"Oh, excuse me," I said awkwardly. "I didn't mean to interrupt."

"Hello, Bill," said Garcia, making my name rhyme with "wheel." "Come in. You're not interrupting."

But I *was* interrupting, I knew; I just couldn't tell exactly *what* I was interrupting. "I was on my way to the research facility," I said to him, "and I wanted to tell you a couple of new things about the Latham case."

"Yes, please," he said. "What is it?"

I told him about going out to the impound lot with Art and Darren Cash, and finding the bits of newspaper in the backseat. I also told him about my trip to the farm, and about finding the wire-cinched blob of material and the small oval of burned grass.

"That's very interesting," he said. But he didn't seem as interested as I'd hoped he would. And I no longer felt as interested as I'd been when I bounded into the bone lab. I'd wanted to ask Miranda what she made of all of this, since she knew Stuart Latham, but this didn't seem the right time or place. A silence hung in the air.

Finally Garcia said, "Was there anything else, Bill?"

"No," I said, looking from his face to Miranda's, then back again. "That was it. I'll see you later." I withdrew, then leaned partway back in. "Did you want this open or closed?" I heard something in my voice—an undertone of suspicion or hurt feelings—that I didn't much like. I hoped neither of them heard it.

"Oh, open of course," said Garcia smoothly.

I turned and retraced my steps down the hall, past the microscope lab, where Miranda's open backpack still sat. It hadn't moved, but it had changed—the map she was sharing with him had been printed in the bone lab, I felt sure, and brought to Garcia in the backpack. I drove back to the stadium feeling suddenly guilty and afraid. Afraid of what? I couldn't have said, but a series of faces flashed in my mind's eye: Miranda's. Jess's. Garland Hamilton's. Stuart Latham's. Edelberto Garcia's. The faces of women I cared for—and men who threatened them, in reality or in my overactive imagination.

CHAPTER 12

THE STREET SIGN WAS HALF HIDDEN BY AN OVER-
hanging tree branch, which doubtless added greatly to the neighborhood's charm in the daylight but subtracted substantially
from the ease of navigation at night. I flipped the headlights to
high beam, but all that did was intensify the shadow on the sign.

I had located North Hills Boulevard without any trouble. A
large subdivision sign, thoughtfully placed down at headlight
level, marked the neighborhood's entrance off Washington Pike.
North Hills was one of three Knoxville "Hills" neighborhoods
dating back to the 1920s. Sequoyah Hills, where I had managed
to find an affordable ranch house amid million-dollar mansions,
sprawled along one bank of the Tennessee River, a few miles
west of downtown and UT. Holston Hills, on the city's east side,
flanked the Holston River, just upstream from the field where
Miranda and I had burned the cars.

North Hills lacked the river frontage and the country clubs

sported by Sequoyah and Holston, but it did not lack for charm. A broad median divided the boulevard winding into the neighborhood, giving the area the feeling of a park. In springtime the emerald grass of the median and the yards that lined it blazed with dogwoods and redbuds and azaleas. But this year's blossoms had shriveled three months earlier, and the summer's heat—and the ban on lawn watering that the drought had made necessary for the past two weeks—had scorched the grass to a pale, crumbling tan. The trees still clung to life and greenness, but it was a dry and desperate shade of green.

The houses were smaller here, tending more toward cottages than mansions, so the neighborhood had remained relatively affordable—the biggest house in North Hills would probably sell for half what a similar place in Sequoyah would fetch. Even so, it would have been a huge stretch for Miranda to afford a house in North Hills. I doubted that her assistantship would cover the monthly mortgage, let alone a down payment. But then again, I realized, her family might have helped her buy a house. Or she might be renting. Or she might have roommates. Or a partner. There was a lot about Miranda's personal life I didn't know—almost everything about it, in fact. Was that because I respected her privacy, or was it because I was uncaring and selfish, interested only in the forty or fifty or even sixty hours of work she did for me every week? But if I didn't care, what was I doing here at nine o'clock at night, trying to find her house in the maze of darkened streets?

I was snooping, that's what I was doing, and the realization shamed me, making me feel like a stalker or a thief.

As I strained to make out the name on the street sign, a car rounded the curve in the boulevard and stopped behind me. Cursing mildly, I rolled forward a few feet and cut the wheel to the right, pulling far enough out of the lane for the car to squeeze past me, and stuck my arm out the window to wave it past. Once the taillights disappeared around the curve, I opened the glove box, took out a flashlight, and aimed it at the green sign. "Kenilworth" was the word I was looking for, but according to the white letters on the sign to my left, Maxwell Street was the name of the cross street, and if I continued straight ahead, I would henceforth be on Fountain Park Boulevard. So what had become of North Hills Boulevard, which had begun with such elegance and promise? Ah, finally, I saw that North Hills took a turn to the right, stealing the thunder of poor little Maxwell Street. I appeared to be at the intersection of North Hills Boulevard and North Hills Boulevard, but how could that be? Confused, I shone the light on the map I'd printed before leaving campus for the day—the very map I'd seen on Miranda's computer and Garcia's desk.

Even though I'd worked closely with Miranda for four years now—and even though I'd sometimes wondered whether there might be more between us than academic collegiality—I'd never been to her house. I knew where she lived, since her address was on file in the department and her assistantship checks were mailed to her house. But anytime we went out on a case together—even once when a body was found less than a mile from her neighborhood—she arranged to meet me at UT. Was there something about me that worried her, that made her guard her boundaries against me? Or was she just one of those people who like to keep work and home completely separate from one another? Probably not the sort of thing I could ask her about, at least not without trespassing in the very manner she was trying to discourage.

I wasn't sure what it was that had bothered me when I'd walked into Garcia's office earlier: the mere fact that she'd handed him the map or the fact that when I walked in, Garcia had folded the map and changed the subject. I'd tried to forget about it, but it nagged at me, like a shred of steak snagged between two teeth. Was it possible that Miranda was getting romantically involved with Garcia? He was handsome, I had to admit, and he seemed smooth and quietly confident. But he had been here for only a matter of weeks. And I was virtually certain I had seen a wedding ring on his left hand.

It's not your business! I shouted at myself. *You're right, it's not,* I answered . . . and then I bent over the map for a closer look. Kenilworth was two blocks beyond this odd corner, where the asphalt straight ahead changed names to Fountain Park; staying on North Hills Boulevard required taking a right. *Jess was killed by a medical examiner,* I added in my own defense to myself. *I know, I know, it was a different medical examiner—a crazy medical examiner. But still, I think I'm entitled to a little paranoia. So could you please cut me some slack here?*

Rightly or wrongly, I cut myself some slack, turned onto North Hills, Part B, and then onto Kenilworth, Miranda's street. Now I was looking for house numbers, and reading house numbers in the dark made reading the street signs seem like a walk in the park. How in the world did police and firefighters find the correct house during an emergency at night? A mental cartoon flashed into my head—a sort of *Far Side* image of firefighters shining a flashlight beam on the numbers on a dark doorpost while flames roar out of the house next door—and I laughed in spite of the complicated and guilty feelings swirling around my clandestine visit to Miranda's neighborhood.

Midway down the block, I glimpsed her white VW Jetta parked in the driveway of a gray bungalow. A yellow vehicle was parked behind the Jetta, and I was startled when I realized it was another Nissan Pathfinder—or the same one I'd seen parked beside the Lathams' farmhouse. I felt a pang of fear, or jealousy, or dread, or shame, or some mixture of them all. I cut the headlights, coasted to the curb just beyond the house, and sat there for a moment. Then I got out, eased the door shut, and walked back toward the driveway. Golden light was spilling from every window on the front and side of the house; the place looked warm and inviting, and a chorus of crickets and katydids sang the praises of cozy domesticity.

I heard the low murmur of voices, then a peal of laughter—Miranda's laugh, floating above the song of the bugs—and then a lower, deeper laugh. The laughter seemed to be coming from the side of the house, and I edged down the driveway, alongside the Pathfinder, toward the lighted windows. As I got closer, I found myself looking into the kitchen. Miranda sat at the table, chatting between bites of food. Eddie Garcia sat catty-corner from her, on her right, smiling and nodding. Then Garcia turned his head away from Miranda and spoke. I heard another voice—another female voice—and a dark-haired woman appeared behind him, holding a dark-haired baby on her hip. Garcia beamed and reached up, taking the baby from her. He nuzzled its cheek, then nibbled at its ear, and I heard the pure melody of baby laughter. Miranda spoke softly, and Garcia handed the baby to her. She sat the child on the edge of the kitchen table, her hands encircling its chest and tucked beneath its arms, and leaned her face close. I caught snatches of her voice, the gentle singsong of baby talk. Miranda looked radiant, and the baby grinned, and Garcia and his wife beamed proudly, and I felt a wave of sadness and loneliness and shame crash over me.

CHAPTER 13

I STILL FELT CAUGHT IN THE SAME UNDERTOW OF feelings the next morning when I walked into the bone lab and saw Miranda poring over brochures extolling the virtues of metal knees and ceramic hips. She glanced up, but only briefly. "I think you should have one of each kind implanted," she said. "Metal bearings on the left side, ceramic on the right. Make a personal investment in your research."

I pointed to a flyer from Smith & Nephew, one of the titans of the artificial-joint industry, and tapped on the word "Oxinium," the company's trademarked name for oxidized zirconium. The term sounded high-tech and exotic—not hokey, the way "cremains" did. Smith & Nephew had probably paid millions for focus-group research on various names for the material, which the brochure said combined the toughness of metal with the hardness and smoothness of ceramics. "I'd rather have Oxinium everywhere."

"Can't," she said. "It's not in the budget."

"Darn. I suppose as Phase Two of the research project you'll be wanting to cremate me?"

"Of course," she said. "It's essential." She paused ever so briefly. "Oh, I had Dr. Garcia and his family over for dinner last night," she said casually.

"That was nice of you." I kept my eyes on the photos of gleaming Oxinium joint surfaces.

"Carmen, his wife, is really funny—she's like this over-the-top, self-mocking version of the fiery Latina. She acts out the stereotype, and then she steps back from it and laughs at herself. She's like a surfer, zipping up and down the face of a giant wave." She smiled. "And their baby—that has *got* to be the world's cutest baby."

"Make you want to have one?"

She looked at me sharply. "Good God, no," she said. "Made me want to babble for an hour or two a week, though. I made them promise to let me baby-sit every Thursday night." She straightened the stack of brochures. "You weren't over in North Hills last night by any chance, were you?"

"Me? What would I be doing in North Hills?" My question wasn't a lie, exactly, but it sure wasn't the truth.

"I don't know. I just wondered." Did Miranda have ESP? Was she that attuned to me? "I went out to pick some mint for the tea, and I heard a car start up. Then a truck like yours did a U-turn and drove past."

"Huh," I said as casually as I could. "Lot of trucks like mine in Knoxville."

"Guess so. I called your name—I was going to invite you to come in and join us. You'd have enjoyed it."

"Maybe we can all get together sometime," I told her. *Serves you right,* I told myself. "Listen," I said, retreating to a safer ground, "I could use your computer-research skills on something."

"Shoot."

"I'm trying to get in touch with the Trinity Crematorium, which is somewhere near Rock Spring, in northwest Georgia. It's the place where Burt DeVriess's aunt was sent to be cremated."

"Did you call 411?"

"I did. There's no listing for them."

"Hmm. That seems odd, unless they're trying to run themselves out of business."

"It gets odder. Guy who runs it is named Littlejohn." I'd gotten the name from Helen Taylor, who'd all but spit when she said it.

"Little John? Like Robin Hood's sidekick?"

"That's his last name, not two names. First name is Delbert."

"Delbert—that's odd, all right."

"Let me finish," I said, relieved that she was back in bantering mode. "Delbert Littlejohn has an unlisted number."

"Ooh, I like this," she said. "It smacks of skullduggery."

"What is skullduggery anyhow? I've heard the word tossed around," I said, "but I've never been sure what it means. Something to do with digging up skulls, I reckon, but what? And how come it's 'duggery,' not 'diggery,' or even 'digging'?"

"What do I look like," she said, "The Oxford English Dictionary?" She swiveled her chair around to face the desk, and her fingers played a fast sonata on the computer's keyboard. "Hmm," she said. "Bizarrely, it has nothing to do with either skulls or digging. According to Dictionary.com, the word comes from an obscure Scottish obscenity meaning 'fornication,' and it means 'trickery' or 'deception.' Both of which, I suppose, are often involved in fornication."

"So young, and yet so cynical," I said.

"I've always been precocious."

"*Any*way," I said, "back to the question at hand. You reckon you could bang around on those keys some more and find out how I could reach this mysterious Mr. Littlejohn, so I can ask him a few questions about Aunt Jean?"

"Shucks, I reckon," she mocked. "I'll call you when I get something. Or when I strike out."

"You never strike out," I said. By the time the door whammed shut behind me, the keys were already clattering.

MY OFFICE phone rang an hour later. Miranda had dug deep into her bag of Google tricks without finding any trace of Trinity Crematorium. She'd also tried AnyWho.com and MapQuest, she said, in a vain effort to track down an address or phone number. "And I'm sure you'll be shocked, shocked, to know that Rock Spring, Georgia, doesn't have an online database of property-tax records." She'd hit a stone wall with the records clerk in the county courthouse but finally hit pay dirt by calling the post office and pretending to be a UPS driver in need of help finding the Littlejohn house. "And," she announced triumphantly, "I got a phone number."

"Miranda," I said, "you are a Jedi master of skullduggery."

But if I thought my quest was over, I was wrong. When I dialed the number she gave me, a machine answered. There was no greeting or announcement, just a beep. I hadn't mentally prepared a message, so I hung up. After collecting my thoughts, I called back, ready to say who I was and simply ask for a return call. Once again I was taken by surprise. "Hello," said a flat, guarded male voice.

"Oh, hello," I said. "Is this Delbert Littlejohn?"

There was a pause. "He's not available right now. Who's this?"

"My name is Dr. Bill Brockton," I began. "I'm a forensic an-thropologist at the University of Tennessee. I've been asked to take a look at some cremains that came from your crematorium—a Tennessee woman named Jean DeVriess. I'm hoping—"

The line went dead. I hit redial, and I got the machine again. I hung up and tried again; again I got the machine. This time I left my name and number. I called once more, and this time the line was busy—or the phone was off the hook.

My next call was to Burt DeVriess. I told Burt about Miranda's near-fruitless research and my unsuccessful phone calls. "This smacks of skullduggery," I said in conclusion. I liked the way it sounded; I could see why Miranda had grinned as she'd said it.

"You're right," he said, "sounds like this place is screwing people over."

Damn, I thought, *how'd he know that?*

"You willing to keep digging, Doc? Or duggering, or what-ever?"

"Keep digging *how*, Burt?"

"Hell, I don't know, Doc—you're the one who's the forensic genius. Maybe go down there, poke around some, see what you stir up?"

I considered the request. I could make a six-hour round-trip to the boonies of Georgia, not knowing if I'd fare any better in per-

son than I'd fared on the phone . . . or I could sit around Knoxville waiting for the phone to ring with news about the search for
Garland Hamilton.

"I'll go dugger around," I said.

"Might be a good idea to take somebody with you," he said.

"I hadn't thought of that," I said, "but Miranda might find it
interesting."

"I was thinking maybe somebody who could watch your
back," he said.

"You're thinking it might be dangerous?"

"You never know," he said, "seeing as how it smacks of skullduggery and all."

ART DIDN'T hesitate when I asked if he'd be willing to accom-
pany me to Georgia. "When you want to go?"

"Whenever you can," I said. "I was supposed to be testifying
this week at Garland Hamilton's trial, but that particular engage-
ment seems to have been postponed for now. And UT doesn't
start fall classes for another couple weeks. How short a leash are
you on with this Internet assignment?"

"If we left early in the morning and could get back by late
afternoon, I can probably swing it," he said. "The chat rooms
don't start heating up till around three or four, and they stay
pretty lively till bedtime. Tiffany needs to be in school all day
anyhow—that's where innocent little fourteen-year-olds are supposed to be between eight and three-thirty. Unless it's the weekend, and then they're sleeping late."

"Tomorrow?"

"Tomorrow," he said.

"How 'bout I pick you up around six-thirty? That would put us down there around eight."

"How 'bout five-thirty," he said, "so we've got time to grab breakfast at a Cracker Barrel down Chattanooga way?"

"Deal," I said. "I'll buy."

"I think your buddy Grease should pick up the tab."

"You're right," I agreed. "Grease'll buy."

"Be good for you to get out of town for a day," he said, "and away from the Hamilton stuff."

He was right about that, too.

CHAPTER 14

FRIDAY MORNING DAWNED HOT AND BRIGHT, AND BY the time it dawned, Art and I had been on the road for an hour already. At seven we bailed off the interstate at the Ooltewah exit, about ten miles north of Chattanooga. The acres of asphalt outside Cracker Barrel were virtually empty.

"This parking lot is nearly as big as Neyland Stadium's," I said.

"An hour from now, it'll be full," said Art. "You'd have to wait thirty minutes to get a table."

"I wouldn't," I said.

"Wouldn't have to?"

"Wouldn't wait," I clarified. "I love the food here. Great breakfast, great vegetables. But I'm not willing to wait half an hour to get it."

"Me neither," said Art. "I might be, though, if they'd ever get the biscuits right."

"You're boycotting them over their biscuits?"

"Not boycotting, exactly," he said, "but less likely to fight the crowd on account of 'em. You'd think a place that prides itself on southern country cooking would make a decent biscuit, but theirs are sorry. Heavy and doughy, too much baking powder, or maybe they're even using Bisquick. The ones at Hardee's are ten times better. Golden and crispy on the outside, light as air on the inside."

"Hardee's does make a better biscuit," I agreed. "We should point that out to Cracker Barrel. In the spirit of constructive criticism, of course."

"I have," he squawked. "I do. Every blessed time I eat at a Cracker Barrel, I fill out one of those customer-comment cards. 'Your biscuits are sorry,' I say."

"That's your idea of constructive criticism?"

"It gets more constructive after that. 'Make better biscuits,' I tell 'em. 'Hire a biscuit maker from Hardee's.' You'd think they'd get the message. But they never do—not unless they've been hiring folks from Hardee's and then making them follow the same sorry Cracker Barrel biscuit recipe. I've pretty much given up now. Always get the corn muffins instead."

"The corn muffins aren't bad," I said.

"They're not," he said, "but at breakfast you really want a good biscuit. And anyhow, you'd think—"

"Yeah, you'd think," I said. "This world is a vale of tears, Art—rife with injustice and disappointment."

"And sorry biscuits," he said.

The peach pancakes were delicious, and the smoked sausage was worth every deadly glob of cholesterol. But I couldn't help wishing for a decent biscuit, soaked in butter and honey, for dessert. I reached for the customer-comment card and wrote. Art did the same.

AFTER CLIMBING East Ridge and dropping down into the broad valley that cradled Chattanooga, we took the Rossville Boulevard exit and headed south on U.S. 27, through the town of Fort Oglethorpe and then the well-tended lawns and woods of Chickamauga Battlefield, where the Army of the Confederacy had won a stunning victory, only to lose the bigger prizes of Chattanooga and then Atlanta not long afterward. South of Chickamauga the highway ran mostly straight and flat through stretches of pinewoods and pastures, punctuated by service stations, hair salons, and Baptist churches. We passed the crossroads of East Turnipseed and West Turnipseed roads, and a few miles beyond those we turned off the highway onto the blacktop road Miranda had marked on the map. The road was a lane and a half wide, with no centerline. Art and I both watched for a crematorium sign, but there wasn't any. When we got to the end of the road, I knew we'd missed it. I turned and retraced the blacktop route, partly because I was determined to find the place and partly because there was no other way back to civilization.

About a quarter mile after doubling back, I saw a gravel driveway on the left. The drive was blocked with a metal farm gate, the kind that resembles a ladder that's four feet high and ten feet wide, the rungs made of tubular galvanized steel. A stout chain and padlock fastened the gate to a fat wooden fence post. A battered mailbox was nailed to the top of the post, and when I looked closely, I made out the name Littlejohn in small, hand-painted letters.

Fastened to the posts at both ends of the gate were large No Trespassing signs. Underneath each of those was another sign, adding Private Property. Under each of those was one that ordered Keep Out.

"Not a very welcoming establishment," I said to Art.

I pulled the truck onto the shoulder of the road, not that there was much risk of traffic, as best I could tell. Art and I clambered out and stood at the gate, peering down a tunnel of trees and underbrush lining the gravel drive. We could see about fifty yards down the narrow drive before it entered a gradual curve and the view was blocked by a wall of trees. I listened for sounds of human activity, but all I could hear was the chittering of cicadas in the summer heat.

"Hello," I called, tentatively at first. When I got no answer, I called again, louder. "Hello there. Can you hear me? Anybody there?" Still no response. I tried once more, this time at the top of my lungs. Nothing. I went to the truck, leaned in the open window, and honked the horn three times. I waited a minute, then laid on it awhile.

"I could be wrong," said Art finally, "but I'm thinking either they're not home or they don't want to be disturbed."

"Could be they're deaf," I said. I studied the six signs posted on either side of the gate. All six encouraged me not to enter the property, but I'd driven three hours to get here and I was seeking answers to what I considered disturbing questions. I looked at Art. "Shall we?"

"Age before beauty," he said, waving me toward the gate. Using the bars of the gate as a ladder, I climbed over, turned around, and descended the other side.

My foot had scarcely touched the ground when I heard a low

snarling sound. I spun. Rocketing down the driveway toward me, mouth agape and teeth bared, was the biggest, meanest-looking pit bull I'd ever seen. He moved remarkably fast for such a big animal, and I found myself moving with surprising swiftness, too, back up the bars of the gate, over the top, and down the other side. I'd just removed my hands from the top bar when a pair of jaws snapped shut like a bear trap, an inch away from my fingers. The dog was too big to get more than his muzzle through the bars, but that didn't stop him from lunging and snapping. I remembered a documentary I'd seen once on Animal Planet, in which a shark attacked the bars of a protective cage so ferociously that it gradually began bending the bars aside, nearly consuming the human quivering inside. Fortunately, this gate was made of sterner stuff; it rattled and strained against the chain, but it held.

Eventually the dog's fury subsided a bit, but not the sense of menace it conveyed, and I decided we'd reached an impasse. I suspected that someone had let him out in response to my honking and calling, since he'd probably have arrived considerably sooner if he'd already been outdoors on guard duty. "Well, I guess that's that," I said. "Sorry we made the trip for nothing." I fished out my handkerchief and mopped my face and neck. Some of the sweat probably came from the adrenaline rush the dog had provoked, but the morning was already remarkably hot. "Let's stop at the nearest gas station and get a cold drink."

Just as I said it, I felt the air stir a bit, whispering from the south—from the woods inside the fence. When it did, I caught a whiff of something familiar, and for a moment I thought I'd had some lapse in consciousness—a blackout that had lasted until I was back in Knoxville, back behind the UT Medical Center. When I realized my mistake, the hairs on my arms and my neck stood up, and I felt a jolt like electricity shoot through me. I was inhaling the stench of death—wholesale human death, Body Farm scale of death—not in Tennessee but here in Georgia, as it drifted lazily across the gate of the Trinity Crematorium.

CHAPTER 15

"I THINK HIS BARK IS WORSE THAN HIS BITE," ART said. He took a step toward the gate, and the dog lunged at him, roaring and snapping.

"*I* think we can't afford to test your theory," I said.

"You're right," he said. He bent down and fiddled with the left leg of his pants, and when he straightened up, I saw a gun in his right hand. He squatted down and aimed through the bars of the gate. "Jesus, Art, you can't just shoot—" I began, but then I saw his finger twitch. Instead of a bang, I heard a loud click; for an instant I thought the gun had misfired, but then the dog crumpled to a twitching heap in the gravel. A pair of thin wires ran from the dog's body back to the barrel of the weapon.

"What the hell . . . ?!"

"Taser," said Art. "Think of me as Captain Kirk from *Star Trek,* with my phaser set to stun."

I stared at the dog sprawled out in the road. "You sure you had that on stun?"

He glanced down at the Taser, which had a fat, round barrel, black with yellow markings—like some high-voltage yellow jacket. "Oops," he said, then, "No, just kidding. It's always on stun. Fifty thousand volts' worth of stun."

"How long will he be out?"

"Don't know," said Art. "Never used one on a dog before. Ten, fifteen minutes, maybe." He scaled the gate and dropped to the other side. "You coming?"

"Isn't he gonna come after us again when he wakes up?"

"Only if he's a really dumb dog," Art chuckled. "And if he does, I've got fifty more shots." He frowned. "Of course, having fired my one set of barbs, I have to actually hold this gizmo against him for the next fifty shots. If he hasn't learned by then, he's got big problems."

"If he comes after us fifty-one more times, we've got bigger problems than he does," I reasoned.

"If he comes after us fifty-one times, we switch to Plan B," Art said, patting his right ankle. He sniffed the air, like a hound seeking a rabbit. "Any guess where that aroma's coming from?"

"Seems like the breeze is blowing from over that way," I said, pointing slightly to the left of the gravel road, on a tangent that would take us into the woods.

"Let's go," he said. "I hope you put on tick repellent before you left home."

"I did," I said. "Did you?"

"Oops," he said again, scratching his left thigh.

The going was slow at first, as we had to tread and trample our way through a tangle of blackberry bushes lining the road.

The leaves hung heavy and orange, laden with dust from the road. Here and there I spotted shriveled berries. "Too bad we weren't here six weeks ago," I said. "This is a pretty good patch. We could've picked enough for a cobbler."

"Maybe if we make friends with the people who own that nice doggy," Art said, "they'll let us come back next year, during blackberry season."

Once we were beneath the shade of the forest canopy, the blackberries ended and the underbrush thinned, leaving us in a pine thicket with widely spaced trunks and a carpet of needles on the floor.

About a hundred yards in, I glimpsed what looked to be a narrow dirt track bulldozed through the woods. I touched Art's arm and nodded in its direction. He changed course, heading for it at a brisk stride, and I followed. When we reached it, I saw multiple sets of tracks, some made by rubber tires, others by a tracked vehicle—a bulldozer or Bobcat. I looked in both directions and spied a rusting bulldozer tucked into a gap in the trees. Just beyond it, half hidden by the yellow dozer, I saw the boxy back end of a black vehicle. I pointed.

"Is that what I think it is?" Art asked.

"If you think it's a hearse," I said.

We passed the dozer, and sure enough, tucked in beside it was a black Cadillac hearse. I'd seen a lot of hearses in my day, but this one was the only one I'd ever seen that was covered with dust and pocked with rust. All four tires were flat, and the windows were nearly opaque with grime.

I waved off a fly that was buzzing around my head, and then another, and another. I noticed Art swatting the air, too. Then I noticed that the entire vehicle was surrounded by flies. I walked to the back of the vehicle, leaned close, and took a sniff, and when I did, I knew what the flies had come for. I tried the latch on the back door, found it unlocked, and pulled it open. The opening door unleashed a wave of odor so strong it almost knocked me down, carried on the wings of thousands of blowflies. Inside the back of the hearse, stacked one atop the other, were half a dozen decaying corpses.

The bodies on the bottom were virtually skeletonized; the ones on top still had tissue on the bones, and I knew—in this heat, with all these flies—that the uppermost bodies couldn't have been here nearly as long as the hearse had been collecting dust and rust and blowflies. They had to be recent additions. Beneath the bodies the floor of the hearse glistened with black, greasy goo, the volatile fatty acids leaching out of the bodies as they decomposed. A writhing mass of maggots covered the entire mess.

Art had stepped away from the vehicle as soon as I opened it, and as the fumes roiled out, he continued to backpedal. "Woof," he said. "I guess we know now what we were smelling, huh?"

"I guess so," I said, but then an unsettling thought occurred to me. "Actually, I'm not so sure." He looked puzzled. "This is part of what we smelled," I explained, "but I don't see how this could account for all the smell. The vehicle was closed, right?" He nodded uneasily. "And we didn't notice a lot of odor till I opened it."

"So you think there's another body or two up near to the edge of the property?"

"Maybe," I said. "Let's see where this bulldozer track leads."

Beyond the hearse the dirt track sliced through the woods toward where I guessed the house or the crematorium might be. I headed the opposite way. Before long I got another whiff of decomposition coming from somewhere ahead. I followed my nose along the red-dirt road, and in less than a minute, in an area where the road ended in a broader circle, I walked into the most surreal scene of my life.

It was as if I'd stumbled into a massacre from Bosnia or Rwanda or Iraq—someplace where ethnic cleansing or mass murder had been unleashed. Bodies—dozens of bodies—lay half hidden in the woods on either side of the bulldozed circle. Some were partially buried in trenches; others were tucked behind trees; still others lay beneath bulldozed brush piles.

"This is very, *very* creepy," said Art.

"If we were anyplace other than the grounds of a crematorium," I said, "I'd swear we'd just discovered the world's worst serial killer. Instead I'm thinking we just discovered the world's worst crematorium."

Some of the corpses were missing arms and legs, and I noticed that a number of the long bones had been reduced to shafts, their ends gnawed away. A few of the bodies were nude, but most wore the tattered remains of what appeared to be church clothes. Funeral clothes. Art and I did a quick count of the bodies ranged around the circle. He counted eighty-six; I counted eighty-eight.

"You think this is it," he asked, "or do you want to look around some more?"

"What difference would it make," I said, "if we found ten or twenty or even fifty more? Let's get out of here while the getting's good."

Art nodded, and we began retracing our steps back through the woods. We were picking our way through the blackberry bushes when I heard a dog baying somewhere down the gravel drive. Then I heard a chorus of baying, from a chorus of dogs.

"I think the getting just got less good," said Art.

We tore through the blackberry bushes and sprinted up the gravel driveway, clearing the gate just as a pack of dogs leaped against the inside of the bars. Art fished the Taser from his left ankle and handed it to me, then pulled a pistol from his right ankle. "Press the end against the dog and hold the trigger for two seconds," he said, without offering any guidance on how to persuade the dog not to rip my throat out during those two seconds. It was difficult to be sure, for all the leaping and lunging, but I counted seven or eight dogs. If they all managed to leap the gate, either Art or I would be dog food. But the dogs stayed on the inside, milling and snarling. We got into the truck and hightailed it for U.S. 27. It wasn't until we'd reached the Tennessee border that either of us spoke.

"I guess we should call the law," said Art.

"You _are_ the law," I pointed out. "Didn't they make you a U.S. marshal when you started tracking down Internet predators?"

"They did," he said, "but I've only got arrest powers in Tennessee."

"Well, damn," I said. "You reckon we can persuade Mr. Littlejohn to haul those bodies across the state line so you can arrest him?"

"Brilliant idea," he said. "I'll let you be the one to climb back over that gate, make friends with the nice doggies, and present that plan." He flipped open his cell phone. "I think it's time to call the friendly neighborhood sheriff."

"Wait a second," I said. "What if Littlejohn's in cahoots with the friendly neighborhood sheriff? Remember Cooke County." Art and I had nearly perished in the mountainous county, not once but twice, both times at the hands of corrupt sheriff's deputies. "If the sheriff's in this guy's pocket, we'd just be giving him a heads-up."

"O ye of little faith," Art said. "Seriously, what do you suggest?"

"I don't know yet; let me sleep on it," I said. "All those folks are already dead. They're not going to get any deader if we wait twenty-four hours before we call the law."

We rode the rest of the way back to Knoxville in silence.

AFTER I DROPPED Art at KPD headquarters, I called Jeff's house. Jenny answered the phone. "Hey," I said, "mind if I invite myself over again?"

"I'd mind if you didn't," she said. "Jeff's coaching Walker's T-ball practice right now, and I'm dashing to pick up Tyler from *his* baseball practice, but we'll all be back under one roof in half an hour. I hope."

"How 'bout I pick up some Buddy's barbecue?"

"You willing to bring some coleslaw and potato salad and baked beans to the table, too? Oh, and a bag of ice?"

"You drive a hard bargain," I said, "but okay, deal."

"What about some batter-dipped, deep-fried corn on the cob?"

"They have deep-fried corn on the cob at Buddy's?"

"Tragically, no," she said. "Only at Sullivan's in Rocky Hill. Breaks my heart I can't get it anywhere out this way. My consumption's fallen way off since we moved to Farragut."

"I'm not sure I believe in deep-fried corn on the cob," I said. "Sounds like gilding the lily to me."

"You've never had it?"

"Not that I can remember."

"If you'd had it, you'd definitely remember," she said. "It's practically a religious experience. Better than sex."

"Remind me to have a talk with Jeff," I said. "Sounds like he could use some pointers."

"He does all right," she said. "But deep-fried corn—that's some pretty stiff competition."

"No pun intended, I hope."

She laughed. "No pun intended."

"Seriously, you've got a desperate craving for fried corn?"

"I do," she said. "But it wouldn't be good by the time you got out here with it. It's gotta be fresh from the grease, so the batter's still crunchy."

"Sounds like you've made a careful study of this," I said.

"I have done *years* of research on Sullivan's deep-fried corn," she said. "I should have a Ph.D. in food science, I've done so much research. I've probably eaten my weight in deep-fried corn by now. That's one reason I still run—to burn off the calories. Otherwise I'd weigh four hundred pounds by now."

"Who knew?" I said. "I'll give it a try."

"It will change your life," she said. "Take me with you when you go. I want to see the look on your face when you taste it for the first time."

"You'll be sitting right across the table when that hot grease scorches my lips," I said.

"Promise?"

"Promise."

An hour later Jeff and Jenny's kitchen was a debris field. The pine trestle table and the tiled floor beneath were strewn with sandwich wrappers, plastic forks, soggy Chinet plates, spilled drinks, melting ice, and stray bits of food: pulled pork, slaw, potato salad, and baked beans. The only thing missing was a pile of ragged corncobs. "Looks like somebody had a food fight in here," I said.

"Doesn't take long to demolish dinner after ball practice," said Jeff.

"I can't imagine what it's going to be like when they're both teenagers," said Jenny. "We'll probably need to contract with a wholesale food distributor to keep them fed."

After dinner the boys spun off to watch a Disney movie before baths and bedtime. As the sounds of singing squirrels and chipmunks wafted through from the living room, I described what Art and I had seen in the Georgia woods earlier in the day. Jeff and Jenny stared in astonishment.

"Did you call the cops yet?" Jeff asked.

"Not yet," I said. "I'm not sure which cops to call, or even what crime's been committed—if any. I don't think it's murder. Maybe just first-degree sorriness."

"Isn't there some law against desecrating corpses?" asked Jenny.

"There is," I said, "but I don't know if dumping them in the woods counts as desecrating them. I'll call Grease—I mean, Mr. DeVriess—first thing Monday morning. He's the one who got me into this, and he's a lawyer. Maybe he can help me figure out what to do."

A short time and some chitchat later, I headed home to bed, feeling more connected with the world of the living than I'd felt twelve hours before, surrounded by corpses in the Georgia woods.

But I hadn't reckoned on what awaited me in my house: emptiness and the looming menace of Garland Hamilton. Nature really does abhor a vacuum, and it wasn't long before the voids in my house and my heart began to fill with sadness, loneliness, fear, and regrets.

I wasn't sure that I could have lived my life any differently or altered its main events. But I was pretty sure I could have stayed with Jeff and Jenny another hour or two. And I was pretty sure that would've been better than this.

CHAPTER 16

"GOOD MORNING," CHIRPED THE VOICE AT THE OTHER end of the phone. "Mr. DeVriess's office."

"Good morning, Chloe. It's Dr. Brockton."

"Hi there. How was your weekend?"

"Let's call it interesting," I said. "Very interesting. How was yours?"

"Also interesting," she said. "I tried speed dating."

"Speed dating? What's that?"

"You sign up and go meet a bunch of other people who are looking to meet Mr. or Ms. Right, and you spend five minutes apiece interviewing a bunch of them."

"Five minutes? And the point of that is what, exactly?"

"It gives you a chance to see whether you like somebody, without the pressure of a fix-up or an actual date," she said. "Actually being out with them, you know? If you like them, you give them your phone number. If you don't, you say, 'Nice to meet you,' you shake their hand, and you move on."

"What if they give you their phone number and you don't really want it?"

"Then you toss it in the trash when you get home," she said.

"What if they ask for your number and you don't want to give it to them?"

"Then you smile sweetly and say, 'I don't think so.' Look, I didn't say it was the perfect system," she said. "I only said it was interesting."

"Just curious." I laughed. "And did you meet the future Mr. Right?"

"As if," she said, which I took to mean she hadn't. "But I did meet a guy who could be Mr. Right Now. A guy who might be a good movie buddy till the real deal comes along."

"Speed dating," I marveled. "It's a whole new world out there. Any old coots like me shuffling amidst the speed daters?"

"Ha—you will *never* be an old coot," she said. "But it did tend to be a youngish crowd. Which is not to say you shouldn't try it."

"Me? I don't think so, Chloe. I'm just curious about the anthropology of it," I said.

"Well, then you should sign up sometime and go study the phenomenon firsthand."

"Maybe I will," I said. "Could I talk to Burt?"

"Sorry, he's not here—he'll be in court all day. His first trial in a month. If it's urgent, I can try to get him a message, though."

"No, I reckon it's not urgent," I said. "They're not going to get any deader."

"Excuse me?"

"Sorry, Chloe, just talking to myself there. I was going to ask his advice on something, but I'll figure it out myself."

After I hung up and thought awhile, I opened my address book to the section headed "F" and dialed another call.

"Hello, you've reached the Federal Bureau of Investigation, Knoxville Division," announced the woman's voice in my ear. "If you know your party's extension, you can dial it at any time." I did not know my party's extension, so I pressed 2, then punched in P, R, I, and C.

"This is Special Agent Price." I tried to recall her first name from our meetings about official corruption in Cooke County—not that I would ever be on a first-name basis with Price, who was a study in cool, brisk efficiency. Andrea? No, not Andrea, but something along those lines.

"Hello there, Special Agent Price. This is Dr. Bill Brockton, from UT."

"Ah, Dr. Brockton. Are you calling to plead guilty to gambling on cockfights, Dr. Brockton?"

I laughed. "Not exactly." Price had sent an undercover FBI agent to gather evidence against a massive cockfighting operation in Cooke County the prior year. Quite by accident, I had found myself an inadvertent spectator as the roosters battled to their bloody deaths. During my brief glimpse at the seamy subculture of cockfighting, I had nearly thrown up on Price's undercover agent. "I admit to second-degree spectating and first-degree nausea, but I did not gamble."

"You sound like Bill Clinton talking about marijuana," she said. "Or sex. What can I do for you, Dr. Brockton?"

"How much do you know about cremation?"

"Do you need help figuring out your funeral arrangements? Or is this a quiz?"

She sounded edgy and tough. Not a bad quality in a federal agent, I realized. "Sorry," I said. "I'm not trying to be cryptic. Suppose there were a crematorium that wasn't doing its job." I paused. She waited. I paused some more. Finally she gave up, unwilling to waste any more time.

"Wasn't doing its job? What does that mean?"

"Well, what's a crematorium's job?"

"Incinerating bodies," she snapped. "What's your point here, Doctor? This is what you mean by trying not to be cryptic?"

"Sorry," I said again. "I'm just in a slightly delicate position here." I was trying to figure out whether I needed to protect the confidentiality of information I had gained on behalf of a client, which is what Burt DeVriess was in this case, since it was his Aunt Jean's cremains that had motivated my trip to Georgia.

"Dr. Brockton, please tell me you haven't stumbled into one of our undercover investigations again."

"If I had," I countered, "how would I know? As you've seen, I'm not too good at spotting your undercover agents."

"True. But let's cut to the chase, Doctor. Are you calling to report a federal crime?"

"I'm not sure," I said, "but I think so. If a crematorium is paid to burn bodies, and if the bodies don't get burned, that would be a breach of contract, right?"

"Breach of contract or fraud, probably."

"And if they're doing business over the phone with people in several states—say, Tennessee and Alabama and Georgia—would that count as interstate wire fraud?"

"Sounds like it."

I struggled to remember what I knew about white-collar crime, which wasn't much. Murder tended to wear a blue collar, or a blood-red one. "And am I right in thinking that interstate wire fraud is considered a form of organized crime?"

"Technically, yes," she said. "I suspect crematoriums weren't tops on anybody's list of dangerous criminal enterprises when the RICO statutes were written. But technically you're probably correct—wire fraud is pretty broadly defined, so what you're describing could constitute wire fraud and an organized-crime enterprise. Technically."

"You keep saying 'technically.' How come?"

"Because there's a fairly high threshold that has to be met before we're going to pursue a federal wire-fraud case."

"What kind of threshold?"

"A financial threshold. The dollar value's got to be around a quarter million dollars to justify committing resources to an investigation and prosecution. The U.S. Attorney has to agree it's worthwhile. It's sort of like speeding—technically, the police can ticket you for doing forty-five in a forty-mile-an-hour zone, but they're not going to waste their time on that. They're going to be on the lookout for the guy going sixty or seventy. So to circle back to cremation, if a crematorium failed to cremate somebody they got paid to cremate, yeah, they committed fraud. If they used interstate phone lines to do it—and these days, unless you're using tin cans and a string to talk to the guy next door, every telephone conversation uses nationwide networks—then yeah, it's interstate wire fraud. But the reality is, we don't have the time or resources to bring the hammer down on some crematorium that didn't cremate a body. That's what civil suits are for."

"How about a hundred bodies? Maybe more?"

Price was silent for longer than I'd ever heard her stay quiet. "What do you mean?"

"I mean, what if this crematorium isn't defrauding one or two people? What if they're defrauding hundreds—everybody they deal with? What if they're not cremating any of the bodies?"

She paused again. I liked it when I could give Price pause. "And what are they doing with these bodies, if they're not cremating them?"

"Piling them in a patch of pine forest."

"You know this for a fact?"

"I've seen it with my own eyes."

"Hundreds of bodies?"

"Technically," I said, "I haven't seen hundreds. Technically, I've seen fewer than a hundred—ninety-four, to be precise. But I didn't exactly do a grid search. That's what I saw in about ten minutes, in one corner of the woods."

"You saw ninety-four bodies piled in the woods?"

"I saw eighty-eight piled in the woods . . . well, not piled, exactly—more like dumped and strewn and half hidden. I saw six more stacked in the back of a broken-down hearse."

"*Damn*, Doc," she said. It was the first time I'd ever heard her sound impressed, or surprised, or anything other than strictly business. "Those folks are giving your Body Farm a run for the money."

"Yeah, except they're not doing the research," I said. "Oh, and they're bringing in a lot more money than I am."

"How much does cremation cost?"

"It costs the consumer about eight hundred to a thousand dollars," I said, "but that includes the funeral home's markup. The crematorium itself doesn't charge that much, more like four hundred per cremation. I hear this place down in Georgia was doing it—or *not* doing it—for three hundred."

"Hmm," she said. "So a hundred unburned bodies—we'll go with a nice round number, to keep the math simple—would represent a thirty-thousand-dollar case of fraud. Have I got that decimal in the right place?"

Put that way—reduced to a bottom-line dollar amount—the shocking scene in the woods sounded insignificant. "But I bet there are more," I said. "Maybe a lot more."

"There would have to be," she said. "I hate to break it to you, Dr. Brockton, but we'd need ten times that many bodies in the woods to justify a federal wire-fraud investigation."

"You're saying you'd need a thousand bodies? You've got to be joking."

"I don't joke, Dr. Brockton." She had a point there, I realized. "My white-collar-crime agents are swamped with cases right now—multimillion-dollar cases. You remember that chop shop we raided last spring over in Grainger County? They were selling stolen-car parts throughout the South, to the tune of seven million dollars a year. Your cockfighting friends in Cooke County? Illegal gambling—hundreds of thousands of dollars every day those birds were pecking each other to death." Technically, I wanted to point out, the roosters spurred or slashed each other to death, but I didn't see much future in interrupting Price just to correct her description of cockfighting. "I don't mean to sound callous," she said, "but I don't think it's big enough for us. Did you call local law enforcement?"

"No," I said. "This a rural county in Podunk, Georgia. They don't begin to have the forensic resources to deal with this."

"If the locals request assistance, we could send in an Evidence Recovery Team."

"There's a whole lot of evidence to recover," I said. "Why not just send in the cavalry now? Eliminate the middleman?"

"It doesn't work that way," she said. "We help if we're asked—it's called 'domestic police cooperation'—but we have to be asked. And despite what you see on television, we consider the 'cooperation' part important. Call the locals."

"That's all you've got for me—'call the locals'?"

"'Fraid so," she said. "Sorry that's not what you wanted to hear. Is there anything else I can do for you?"

"I guess not," I said. "Thanks."

She clicked off without saying good-bye.

Angela: that was her name. "Thanks for nothing, Angela," I said to the dead receiver.

Call the locals? I didn't even know who the locals were. I had an atlas in my truck, so I went out and got it and traced my route from Chattanooga down into the northwest corner of Georgia. It didn't take long to pinpoint what county the crematorium was in, and I knew that it wouldn't take a genius to track down the number for the county sheriff. But I found myself hesitating, re-sisting the idea of calling 411. As I took a mental step back and analyzed the reasons for my hesitation, it came clear. Over the years of my work, I had come to know and respect many sher-iffs in rural Tennessee. But within the past year, I had survived a couple of near-death experiences with deputies in Cooke County, where Chief Deputy Orbin Kitchings was a regular at the cock-fights—and where Deputy Leon Williams had used dynamite to entomb Art Bohanan and me in a cave. On the one hand, I had no reason to suspect that the sheriff in northwest Georgia was looking the other way as bodies piled up in the woods. But then again, I had no particular basis for confidence either. And if the sheriff did happen to be in cahoots with the crematorium, my call might actually trigger a quick cleanup and a massive cover-up. The more I thought, the less I wanted to call the locals.

But if not the locals, then who could I call?

I glanced idly at the atlas again, and my gaze strayed south-ward, to Atlanta. "Sean Richter," I said out loud. "I can call Sean."

Sean Richter was one of my former graduate students. After completing his master's degree, he had spent a year in the rem-nants of Yugoslavia, helping excavate mass graves and identify victims of ethnic-cleansing massacres in Kosovo. Now he was working in Atlanta as the staff forensic anthropologist for the Georgia Bureau of Investigation. As an interstate wire-fraud case, the crematorium might be too small for the FBI to bother with. But as a Georgia fraud case, it might be big enough to interest the GBI. And I was certain it would interest Sean, with its simi-larities to the mass-fatality identifications he'd done in Kosovo. I fished out my pocket calendar, which had a small address book tucked in the back, and looked up his number.

"Anthropology lab, this is Richter."

"Sean, this is Bill Brockton."

"Dr. Brockton, how are you?"

"I'm fine, but I'd be better if you quit calling me Dr. Brock-ton, Sean. You're my colleague now, not my student. It's time you graduated to calling me Bill."

"I'll try," he said. "That's gonna be a tough habit to break, though. Once a forensic god, always a forensic god."

"Well, once you break this case wide open," I said, "you'll be a legend yourself."

"What case?"

"How would you like to lead the recovery and identification of a hundred decomposing bodies, maybe more? Maybe lots more?"

He laughed. "You're one of the few people who actually find that an irresistible temptation," he said. "But I'm one of the others. Unfortunately, I doubt that I could get a leave of absence right now to do that. I fear my traveling days are over, for a while at least."

"You wouldn't have to travel. At least not outside your jurisdiction."

Sean didn't say anything for a long time. When he did speak, his voice sounded unnatural and forced, as if he were pushing the words out by sheer willpower. "Are you telling me you think there's a mass grave here in Georgia with a hundred or more bodies in it?"

"No, and not exactly," I said. "I don't think—I know. But it's not a grave, it's surface. You wouldn't even have to dig." As I described what I'd seen in the woods, he interrupted me often, asking me to repeat or confirm or elaborate on some detail. The shakiness in his voice gave way to a mixture of excitement and anger. Sean was smart enough to realize that this case would be forensically fascinating, as well as a watershed in his career. But his anger at the indignity inflicted on the dead—dumped in the woods like refuse—was genuine, and I knew that Sean would do whatever it took to make the case a priority for the GBI.

His eagerness was tempered by one very legitimate concern. The GBI's anthropology lab was small, and Sean's resources—

equipment and personnel—were nowhere near adequate to re-cover and identify so many bodies all at once. "You might want to ask for help from DMORT," I said. DMORT—the Disaster Mortuary Operational Response Team—was a federally de-ployed unit designed to assist with mass fatalities. The team members, who included forensic anthropologists, dentists, fu-neral directors, and other professionals skilled at identifying or handling corpses, were volunteers, but they were highly trained and extremely capable. DMORT teams had performed heroically at Ground Zero after the World Trade Center attacks, and they had worked for months to identify the hundreds of victims of Hurricane Katrina. Sean agreed that DMORT could be a valu-able resource.

"You might also want to ask the FBI for an Evidence Recovery Team," I said. Then, and only then, did I recount the gist of my conversation with Special Agent Price. "They don't want to run the case," I said, "but I gather they'd be willing to roll up their sleeves and help with the fieldwork. If you ask."

"I'll certainly recommend that we ask," he said. "This is going to be huge, and we'll need all the help we can get." He paused, then said, "Hmm." I waited, figuring he was working up to an-other question, and I was right. "So when my bosses ask me how I know about this mess, what do I tell them?"

"Tell them the truth," I said. "I don't see how it can hurt. Might give them a little more confidence that it's not a wild-goose chase if they know the tip came from a guy who has a reasonably good idea what bodies in the woods look like."

He chuckled at that. "True. Be hard for them to doubt the ac-curacy of the report if they know it comes from you."

"I don't particularly want my name in the news, though, if

you can keep me out of it," I said. "Any chance y'all could say the GBI received a call from a 'concerned citizen' or some such?"

"I'll suggest it," he said. "Politically, that might have some appeal—if we say, 'It took an anthropologist from Tennessee to sniff this out,' the GBI doesn't look real bright. But if we say, 'We acted swiftly in response to a tip,' we look semicompetent."

"Semicompetent nothing," I said. "Y'all'll be heroes. But only if you quit yakking and get busy."

"Right," he said. "Thanks, Dr. Brockton."

"Excuse me—who?"

"Oh. Sorry. Thanks . . . Bill."

His teeth were nearly clenched as he said it. But at least he said it.

CHAPTER 17

DOWN IN GEORGIA I'D STUMBLED UPON A BUNCH OF bodies that should have been burned but weren't. Here in Knoxville, I reflected, I was obsessed with a body that shouldn't have been burned but was. *I guess the universe is in balance,* I thought. *Except that Garland Hamilton's still out there somewhere.*

Darren Cash answered his cell phone on the third ring.

"I think I know how he did it," I said.

"How who did *what?*"

I laughed. "Sorry. It's Dr. Brockton from UT. I think I know how Stuart Latham set the car on fire while he was in Vegas."

"Do tell," said Cash.

"I'm not sure you'd believe me if I told you," I said. "I'd rather show you. Any chance you've got some free time late this afternoon or tomorrow?"

"Since you ask so nice," he said, "and since you're about to help me blast a killer's alibi out of the water, I'll make time. I've

got some folks to interview this morning and after lunch, but I
should be through by four o'clock or so."

I checked my watch. It read 8:37.

"Can you meet me at the Anthropology Department around
four-thirty? We'll take a little field trip from there."

"You're being mighty cryptic," he said, "but you've got me
hooked."

I told him how to find my office, and then I called Jason Story,
one of my master's-level graduate students. Jason sounded sleepy
when he answered the phone, which wasn't surprising considering he'd sent me an e-mail in the middle of the night describing
the experiment he'd just finished.

"Sorry if I woke you up, Jason," I said. "We need to do another run today."

He yawned. "So soon? I've already done six in the past two
days."

"'Fraid so," I said. "The stakes are higher on this one, though.
This one's the dog and pony show for the D.A.'s investigator."

Suddenly he sounded much more alert. "Okay, no problem,"
he said.

"Can you get it started by ten?"

"A.M. or P.M.?"

"A.M."

"Wow," he said. "That's cutting it close. But okay, yeah. You
might want to stay upwind of me, though—it's been pretty hot
out there, and I won't have time to take a shower."

"No matter how bad you smell, Jason? I've smelled worse
things."

"I guess so." He laughed. "What time are you bringing the guy
from the D.A.'s office out?"

"Around five, five-thirty. That should be about right, shouldn't it?"

"Should be. Gotta go. See you then."

Jason was getting ready to enter his second year in the graduate program. Like countless other high-school and college kids who'd gotten hooked on *CSI,* Jason aspired to be a forensic scientist. Unlike most, though, Jason had gone out and gotten real-world experience. He'd spent three years as a volunteer with a Knox County Rescue Squad. The rescue squad didn't handle criminal cases, but Jason had worked enough death scenes—car crashes and drownings, even a plane crash—to get past the jitters, and as soon as he took osteology, I was sure he'd be a valuable addition to my Forensic Response Team. He was good with gadgetry, too—Jason felt as comfortable with a GPS or with a topographic map and a compass as I felt with a mandible or a femur. And if I ever needed to tie somebody up and be sure they couldn't get loose, Jason would be the one whose knotcraft I would call on. He was steady and reliable, and, maybe more to the point, he was in the market for a thesis topic, so he'd jumped at the chance to help with some research.

At 4:20, Cash knocked on my door. "You're early," I said. "Good man."

"I finished up a little sooner than I expected," he said, "and I didn't see much point in just killing time. If you've got things to do, though, tell me, and I'll make some phone calls till you're ready."

'No, this is fine," I said. "Let's go. Do you want to ride with me or follow me?"

"Let me follow you, so I can just head home when we're done. You ready to tell me where we're going?"

"One of the Ag farms," I said. "By way of Burger King, if you don't mind?"

"I never got lunch," he said. "Burger King sounds great. At this point Purina Dog Chow would probably sound pretty good."

"Let's say Burger King."

"WELC . . . BRRGRR . . . KI . . ." crackled the voice through the loudspeaker. I couldn't even tell if the person was male or female. I hoped they'd be able to hear me better than I could hear them. *"W . . . LIKE . . . TRY OUR zzttzztt COMBO . . . DAY?"*

I didn't know what I'd just been offered, but I did know that I didn't want a combo. "I'd like a Whopper and a sweet tea, please," I said. I spoke up, because the sound system didn't seem to be working well.

"zzttzztt TEA?"

"Sweet tea," I said loudly. "Do you have sweet tea?"

"zzttzztt TEA?"

"Sweet tea!" I shouted. "Sweet tea! If you don't have sweet tea, regular tea's okay!"

"zzttzztt TEA . . . ELSE?"

"That's it!" I yelled. "Just the Whopper and the tea!"

A young man walking into the restaurant, a backpack slung over one shoulder, looked at me oddly and gave me a wide berth.

"YOU SAID A . . . zzttzztt AND . . . zzttzztt . . . TOTAL COMES . . . zzttzztt . . . WINDOW."

Just as I was pulling away from the speaker, I noticed a display mounted underneath. It read Whopper, sweet tea, $3.87. Clearly I wasn't the only one who'd had trouble with the audio system. Funny, I thought. Instead of fixing the microphone and the speaker, they'd installed a whole 'nother gadget. I fished my wallet out of my hip pocket and extracted a five-dollar bill as I eased around the building to the drive-up window.

I waited several minutes, but the window remained tightly closed. I gave a quick tap on the horn. Still no response. Behind me another horn blared, louder and longer than my polite little toot. I checked the mirror and saw two more vehicles idling behind Cash's car. Now both of them blasted their horns at me. Frustrated, I decided to forego the Whopper, and gunned the gas. Suddenly an arm emerged from a window—a second drive-up window, which I hadn't noticed—and waved frantically. I nearly clipped the hand with my outside mirror.

A pleasant young woman, probably a UT student, opened the window and smiled. "I was about to send out a search party for you," she said brightly. "Your order comes to three eighty-seven." I held out the five. She made change, then handed me a white paper bag and a heavy cup. "Enjoy your meal," she said.

"THANK . . . *zztt* . . . MUH," I said, delivering my best imitation of the faulty loudspeaker.

She looked startled, maybe even alarmed. The window snapped shut.

I'd meant to save the Whopper until Cash and I got to the Ag farm, but the smell of charbroiled beef came floating up out of the bag, almost like one of those beckoning fingers of aroma in an old cartoon. I held out as long as I could, which wasn't long—just long enough to get from the Strip back to Neyland Drive. Steering with my left knee along Neyland's slight curves, I fished out the burger and unfolded the wrapper to expose half the sandwich. My mouth was watering, despite what Jeff had told me about the carcinogenic chemistry of flame broiling—or maybe *because* of what Jeff had told me. Did knowing that the Whopper had a dark side beneath those grill marks make it more appealing? I'd never been particularly attracted by the idea of illicit sex, but I knew that some people were, and I wondered if this was anything like their experience. *Maybe this,* I thought, taking a greedy breath, *is the sweet smell of forbidden fruit. Brockton, you are one reckless daredevil.* The truck swerved as my knee slipped, and I made a quick grab for the wheel with my right hand. *See?* Once I was tracking straight again, I hoisted the burger with my left hand and bit down. "Mmm-*mmm,*" I moaned, as a symphonic chord of hot grease, smoky beef, mayonnaise, ketchup, pickle, onion, and carcinogens crescendoed in my mouth.

Chewing contentedly, I led Cash up the ramp onto James White Parkway, down the ramp to Riverside Drive, and then along Riverside to the Ag farm above the river confluence. As we passed the barn and the equipment shed, I noticed that the water truck's windshield had been replaced but the deep dent in the hood remained. Then again, the fenders were rusting and the silver paint was peeling off the water tank, so I didn't feel too bad. Besides, I'd done some serious groveling to the farm's employees–and underscored the apology with a couple of cases of beer.

Cash and I bumped along a pair of ruts to an unburned part of the pasture and pulled to a stop beside Jason Story. Jason was reclining in a folding camp chair, the geometric, NASA-looking kind, with a footrest and drink holders and probably a mini-fridge and a television set tucked away somewhere. He was slouched, a floppy hat pulled low over his eyes, his chin practically on his chest, and when I saw him, I thought, *Oh, Lord, he's fallen asleep.* But then I saw his right index finger twitch, and he raised a handheld electronic display from his lap to his face. His left hand came off the armrest and gripped the top of a large fire extinguisher standing in the grass beside him.

Jason barely glanced in our direction when we got out of our vehicles and slammed the doors. His attention alternated between the electronic display in his hand and the 2006 Lexus SUV that idled in the grass ten feet in front of him.

"Jason, this is Darren Cash," I said, "an investigator with the Knox County D.A.'s Office. Darren, Jason Story."

"Pleased to meet you, Jason," said Cash.

"You, too," Jason said, not making a move. "Sorry if I seem rude. I need to keep a pretty close eye on this thermocouple monitor." I was just about to ask Jason what the readout was saying when a series of earsplitting beeps came from beneath the car.

Jason snatched at a lanyard hanging around his neck and grabbed a stopwatch, then punched a button. "Wow, that is right on time," he said. He lurched out of the chair, hoisted the fire extinguisher, and discharged a cloud of vapor at the underside of the Lexus. Then he flung open the driver's door, hopped in, and pulled the car forward about twenty feet.

When he did, he exposed a still-smoking circle of burned grass about two feet in diameter, along with a partially melted smoke detector lying near one edge and a pair of wires stretching to the thermocouple monitor now lying beside the chair. Jason shut off the car and clambered out, then gave the grass another shot with the extinguisher. He consulted the stopwatch dangling from his neck again. "Seven hours, forty-three minutes," he said proudly.

I turned to Cash. "Seven hours, forty-three minutes. You think that gives your guy enough time to get to Las Vegas?"

"He flew direct on Allegiant," Cash said. "Flight's four hours and a quarter," he said. "Thirty-minute drive to the airport; check-in and boarding takes another thirty, if you shave it close. I'd say it would." He studied the charred circle, studied the Lexus, and then studied Jason.

"Okay, I give," he said. "How'd you do it?"

"Take a look in the grass," I said.

He squatted down beside the blackened circle, then dropped to one knee and leaned forward, almost like a football player on the line of scrimmage. He plucked something from the ground and held it up between his left thumb and forefinger. It was a piece of heavy steel wire, cinched tight around a ruffle of ragged plastic.

I nodded at it. "Recognize that?"

He scrutinized it. "It's like the thing you found in the burned grass at the Latham farm," he said, "but this plastic stuff is different."

"Exactly," I said. "It's not melted. That's because we put the fire out before the car burned."

"I hate to say it, but you've still got me," he said. "What is it?"

"That," I said, "is the end of an eight-pound bag of ice."

"A bag of ice?"

"A bag of ice," I said. "I realized what it was the other night when I picked up a bag on the way to my son's house. It's how Latham delayed the fire. He dumped a bag of ice on the grass, drove the car so the catalytic converter was right over the ice, then skedaddled for the airport."

He looked dubious. "Come on, Doc. How's he gonna control that? How's he gonna know it'll work at all, and how's he gonna know how much time it buys him?"

"You remember that smaller burned oval in the grass at the Lathams' farm, the one near the barn?"

He nodded. "Actually," he said, "we found two more of those after you pointed out the first one."

I could see the light beginning to dawn. I pointed at the scorched grass, frosted with powder from the fire extinguisher.

"We're not the only ones who do experiments. Stuart Latham might've made a good scientist." I turned to Jason. "You want to summarize the data for Mr. Cash, Jason?"

Jason cleared his throat nervously. "Well," he said, "we've only got six data points—actually, seven now—so statistically the data set isn't robust. In fact, if you remove the two outliers—"

"Jason," I interrupted, "just cut to the chase. Tell the man what you found."

"Okay, sorry," he said. "On average, it takes the ice about ninety minutes to melt, plus or minus ten percent, depending on how consolidated the ice remains and how close to the catalytic converter it is. But then the grass is wet and the ground's cold, so it takes about another six hours for everything to dry out, and another fifteen minutes or so for the grass to reach its flash point and catch fire."

"In the seven runs you've done," I asked, "how much variation did you see in the total elapsed time between parking the car and seeing the grass catch fire?"

"Less than thirty minutes," he said. "It's surprisingly consistent. Now, if the grass were shorter or taller or a different type or—"

"Thank you, Jason," I interrupted again. I regarded Cash. "Does this look pretty similar to the grass in the pasture at the Latham farm?"

"If I were a cow," he said, "I'd think I was eating at the same restaurant."

"And you've got pictures of the Latham's pasture, taken the day the car burned?"

"Sure," he said. "Dozens."

"Any good close-ups of unburned grass?"

"Well, we weren't actually focusing on the grass as a murder weapon," he said. "We took close-ups of the burned cigarette butts under the driver's window, but the grass in that area was burned, obviously." He frowned, then he brightened. "We do have wide shots that show the whole circle of burned grass, including the unburned grass around the edges. Come to think of it," he added, "one of them shows a uniformed officer standing in the field. The grass comes up about yea high on him." He bent down and sliced a hand across his lower leg, midway between the knee and the foot. As he did, the tops of the Ag field's grass grazed his fingers.

I grinned. "Jason, you took a bunch of pictures of the first couple experiments, didn't you?"

"Oh, yessir, Dr. B.," he said. "I've got probably three hundred. I filled up the memory card on my camera, and it holds a gigabyte."

"A jury'll like this," I said.

"I sure like it," said Cash.

CHAPTER 18

THE PHONE RANG THE NEXT MORNING, JUST AS I WAS hoisting a spoonful of Raisin Bran to my mouth. I had the newspaper open to the comics; the combination of crisp cereal and corny cartoons was my favorite way to start the day. I looked at the clock on the wall above the stove; it read seven-thirty. "Well, damn," I said—not because it was early (I'd been up since six) but because the cereal was sure to be soggy by the time I got off the phone. I figured it must be Jeff, Miranda, or Art calling.

"Turn on CNN right now," said Art, and hung up.

I stared at the phone as if further enlightenment might be forthcoming from the dead receiver in my hand. When none came, I went to the living room and switched on the TV, flipping to channel 22, CNN. The screen was filled with an aerial view of a patch of pine forest, filmed from a circling helicopter. The woods framed a clearing containing a brick ranch house, a garage, a couple of ramshackle sheds, and a small garage-type building with a rusted flue projecting from the roof. The clearing was filled with law-enforcement vehicles, a few black-and-white cruisers and SUVs, but mostly the unmarked Town Cars and Crown Victorias favored by the FBI and their state-level counterparts. The caption crawling across the bottom of the screen read, *"Hundreds of bodies found in Georgia woods."*

I found the scrap of paper where I had written Burt DeVriess's cell-phone number—a number he'd never given me when I was his client, only after I took his Aunt Jean's case. He sounded sleepy and pissed off.

"Hello?"

"Burt, Bill Brockton. Turn on CNN right now," I said. Then I hung up with a smile, probably just as Art had.

My phone rang five minutes later, just after CNN cut to a commercial break. It was DeVriess. "Damn, Doc," he said, "when you take a case, things happen. I should've teamed up with you years ago."

"You were too busy busting my chops on the witness stand," I said. "Anyhow, maybe now that it's out in the open, those folks will be held accountable."

"I can promise you they'll be held accountable," he said. "I'm dedicating the full resources of this law firm to holding them accountable."

The full resources of the firm, as far as I knew, were Burt and Chloe. But then again, the full resources of the firm had rounded up the video expert who'd cleared me of Jess's murder. Even so, Burt's declaration struck me as odd. "You're a criminal defense attorney, Burt, not a prosecutor," I pointed out. "You *defend* people like this."

"Mostly," he said. "But I've decided to branch out—try my hand in the civil courts, as a plaintiff's attorney."

"Plaintiff's attorney? You're going to start suing people?"

"I believe so," he said. "And now seems like a good time to dip a toe in the water."

"You're going to sue the crematorium for not cremating your aunt?"

"My aunt and a whole bunch of other folks."

A lightbulb flickered on above my head. "Ah. A class-action lawsuit. But how you gonna track down all the families of these people?"

"I won't have to," he said. "They'll track me down."

"How will they know to do that?"

"You forgetting what a master of the media I am, Doc?"

I had a quick flashback to the press conference Burt had held— had orchestrated, scripted, and choreographed—the moment the video expert had found the evidence that cleared me of Jess's murder. "Silly me," I said. "What was I thinking? You'll probably be on *Larry King*, and I should hang up so you can start working the press and taking phone calls."

"Before you do," Burt said, "can I ask you for another favor?"

"You can always ask," I said.

"I know you must have called in some markers to set those wheels in motion down in Georgia," he said.

"I've helped a few people in law enforcement over the years," I said. "They're pretty willing to help me in return, if they can. Besides, it was the right thing to do."

"Whatever string you pulled down there to blow the lid off that thing—any chance you could tug on it one more time?"

I felt my guard go up, knowing he was probably already laying plans for a class-action suit that could net him millions in contingency fees. "What do you want, Burt?"

"I want my Aunt Jean, Doc," he said. "I know she's one of those three hundred bodies they're hauling out of the woods. It's gonna kill my Uncle Edgar to find out how she was treated. If there's any way you can go back down there and find her, so we can get her home and try to set this thing right, I'd be forever grateful."

The request surprised me, and impressed me. "I'll see, Burt," I said, "but I can't promise anything. Everybody who ever sent a loved one there is going to be clamoring to get in, you know."

"I know," he said. "But you're the guy who uncovered the truth."

"I'll see, Burt," I repeated. "That's all I can do."

"I understand. Thanks, Doc. I 'preciate you."

CHAPTER 19

WHEN I DIALED SEAN RICHTER, I GOT HIS PAGER, which didn't surprise me. Sean would have his hands full, and then some, for quite a while. During their first day's search of the woods surrounding the crematorium, the GBI and FBI evidence teams had found nearly three hundred bodies and skeletons. Recovering them could take weeks; identifying them could take months, if not years. DMORT had brought in a couple of inflatable morgues, and the GBI had trucked in a small fleet of refrigerated trailers to house the bodies while they figured out how to process them. My guess was they'd end up building a massive new morgue and DNA lab dedicated to this one case.

The gruesome scene in the Georgia backwoods was the lead story on every major television network, wire service, and Internet news site in the country. It was also, I learned from the stack of printouts Miranda had put on my desk, the topic of dozens of international headlines—variations on the theme of "Americans are barbarians," many of them. Atop the stack Miranda had left a sticky note: *"How come you couldn't have found this in Tennessee instead of Georgia? Jealous Junior Anthropologist."*

Sean returned my page within ten minutes, which did surprise me. "I didn't think you'd get a chance to call me back for . . . oh, about ten or twenty years."

"It's a zoo," he said, "and it'll stay that way for a long time. But since you're the one who steered us to this, I figure if you page me, I return the call. You're number three on my priority list, right after the GBI director and my wife."

"She outranks me now? You're obviously not under my thumb anymore," I said.

"Yet here you are," he said good-naturedly, "still pulling my strings." He took a deep breath and puffed it out. "You're not calling to tell me about another big batch of bodies somewhere in Georgia, I hope?"

"How'd you guess?" I laughed. "No, not today. I'm calling to ask a favor—to see if you can pull a string or two for me."

"You want us to just ship everything up to the Body Farm, right?"

"I hadn't thought that far ahead," I said. "But now that you mention it, I'd love to add another three hundred skeletons to the collection. Can you have 'em here tomorrow?"

"Sure," he joked, "piece of cake." We both knew that eventually—once the bodies were identified—they'd need to be returned to their families, or to whoever had sent them to be cremated. "Anything else on your wish list?"

"This might be nearly as difficult to arrange," I said, "but if you can't bring the mountain of bodies to Mohammed, how about if Mohammed comes down to the mountain? I'd love to take a quick look around. Not just for curiosity," I hastened to add. "You know the woman whose bogus cremains caused me to start poking around in the woods? I'm wondering if you'd be able and willing to let me take a quick look for her." I was pretty sure Burt's Aunt Jean was one of the hundreds of bodies chilling in those refrigerated trailers, but it might be months before Sean got to her. To him she was just one among hundreds, but to me—and to Grease, who'd asked whether I could get into the makeshift morgue and find her fast—she was a priority.

"Ah," he said. "I understand. I'd certainly have no problem with that. But it's not my call. This is the highest-profile case anybody around here can remember, and the director and the public-affairs people are pretty touchy. So far, access is limited to the GBI, FBI, and DMORT teams. Hell, we even turned away the governor, who wanted to come up and hold a press conference in the woods with that grungy crematorium in the background." He paused, and in the distance I could hear the hum of refrigeration units, the beep of a truck backing up, and the squawk of a public-address announcement asking somebody or other to report to the command post.

"Well, I'd appreciate it if you'd give it a shot at least," I said. "Could save you a little time and money," I added. "If I find her, that'd be one less person for you to ID. One less DNA test to pay for."

"Good point," he said. "We're at three hundred twenty-seven bodies already, and we haven't finished searching. Can you maybe help us ID another fifty or sixty?"

"If I say yes, does that give me a better shot at getting in to look for Aunt Jean?"

"You bet," he said.

"I'd love to pitch in for a week or two," I said, "but I want to stay close to home until Garland Hamilton's back in custody. It's not like I'm out beating the bushes myself, but I do want to stay near the phone."

"I understand," he said. "Dr. Carter was a good M.E.—she worked with us on a couple of cases that crossed jurisdictional lines—and I was sorry to hear she'd been killed." There was an awkward pause, and then he added, "I was also sorry to hear the police suspected you at first."

I appreciated Sean's sentiments, but I suddenly wished the conversation hadn't taken this particular turn.

"Listen, Sean, I bet you've got half a dozen people clamoring for you," I said. "I'd better let you get back to work. Call if you get the okay for me to come down in the next couple days."

"I will," he said. "I'll give it my best shot."

His best shot must have been pretty good, because two days later a Georgia state trooper swung open the gate and waved me into the driveway of the Littlejohn property. The watchdogs inside the fence were gone, replaced by a pack of television crews patrolling the outer perimeter. Several cameramen jogged toward my truck, cameras bobbing on their shoulders, but by the time they reached the gate, I was already crunching down the driveway in a cloud of dust.

After threading through the pines for a quarter mile, the driveway emerged into a yard the size of a football field. To the left was a pond measuring maybe fifty yards across; to the right was a single-story brick ranch house with a small front porch at the center, framed by two white columns. I'd probably passed a dozen such houses, I realized, flanking the thirty miles of two-lane highway between Chattanooga and here. Next came a small prefab wooden building, roughly ten feet square—the sort of thing that might house a snow-cone stand for a few months in the summer. Beyond that was a big, barnlike shed. Inside, I glimpsed a tractor, a bushhog mowing attachment, a battered old pickup, and—the first indication that this was anything other than an ordinary rural farmstead—a handful of concrete burial vaults.

The next odd thing I saw, as I passed the shed, was the row of stainless-steel refrigerated trailers parked behind it, their cluster of diesel generators and compressor motors combining to produce a roaring, clattering chorus. From here on, the driveway was lined with police vehicles—county, state, and federal cars, marked and unmarked—plus crime-lab vans and DMORT trucks. The final building was tucked beside a large turnaround area at the end of the drive. This building resembled a dilapidated garage with a rusty metal flue at one end, and I recognized it as a smaller, shabbier cousin of the immaculate crematorium I'd visited in Alcoa. Beside it, I noticed with a jolt, was a huge barbecue grill.

A woman in a white biohazard suit labeled GBI was headed toward the building, a trowel in one hand, an evidence bag in the other. "Excuse me," I called, "I'm looking for Sean Richter. Do you know where I might find him?" She glanced at me and seemed surprised to see a middle-aged, bespectacled guy in khakis and a polo shirt.

"He's in there," she said, cocking her head toward the building's open garage door and the darkness within. She glanced at my feet and seemed about to say something but didn't. I guessed that my shoes—rubber-soled Doc Martens—had passed muster, showing that I knew enough to leave my dress shoes at home in the closet. I thanked her, and she nodded, then walked around the end of the small building and disappeared behind it, leaving me alone at the entrance.

After my eyes adjusted to the dimness inside, I found myself face-to-face with a cremation furnace that looked slightly archaic and more than a little sinister. My first thought was, *Auschwitz.* Unlike the lustrous steel control panels I'd seen at the Alcoa crematorium, this furnace had a massive door of black cast iron bolted directly to the brickwork, with huge hinges to support its weight. The furnace door was open, but the interior was utterly dark. My key ring had a tiny flashlight on it; I fished it out and shone the feeble light into the arched cavity. The firebrick was jagged and crumbling, completely caked with soot and cobwebs.

Sean was nowhere to be seen, but I heard voices, so I called his name. From somewhere behind the furnace, I heard him answer. "Bill Brockton, is that you?"

"It is," I said. "Somebody told me you were in here. When I didn't see you, I thought maybe you'd crawled into the furnace and burned up."

"Not a chance," he said, emerging from the rear of the cramped building. "Nothing to burn. Guy at the gas company says they stopped taking propane deliveries about eighteen months ago. He actually smelled something the last time he was out there; got suspicious and called the cops. Whoever he talked to told him it was a dead cow and suggested he mind his own business." *So much for "call the locals,"* I thought, wishing Agent Price were standing beside me to hear this. "Let's head on up to the coolers, and we'll get you started," he said. "Do you need clothing?"

I shook my head. "I've got everything I need in the truck."

We trudged up the drive and toward the row of refrigerated

trailers. Sean's white biohazard suit, I noticed, was covered with soot and cobwebs from the filthy building.

"We've divided them by sex," he shouted over the rising din of the generators. "Males in trailers one and two, females in three and four, and unknowns in five and six."

"Roughly how many in each?"

"Fairly evenly divided," he yelled. "Not a whole lot of soft tissue on any of these—it's Georgia and it's summertime, so anybody who's been here more than a week or two is pretty well skeletonized or mummified. The clothing seems to have held up better than the tissue, so that helps."

I nodded; I had expected as much from the bodies I'd seen.

A set of bare wooden steps, assembled from fresh lumber, led up to the back of each trailer. I followed Sean up the steps of the third trailer. He unlatched the door, and a blast of frosty air rolled over me, chilling the sweat on my face and neck. Even cold, the air was ripe with the odor of decomp.

The interior was lit by a string of fluorescent work lights, jury-rigged to the ceiling. Both sides of the trailer were lined with metal shelving units, four shelves high. Every shelf held a body bag—some black, some white. The topmost shelves were head-high; at the far end of the trailer, I noticed a stepstool, which I'd need to stand on to inspect the upper row of bodies. Sean walked to the nearest bag, on a shelf at chest height, and tugged the zipper around the C-shaped opening. He folded back the flap, revealing a head, the skull and cervical vertebrae exposed. The skull was small and smooth, with a pointed chin and sharp edges at the top of the eye orbits—a classic female skull. A mat of long, tangled brown hair lay beside the skull. "Well, she's in the right trailer, whoever she is," I said.

Sean laughed. "Be kinda embarrassing if I'd unzipped one that we'd gotten wrong," he said. He tugged the zipper farther toward the foot of the bag so he could fold back more of the flap. "We've tagged the upper left arm and the left ankle of every body," he said. "Numerical tags, starting with one." He checked the tag on the skeletal arm. "This is number forty-seven," he said. "If I remember right, she was one of that batch you found over near the bulldozer. We started with the ones in the hearse—no particular reason; it was just someplace to start—then tackled the big group by the dozer. There were bodies everywhere, Bill. Bodies stacked in burial vaults in the shed, bodies dumped in a shallow pit—hell, even a couple bodies stuffed in an old chest-type freezer out by a trash pile."

"What on earth were they thinking?"

"I'm not sure they *were* thinking," he said. "Guy said the furnace quit working and he just got behind and overwhelmed. But we had a technician check it out, and it seemed to be working fine once we got some propane in the tank. I'm not sure we'll ever know the whole story. My theory? It's like those folks out in the country that strew junked cars and washing machines and bedsprings all over their property. Only difference is, this guy wasn't strewing around broken-down vehicles or appliances—this guy was accumulating broken-down human beings."

"Any idea how much money he saved by not cremating the bodies?"

"Seventy, eighty bucks apiece, best we can tell. Less than a hundred. Not near enough to justify this mess, that's for sure."

I couldn't imagine what might be enough to justify this mess. It would cost millions of dollars, I felt sure, to clean up the site and identify the bodies, and many millions more to settle the lawsuits that aggrieved families were bound to start filing. I had long since given up on trying to predict the oddities that turned up in murder cases and death investigations, but this—the sheer scale and stupidity of it—stunned even me. "Sean, I'm going to suit up and start looking for Aunt Jean," I said, "so you can get back to work."

He nodded, suddenly looking weary. When he opened the trailer's door, the blazing heat and blinding light outside nearly knocked us backward.

"Listen, I really appreciate your getting me in here to take a look," I said as we thudded down the wooden steps. "If I find her, I'll let you know. And if I don't find her, I'll let you know that, too."

He peeled off his glove to shake my hand again—I wished I owned stock in the company that was providing the gloves and body bags for this operation—and thanked me once more, then headed for the command post. As he walked, I saw him checking his pager and shaking his head.

I walked to the back of my truck, lifted up the hard cover over the bed, and dropped the tailgate. Sitting on the gate, I shucked off my Doc Martens, then wiggled into a pair of insulated ski pants to keep my legs warm. Next I threaded my legs into a baggy Tyvek jumpsuit, then put my shoes back on and stretched paper booties over them, since there was likely to be goo here and there on the trailer floors. I stuffed a few pairs of nitrile gloves into the hip pockets of the jumpsuit, slung my camera around my neck, and tucked a thick sweater under one arm. I'd need the sweater in the coolers, but I wasn't ready to put it on just yet. Before waddling back to trailer three, the empty sleeves of the jumpsuit dangling from my waist, I took another look at the picture

I'd gotten from Burt DeVriess. Burt's Aunt Jean smiled up at me from the photo. She wore a sky blue dress with a strand of black pearls—an anniversary present—around her neck. This had been her summer church outfit for years, Uncle Edgar had said. In the South, church clothes eventually became burial clothes. Uncle Edgar had kept the pearls as a memento after the memorial service, but I hoped the dress or its black plastic buttons would have survived.

I reentered trailer three, latched the door behind me, then squirmed into the sweater and zipped up the suit. Where to begin? "Eeny, meeny, miney, moe," I said, pointing in turn to each of the trailer's corners. "Moe" was back in the far right corner—up near where the cab would be when the trailer was being towed—so I headed that way. The stepstool was already back there, so I decided to start with the uppermost body, then work my way down toward the floor. Each shelving unit consisted of four shelves, and there were seven units along each wall. Twenty-eight bodies per side, fifty-six in this trailer. I'd need to hustle. For efficiency and thoroughness, I decided I'd work in a regular pattern: down four, over one, up four, over one, down another four, and so on, till my vertical zigzags brought me all the way back to the rear door. Then I'd work the other side, the other twenty-eight bodies in the same pattern. "Okay, here we go," I said, scooting the stool into position, climbing to the upper step, and pulling down the zipper.

The body in the right front corner of the trailer was number 28, according to her arm tag, her leg tag, and a computer-generated tag stuck to the front of the metal shelf she lay on. She was dressed in what had once been a cream-colored suit, which had probably contrasted nicely with her skin tone, as she was an

African-American woman. I couldn't tell that by the skin—there wasn't much left, and even white people's corpses tended to turn black as they decayed. But her hair was characteristically kinky, and her jaws and teeth jutted forward in the distinctly Negroid feature called prognathism. I zipped her up and dropped down a level.

Body 107, the second I looked at, appeared to be an elderly white woman, with wispy, thinning hair. My pulse quickened when I saw that she wore blue—it looked closer to navy than to sky blue, but photos can be misleading. It only took a moment, though, to realize that she wore dentures, and I knew from Burt and his uncle that I was looking for a woman with all her teeth. *Almost* all her teeth, I corrected myself.

And so it went, up, across, down, across, up again: body after body, skeleton after skeleton, all of them female, none of them possessing quite the combination of features that, collectively, had once been called Jeannie by her husband, Aunt Jean by her nephew, and Mamaw by her grandchildren and great-grandchildren.

It took me over an hour to look at the first twenty-eight bodies, only twenty minutes to work my way down the second side of the trailer. I studied the first dozen bodies closely, looking for markers of their age and race. By the second dozen bodies, I was already getting jaded, by the fourth dozen ruthless and impatient, as my stomach began rumbling and my feet started hurting. I found myself yanking each zipper down, casting a quick, exclusionary glance under the flap, and then pulling the zipper closed impatiently.

I was halfway down the first side of the second trailer—the trailer with the big black 4-F painted on the doors—when I froze, halfway through the reflexive upward tug that would zip the body bag closed. The dress I had glimpsed was nearly black in the center, but my peripheral vision, and then my brain, noticed that the dark color was limited to the chest and neck region. In the sleeves, enough of the original color showed through the dark stain to suggest that the fabric itself was light to medium blue—or once had been, back when a farm wife wore it to a white clapboard church. It would have been the kind of church where the Sunday service was followed by dinner on the grounds, a potluck where the world's best cooks—southern church cooks—competed sweetly but fiercely to be the acknowledged winner: the one whose baked beans or fried chicken or peach cobbler was the dish that was emptied first, scraped cleanest, and then eyed most sadly by those who'd ended up too far back in the line.

I peeled off my right glove and unzipped my jumpsuit partway, then threaded my hand down the neck of my sweater and fished the photo out of my shirt pocket again. It showed a blue-dressed, silver-haired woman in her seventies. She was holding a toddler on her lap, probably a great-grandchild. She had kind eyes, with a big smile on her face. She also had a big chip out of her upper left lateral incisor. "Her pie injury," Burt had said when he'd pointed it out to me.

"Pie injury?"

"Pie injury. My Aunt Jean loved pie," he'd said. "Lord, Doc, that woman could knock back half a pie at one sitting and still want the other half. It's a wonder she didn't weigh four hundred pounds. Anyhow, years ago—I was just a kid then—she was eating a piece of cherry pie, and she bit down on a pit and broke a tooth. She could've gotten a crown put on, but I think she liked the attention. All the little kids in the family loved to hear her tell the pie story. Every time she told it, that cherry pit got bigger and harder. I swear, by the time she died, that pit was the size of Mount Rushmore and as hard as the Hope Diamond." As he'd told the story, I'd heard things in Burt DeVriess's voice that I'd never heard before—warmth and unguardedness and innocence and maybe even love. Funny how a dead woman's pie story could bring something to the surface through years of cynicism and bare-knuckles courtroom battles.

"Okay, Number Ninety-nine," I said to the rotted corpse on the shelf, "let's have a look at your upper left lateral incisor." I leaned down—the body was on the second shelf up from the floor, at waist level—to study the teeth. The head was in shadow, partly from the shelf above and partly from me, making it difficult to see the tooth's contours, so I reached in and ran the tip of my left index finger over the biting surfaces of the upper teeth. Where the edge of the incisor should have been, I felt a quarter-inch notch instead. I retrieved my key chain again and shone the tiny LED light on the teeth. Years of wear had softened the edges, but half the tooth had broken away. This had to be Aunt Jean, but I needed to make absolutely sure. Unzipping the body bag completely, I folded back the entire C-shaped flap that constituted the bag's upper surface. I gave the key-chain light another squeeze and swept the faint beam down from the face, down across the shipwreck of the rib cage, across the collapsed abdomen and jutting hipbones, and along the legs. When I got to the knees, I stopped. The light bounced back at me with a dull silvery sheen. Number 99 had two metallic knees—knees made of titanium-662, I felt certain.

"Hello, Aunt Jean," I said. "I've heard a lot about you. I'm glad I found you."

A dozen photos, a quick conversation with Sean, and a three-hour drive later, I rolled into Knoxville, feeling exhausted but accomplished. I took a long, hot shower to wash away the smell of death and the aches of bending, then tumbled into bed and fell swiftly asleep. In my dreams I shared a cherry pie with a skeletal woman who flashed me a crooked smile. "Watch out for the pits," she said, "they'll break a tooth if you bite down on 'em. Did I ever tell you about the pie that broke my tooth?"

"Tell me again," I said to her. "Tell me the pie story."

When I woke up, daylight was streaming in the windows, and I called Burt DeVriess to tell him I'd found her.

CHAPTER 20

AFTER CALLING DEVRIESS, I HEADED TO CAMPUS. IT
was early yet—not quite 7:30—and all the offices in the Anthropology Department were still dark and empty. Even the osteology lab, where Miranda often arrived by 7:00, remained locked.
I was intrigued to find a vase of flowers—red roses—sitting in
the stairwell just outside the lab's door. A small card was nestled
amid the flowers; the envelope was unsealed, so I slid out the card
to see who was getting roses. I doubted that it was me, but then
again, you never know.

"For Miranda," the neat block letters read, "my new favorite."
Below the inscription was a drawing of a heart pierced by an arrow. I felt a pang of jealousy the moment I read the words. But
what disturbed me more was the blood dripping from the heart
and pooling beneath it.

An hour later, Miranda answered when I phoned the lab. She

sounded jangled and edgy, and I wasn't surprised. "I saw the flowers," I said. "Who do you think sent them?"

"I don't want to think about it," she said. "It creeps me out."

"Better to figure it out than not to know," I said.

"You're probably right," she said, "but I hate to get upset about it, because that gives whoever it is more power over me than I want." I didn't say anything, and after a moment, she went on. "I'm afraid it's Stuart Latham," she said. "He called yesterday, asking if I was involved with the investigation into Mary's death."

This revelation stunned me. "My god," I said, "what did you tell him?"

"I told him I couldn't discuss any forensic cases with him. But—true to form—he didn't want to take no for an answer." She laughed a brief, bitter laugh. "First he tried to charm me, and when that didn't work, he played the grieving widower—the real victim in the case—and tried to guilt it out of me. Finally, when *that* didn't work, he started getting mean."

"How so? Did he threaten you in any way?" I felt my pulse getting faster and my blood pressure rising.

"No, nothing overt," she said. "Just talking about how selfish and heartless I am." She paused. "How I flirted with him and led him on back when I used to see them. How unhappy that made him realize he was in his marriage. How hard a time he's had getting over the rejection." She fell silent again, except for her breathing. From the sound of it, I wondered if she was crying. "The thing I'm ashamed of, Dr. B., is that I *did* flirt with him. I don't know why. No, that's not true; I do know. He was handsome, and he was a grown-up, and it was obvious that he was attracted to me. I think it was the seductiveness of being desired, you know?"

I did know; what surprised me was that Miranda knew, and that she'd found it out from the likes of Stuart Latham.

"Anyhow," she said, "I never meant to cause trouble in their marriage, and I stopped flirting with him when I realized it was starting to."

"So how did the phone call end?"

"Abruptly," she said. "I told him never to call me again, and I hung up on him."

"You think he sent the flowers as an apology?"

"Did you see the card?"

"Yes," I admitted.

"Did that look like an apology?"

"If it was an apology," I said, "it was a kinda scary one."

"Kinda," she said. "Like the pope is kinda Catholic."

"Are you okay?"

"I will be," she said. "Soon as I get a chance to take a long, hot shower and wash the scum off."

"If he contacts you again, tell me," I said. "We'll call the campus police or KPD. The last thing he needs right now is to be any higher on the radar screen of the cops."

She thanked me and hung up. From what she'd said, it sounded plausible that Stuart Latham had sent the flowers, and the possibility was troubling. Two other possibilities—two other suspects, as I thought of them—had occurred to me, and both of those were troubling as well.

One possibility was Edelberto Garcia, who I still feared might be interested in Miranda as more than a colleague or occasional babysitter. There was something about Garcia's cool smoothness I didn't fully trust, although I recognized that it might be jealousy rather than logic that lay behind my suspicions.

The other possibility was Garland Hamilton, and the thought that Hamilton might have sent Miranda the flowers chilled me to the bone. A few months before, Hamilton had locked his sights on Jess, and now Jess was dead. When I considered this possibility, I couldn't help praying that the flowers had come from Stuart Latham.

By midmorning I was lost in the pages of the latest issue of the *Journal of Forensic Sciences*—one of my colleagues was fine-tuning a way to estimate age by studying cranial sutures—when I gradually became aware of a soft, insistent tapping sound and then a familiar voice saying, "Doc, mind if I come in?" I roused myself back to the present.

"Sorry. Sure, come on in." I looked up at the same moment I placed the voice. Steve Morgan walked in, and the sight brought a smile to my face, despite the stress of the past two days. Steve was a TBI agent who'd been a student of mine years before; more recently he'd been part of a joint TBI-FBI investigation into official corruption in the Cooke County Sheriff's Office.

"I hope you're here to tell me y'all have caught Garland Hamilton," I said.

He winced and shook his head. "I wish I were, but I'm not," he said. "I think you'll find this interesting, though. We've been watching his bank accounts and looking at his credit cards."

"And?"

"We found a storage unit he rented about six months ago, and inside was something that belongs to you." He stepped back into the hallway, then reappeared, cradling a cardboard box in his arms. The box was 36 inches long, 12 inches high, and 12 inches deep. I knew the exact dimensions because I had spent years putting skeletons into boxes just like this one. I had a pretty good

idea whose skeleton was in this particular box, too: I'd have bet a
year's salary that the box contained the postcranial skeleton—the
bones from the neck down—of Leena Bonds, a young woman
killed in Cooke County thirty years earlier. I had recovered the
woman's body from deep in a cave in the mountains, where the
combination of cool air and abundant moisture had transformed
her soft tissue into adipocere, a soaplike substance that preserved
her features remarkably well over the decades. Midway through
the investigation into Leena's murder, someone had broken into
my office and stolen the box. That someone had been Garland
Hamilton.

I motioned toward my desktop, and Morgan set the box down.
I raised the lid, which was hinged along one of the three-foot
sides. Inside, I saw the bones of a young white female, each bone
bearing the case number in my writing. Two parts of the skeleton
were missing, as I knew they would be: the skull and the hyoid,
both of which I had taken to show my anthropology class the
day the box was stolen. The woman's skull—Leena's skull—and
the fractured hyoid bone from her throat had been buried eight
months ago up in Cooke County by Jim O'Conner. O'Conner
was now the county's sheriff, but thirty years earlier he'd been
simply a young man who loved Leena, when she was still an innocent girl. Before her uncle had molested her and her aunt had
strangled her.

The bones took me back in time, the way the smell of baking
bread or fresh-mown grass can take you back to your childhood.
For me, seeing a skeleton was like reading a diary—a diary recording injuries, illnesses, handedness, and a host of other parts
of life that remained written in the bones long after death. In the
room that adjoined my office, I had a library full of such dia-

ries—diaries of life and death. Every one was uniquely fascinating, and I always remembered its details. Every one was uniquely sad, too—Leena's doubly so. I shook myself free of the memory and looked up at Morgan.

"Sorry," I said. "I was just taking a quick trip down a dark stretch of memory lane."

He nodded. "I understand," he said. "Take your time."

"I'm done," I said. "You mentioned you were looking at Garland Hamilton's credit-card receipts. Anything that points to where he is now?"

"No," he said. "The storage-unit rental was about six months ago, and he paid for a whole year up front. Latest activity"—he hesitated—"was a couple hours after he escaped. A security camera at a SunTrust ATM on Hill Avenue shows him using the cash machine. He got a four-hundred-dollar cash advance and four hundred dollars out of checking. The most the machine would let him get."

"Where'd he get the cards?"

"I don't know," said Morgan. "He didn't have them in jail, so he must have had them stashed someplace safe and easy to get to. Maybe the storage unit."

"Weren't his accounts frozen?"

Morgan shook his head. "If he were bankrolling international terrorism or embezzling millions, the feds would freeze his accounts. Otherwise there's no legal basis for it. He won't get real far on eight hundred bucks, but it lets him drop off the radar at least for a while."

"Any idea where he might be? You think he's staying put, or do you think he's on the run?"

Morgan frowned. "Hard to tell. Typically, escaped murderers

run, but he's not typical. He's smarter than most, and he knows how cops think."

"So he might run after all," I said. "Figuring that you guys would expect him not to."

"Hell, you can chase your tail in circles second- and third-guessing that way. Doesn't get you anything except dizzy, though. His picture's all over the media, and we've sent an APB to every law-enforcement agency in the country. We'll get him."

"I hope sooner rather than later," I said.

"It'll be sooner," he said. "Meantime, though, I was wondering—have you thought about carrying a gun?"

"Me? A gun? When I'm out in the field, I'm generally on all fours, with my butt sticking up in the air." The description got a laugh from Morgan. "What good would a gun do me?"

"I meant for when you're not in the field," he said. "When you're in the office, or at home. I know you're not a gun-totin' kind of guy. But maybe for now, till we catch him."

In fact, I had already considered it. "You think I'm in danger?" I asked.

He considered that. "Depends on which matters more to Hamilton," he said, "getting away or getting even. He already tried to kill you once. He might consider that unfinished business—a score he's got another chance to settle, now that he's on the loose."

"Gee, this is making me feel better," I said.

"I'm not trying to scare you," he said. "I'm just being realistic. Get a weapon. Hell, you're a TBI consultant; I'm sure we can get you a permit. We'd just need to take you out to the firing range and get you qualified."

"Damn," I said. "I hate this. But if you can make it happen, I'll do it."

"Good," he said. "I'll see what hoops we need to jump through. And I'll let you know as soon as we find anything on Hamilton." He shook my hand and turned to go. "Be careful," he said.

"Sure."

After Morgan left, I picked up the phone and dialed.

"Cooke County Sheriff," said a brisk voice in an East Tennessee twang. "Kin I hep you'uns?"

"Yes, ma'am. I'm wondering if the sheriff's in."

"Kin I tell him who's calling?"

"It's Dr. Bill Brockton from UT."

"I'll tell him, hon," she said. I felt like I was in a truck-stop café rather than on the phone with a law-enforcement agency. "Hang on, if you don't care to." The expression—which actually meant "if you don't mind"—made me smile.

Ten seconds later, I heard Jim O'Conner's voice. "Doc, you all right? I hear things have gotten exciting down there."

"I've had better times, but I'm okay," I said.

"I'm sorry he's loose."

"Not half as sorry as I am," I said. "Listen, you gonna be around late this afternoon?"

"Should be," he said. "Unless somebody does some spectacular lawbreaking up here in Cooke County. Which," he added, "is always a distinct possibility."

"Mind if I come see you?"

"Come on up. Any particular occasion?"

"Got something to show you," I said.

"I'll be here. You remember how to find us?"

"Sure," I said. "Drive east till civilization ends, then follow the sound of the gunfire."

He laughed. "Yup, you remember. If something comes up and I can't be here, I'll give you a call."

"Same here," I said. "It'll be good to see you, Jim."

"Be good to see you, too, Doc."

TWO HOURS later and fifty miles to the east, I took the I-40 exit for River Road, the winding, two-lane blacktop that snaked along a tumbling mountain river and into Jonesport, the county seat of Cooke County.

The sheriff's office was tucked into a granite courthouse that looked more like a small fortress than a seat of county government. As I parked, I noticed a couple of stoop-shouldered whittlers occupying a bench on the courthouse lawn. Shavings were heaped almost knee-high between the feet of each man. I had seen these same whittlers on that same bench in the exact same postures some nine months earlier when I'd been up in Cooke County. I wondered if they had even left their post, or were they permanent fixtures, like the Civil War cannon and the statue of Obadiah Jones, the town's founder and namesake? I tucked the box of Leena's bones under one arm. As I passed the bench, I lifted my other hand in greeting. Neither man spoke or waved, but there was a flicker of eye contact and the barest hint of a nod from each aged head, and both pairs of eyes swiveled to the box under my arm.

"That's a mighty good pile of shavings you-all got there," I said. "Just be careful you don't drop a lit match. I'd hate to have to come identify your burned bones."

"Is them bones you got in that box?" one of the men asked.

"From that Kitchings girl?" asked the other.

"She weren't a Kitchings," corrected the first one. "She were a Bonds."

"Bonds. I knowed that," said his friend. "I just disremembered."

"Are them bones? That Bonds girl's bones?" persisted the first one.

"You'd need to ask the sheriff about that," I said.

"Sheriff's inside," said Whittler Number Two.

"Is he doing a pretty good job cleaning up the county?" I asked.

"View from here is pretty much the same all the time," said the first whittler. "Don't too many folks commit their crimes right here in front of the courthouse."

The second one laughed, exposing toothless gums. "They was a lot of crime going on *inside* the courthouse," he said.

The first one wheezed out a chuckle at that.

"Course we didn't know about some of it at the time. New sheriff might be doing stuff we don't know about neither."

"I don't think so," I said. "Jim O'Conner isn't that kind of guy. Anyway, I'd best get in. Y'all don't cut yourselves." They nodded, bent low over their whittling again.

Jim O'Conner's head was barely visible behind the immense pile of papers, files, and folders on his desk. I knocked on the door. He raised up, peering over the stack.

"Thank goodness," he said. "This paperwork's driving me nuts, and I was desperate for a break. Come on in."

"Not quite how I imagined I'd find you," I said. "Figured you'd be out chasing thieves and bootleggers and poachers and such things."

"Well, the job is mostly administrative," he said. "Got training logs to fill out, grant requests to write, grant *reports* to write, court cases to get ready for, hiring requisitions."

"You're hiring? Business booming?"

"Well," he said, "we didn't have many people to start with. I had to let some of them go, 'cause they were sort of in Orbin Kitchings's vein," he said. "Law enforcement for personal profit."

I grimaced at the mention of the name. Orbin Kitchings had been the county's chief deputy, and he'd used his badge and his authority to commit crimes with impunity. I'd never forget the interaction I witnessed between Orbin and a small-time marijuana farmer—the deputy had extorted money from the man and had cruelly shot the poor fellow's dog.

"I'm not surprised you're having trouble with that," I said. "It's a small county, with a frontier mentality. The line between the good guys and the bad guys gets kind of fuzzy sometimes, especially when money's involved."

"Oh, I didn't mean to be rude," O'Conner said. "Here, let me clear a spot for you to sit down." He stood up and came around the desk to remove another stack of papers and files from the one chair in the office. That's when he saw the box. He looked from the box up to my face, just as I'd done when Steve Morgan brought it into my office at UT. I read the question in his eyes. "Is that what I think it is?"

"Yeah," I said. "TBI found this when they were searching a storage unit Garland Hamilton had rented."

The sheriff sucked in a deep breath and blew it out, then started grabbing armfuls of folders and setting them in the corner.

After he'd cleared off one end of the desk, I set the box down and stepped back to give him space, physically and emotionally. He reached out, folded up the lid, and eyed the bones with a mixture of sorrow and tenderness that thirty years seemed to have done little to diminish. One by one, he picked up the bones and turned them over in his hands. A femur. A hip bone. A handful of ribs. His eyes got a faraway look in them.

"Funny thing," he said. "She's been gone so long. These bones aren't her, but they *were* her. Part of her, anyhow. I couldn't pick these out of a lineup. I mean, I can't tell one skeleton from another. But because you say this is her, I know it's true, and that brings the whole thing back. Does that sound strange?"

"Not at all," I said. "I've seen hundreds of people react this way. We humans seem to have a deep need for closure when somebody we love dies. That's why when a child goes missing, the parent can never finish their grieving unless or until the body's found. We want our stories to have endings, even if the endings break our hearts."

He didn't say anything, but he nodded, his eyes glistening. Then he noticed the paper bag nestled in one end of the box. He hesitated, but only briefly, then unrolled the top and peered inside. He looked up at me and said, "Do you mind?"

I picked up the bag and gently tipped its contents into his cupped hands: the tiny bones of a half-formed baby, which Leena had been carrying when she was killed. The biggest of the bones, the femur, was smaller than a chicken drumstick. "Damn it, Doc," he said. "I don't know who to hate more, her aunt for killing her or her uncle for getting her pregnant."

"I'm not sure there's a lesser of those two evils," I said. "And it probably doesn't change the equation that the uncle's dead and the aunt's in prison."

"Not a bit."

"You said a while back that if we ever recovered these bones, you'd like to bury them with the skull. You still feel that way?"

He nodded.

"What about the fetal bones—do you want to bury those with Leena's bones?"

"Of course," he said. "This was Leena's baby." He paused. "Even if it was fathered by a hypocritical, abusive son of a bitch."

"Yeah," I said.

He drew another deep breath and then shook himself. He looked at the clock on the wall over his door. "I'm thinking maybe that now would be a good time to call it a day," he said. "It's after five, and I don't think my heart's in this paperwork anymore for today. You got to hurry right back to Knoxville?"

"I'm not in a big rush," I said.

"Come on up to the farmhouse with me."

"I was hoping you'd ask."

"You want to ride with me, or would you rather follow me up?"

"I'll follow you," I said. "That way you don't have to drive me back to town."

We walked out together, past the bench, past the whittlers. This time O'Conner had the box of bones under his arm.

"Evening, Sheriff," said Whittler Number One. Either O'Conner ranked higher in their esteem than I did or they were sufficiently curious to speak first.

"Evening, fellas," he said.

"Are them there that girl's bones?"

O'Conner didn't say anything at first. I could see a couple of different emotions working in his face, then it smoothed out, and he said, "Yes, sir. They are. We're going to give her a decent burial finally."

"That's good," said the old man. "That was a shame what them Kitchingses done to her. She deserves a decent burial."

"You all have a good evening," said O'Conner. "I'll see you in the morning."

"Night, Sheriff," the two men chorused together.

O'Conner placed the box in the backseat of a black-and-white Jeep Cherokee that had a seven-pointed star on the side.

I got into my truck, and together we backtracked along River Road a couple of miles back toward I-40, then turned up a gravel road through dense forest, along a small stream that fed into the river on the other side of the blacktop. My first trip up this gravel road, I'd been blindfolded and bound with duct tape—shanghaied by a giant mountain man named Waylon—and brought up this road to see Jim O'Conner. I hadn't known what lay along either side of the gravel at the time. My second trip up, I'd been able to see, and I had seen the gravel end at a wall of vegetation—or *seem* to end. In fact, it plunged beneath a cascade of kudzu vines. We had snaked through a tunnel of kudzu and then emerged into a small hanging valley, where O'Conner was conducting a secret experiment in agriculture. Not marijuana, as I had suspected at one point, but ginseng: he'd found a way to replicate wild black ginseng, the sort prized by poachers, the sort that commanded top dollar in Chinese markets. This trip, I noticed that the road had recently been regraveled. It looked slightly wider, and a film of dust on the weeds alongside hinted at heavy traffic. When we got to the kudzu tunnel, I saw that the vines hiding the tunnel's mouth had been cut back, transfering what had once been a secret entrance to O'Conner's little valley into a shaded arbor. The vines had been thinned, which took some frequent attention, I knew, given kudzu's prodigious ability to grow by several feet a day. Sunlight filtered through. It still wasn't cool under here, but it was a brief respite from the baking sun of the late-summer afternoon. When we emerged out the other side, into a large clearing with a frame farmhouse at one end, I was surprised at the transformation. Half a dozen vehicles, pickup trucks, and late-model cars were tucked into a small parking lot of gravel. The kudzu vines that had wrapped the back of the house—forming another tunnel connecting with the giant ginseng patch—had also been trimmed back, and the house had been freshly painted. I saw a small satellite dish and junction boxes, where underground telephone wires and television cable emerged from the ground.

As I got out, I said to O'Conner, "I see you've made some changes around here."

He smiled. "A few," he said. "My cover was blown, so I figured we needed to go ahead and get into the market with this fall's crop, which'll be our first. We took some samples to buyers, and we've got contracts for all we can produce. Should be several thousand pounds of top-grade ginseng root. We're not getting quite what the poachers get for the stuff from the national park," he said, "but close. If we can keep things from drying out in the heat of the summer, we should have several thousand pounds, at almost two hundred dollars a pound."

I did the math. "So you're looking at six figures?"

"Should be," he said. "Seven if we get real lucky. But you know what? It doesn't matter all that much. It's been an interesting experiment. Maybe it'll help lessen the demand for the poached 'sang, which would be good. And I've got half a dozen people working for me, doing honest jobs, which is also a good thing here in Cooke County. But I don't really need the money, so if this doesn't work, I'm not hurting. "

I laughed. "Yeah, I know how big that sheriff's paycheck is," I said.

"Well, yeah, I'm not gonna get rich off that," he said. "But I've got almost no overhead, apart from the ginseng operation here. My car's provided. I've long since owned this farm outright. I live like a monk when I'm not at work. Hell, I don't even spend everything the county pays me."

"You sound like a man whose life is in balance," I said. "Of course, even when you looked like an outlaw, you seemed pretty balanced and content."

"It took me a while to get there," he said. "But yeah. I mean, you are who you are, you aren't what you do."

He motioned me up toward the wide wooden porch, where a pair of weathered wooden rocking chairs sat side by side, like an old couple.

"Come on up," he said. "Sit a spell. You want some iced tea?" I nodded.

The wooden screen door had been freshly painted, too, but the spring still creaked when O'Conner pulled it open. He grinned.

"Always did like that sound," he said. "The guys working on the house replaced the old spring with a new one that didn't make any noise. I made them take the new spring off and put the old one back on."

O'Conner disappeared, then emerged from the kitchen several minutes later, bearing two tall ceramic tumblers. The one he handed me was ice cold and frosted at the top—fresh from the freezer. I took a sip. I'd had O'Conner's hot ginseng tea once before, but never iced ginseng. I liked it cold. It had the slightly earthy, tangy taste I'd remembered, and hints of honey, plus maybe a little fruit juice in it, too.

"It's good," I said. "You ought to bottle this stuff."

He smiled. "It's in the business plan—year two," he said. "You've got a good head for business, Doc."

I took another sip. "No, I just know something tasty when I get a swig of it," I said.

O'Conner sat in the other chair and began to rock in time with me. A small end table separated the rockers, a remote control rested on the table. O'Conner pressed a button on the remote, and a ceiling fan stirred a breeze down onto us.

"Another new addition," I said.

"Yeah," he said. "Usually there's a pretty good breeze, but this summer's been so hot I finally broke down and hauled in some technology. I can't remember how I did without it. I got a house in town now, but sometimes, if the night's not too hot, I'll come up here and sleep on the porch." He opened a drawer in the end table and pulled out a small silver flask. "You want a little nip of Jack in there?" he said.

"No thanks," I said.

"That's right, you don't drink," he said. "You mind if I add a little nip to mine?"

"Go right ahead," I said. "I'm not sure you'll be helping the taste any, but you probably know what you're doing."

"I've done rigorous experiments," he said. "I think I've perfected the ratio." He poured in a small splash—it couldn't have been more than an ounce—then screwed the cap back on the flask and replaced the flask in the drawer. "Different," he said, taking a sip and assessing it. "But mighty good."

"You gonna bottle that version, too?" I asked.

He laughed. "Year three. Good thing I'm not trying to keep any trade secrets from you."

We rocked until sundown, and beyond, the sheriff and I. As the daylight dwindled, so did our words, and the night wrapped us in a blanket of comfortable silence. After a while I realized that Jim and I were not the only two people present on the porch. Leena Bonds—Jim's murdered love—was with us, too, somewhere in the darkness beyond him. So was Jess Carter, I realized—with me in the way that everyone you ever love remains with you, no matter what happens to either of you.

As the rockers creaked and the stars came out, I felt the pain and the fear inside me subside. In their place, I was amazed to find—at least for this moment—peace and a feeling I could only have described as quiet, unexpected joy.

CHAPTER 21

IT WAS RARE FOR ME TO STAY UP LATE ENOUGH TO watch the eleven o'clock news, but I was late getting home from Cooke County. Besides, Channel 10 had promised an update on the manhunt for Garland Hamilton. I'd heard through the Knox County prosecutor's office that the Tennessee Association of District Attorneys General had offered a twenty-thousand-dollar reward for information leading to Hamilton's arrest and capture, and Channel 10 was promising to lead off the newscast with more details. Jess Carter had worked closely with district attorneys, so the D.A.'s had taken a special interest in recapturing her killer.

The newscast's theme music had just started when my phone rang. I checked the caller ID display and saw the main number for the UT switchboard. I knew there were no operators on duty this late at night. That meant the phone call could have come from any one of thousands of extensions scattered across the campus.

"Hello?"

"Is this Dr. Brockton?"

"Yes, it is."

"Dr. Brockton, this is Officer Sutton from the UT Police calling. We have an alarm going off in the Anthropology Department. Our protocols call for us to notify you when that happens."

I lunged for the remote and switched off the television. We'd had the alarms installed only a few months before, after a break-in and the theft of two sets of bones from the forensic skeletal collection.

"We've got alarms in two places," I said, cradling the phone with my shoulder and jamming on a pair of shoes. "One's in the collection room, the other's in the bone lab. Which one's going off?"

"I'm not sure it's either one of those," he said. "It's labeled 'Osteology.'"

"That's the bone lab. Damn. I'll be right there." I hung up and dashed out the door.

My tires squealed as I careened around the serpentine streets leading out of Sequoyah Hills. The speed limit here was twenty-five, but tonight I was doing twice that. As soon as I turned onto Kingston Pike and had a straight stretch of road, I dialed Miranda's cell phone. She'd been planning to stay late and work tonight, whittling away at the backlog of skeletal measurements awaiting entry into the Forensic Data Bank. She didn't answer, which was unlike Miranda, whom I'd seen juggle four or five calls at once. The fact that I got her voice mail alarmed me.

"Miranda, it's Bill. It's just after eleven. Give me a call as soon as you get this."

I skidded around the corner from Kingston Pike onto Neyland and then floored the accelerator. Flying past the sewage treatment plant, I nearly rear-ended a street sweeper that was poking along at twenty or thirty miles an hour. As I yanked the wheel to avoid the machine, I fishtailed into the oncoming lane and nearly hit another car head-on. The oncoming car veered onto the shoulder and fishtailed slightly, too, then corrected and sped away, its horn blaring. Only after the other car was out of sight did it register that I'd nearly crashed head-on into a yellow SUV. A yellow Nissan Pathfinder, I realized.

I could see the blue strobes of the police lights long before I threaded my way down the drive to the foot of the stadium. The lights throbbed up through the tracery of girders, transforming the stadium into an ominous set for a suspense movie. Another set of strobes, red ones, was pulsing too, and I nearly threw up when I realized that the red strobes belonged to an ambulance, backed up to the double doors behind a white Jetta. The truck was still skidding forward when I slammed the transmission into Park and leaped out. I left the door open and sprinted the fifty yards to the ambulance.

A figure in dark blue stepped toward me. "Police!" he shouted. "Stop right there!"

"It's Dr. Brockton," I yelled. "I think I've got a student in there. I've got to see."

"Hold on. Hold on, " he said.

I kept running. He stepped directly into my path and spread his arms wide.

"Hold on, Dr. Brockton. Wait just a minute. "

I tried to sidestep him, but he was too quick. He wrapped both arms around me.

"I can't let you in there until I know it's safe," he said.

I struggled to break free of his grip. "I've got to check on Miranda," I said. "I have to see about her."

"Dr. Brockton, listen up now. You have got to calm down. You have got to stop struggling, or I will handcuff you, sir. Do you understand me?" He gave me a powerful squeeze. He was no taller than I was, but he was twenty years younger and probably outweighed me by forty pounds, all of it muscle. "Dr. Brockton, please don't make me handcuff you. Do you understand me?"

I went limp. "Yes," I said. "I understand. Tell me what's going on. Is Miranda in there?"

"We do have someone in there," he said. "I don't know the status. If I can turn loose of you, I'll radio and ask what's going on and if it's all right for you to come in."

"Please," I said.

"Have you got ahold of yourself?" he asked. "If I let you go, you're not gonna go charging in there to be a hero, are you?"

"No," I said. "If you turn me loose, I'll step back so you can make the radio call."

It wasn't until he released me, and I was able to breathe again, that I realized how hard he'd been holding me.

He pressed the "transmit" button on his radio. "This is Markham," he said. "I've got Dr. Brockton out here, just outside the basement door. Is it all right if he comes in there now?"

The answer came into his earpiece, so I couldn't hear it, but he nodded and motioned me in. I broke into a run, but he quickly called, "Walk! Don't run! We've got officers with weapons. You go running in, they're liable to shoot you."

I forced myself to slow to a walk. When I reached the metal door leading into the building, I heard Markham say, "He's coming in the door right now." A second officer was standing in the stairwell between the exterior door and the bone lab's door. The metal door to the lab was propped open—a disconcerting sight, as we always kept it closed. The door was steel, fitted with a small window that was kept covered by a piece of paper so no one could look inside. The paper was gone. So was the glass. A smear of blood ran down the door, reaching halfway to the floor.

I stared around the bone lab, wild-eyed. Two uniformed officers stood to my left, by the desks and the tables where graduate students worked. To the right was the storage area that held row on row of boxed Native American skeletons—several thousand of them—stacked on shelves three feet deep.

An EMT backed out of the aisle between the rows of shelves, pulling a gurney with him. A motionless figure lay on the gurney; beneath a sheet I saw the contours of feet, legs, torso. I'd seen that body nearly every day for years now in various postures—sitting, standing, crawling on all fours, bending over to pluck a bone from the ground. I'd never seen it lying motionless, but I recognized it instantly as Miranda's.

"Dear God," I said. "Tell me what happened."

"It's about time you got here." Miranda sat up partway, propping herself on her elbows.

"Jesus," I breathed, "Miranda! Are you okay? You're hurt? What happened?"

"Could you repeat the questions one at a time? On second thought, never mind. I'm okay—I think it's just a sprained ankle—but there's a guy out there I don't want a second date with."

"Who? Tell me. Tell me everything."

"I was putting measurements into the data bank, over at that table by the windows, using the digitizing probe. I'd just gotten to that really huge skull, and I was halfway through the cranial measurements when I got a creepy feeling, like maybe somebody was watching me. I looked up, but all I could see was my own reflection."

"Remind me to get some floodlights put in outside tomorrow," I said. "Or a video camera. Or an electric fence."

"I went back to measuring," she said, "but a minute later I heard the outside door open and close. I was jumpy already, so I listened closely for the sound of someone going up the steps to the second floor. Nothing. I turned around to look and listen, and I saw a shadow fall across the piece of paper covering the little window in the door. I got a really bad feeling, and it got worse when the knob started to turn, very slowly—first one way, then the other—and the door started rattling and shaking as somebody pulled on the knob.

"I yelled, 'We're closed!' and the door just started shaking harder. 'I'm calling the police!' I said, and it shook even harder. I picked up the phone and dialed 911, but right then the glass shattered and an arm reached through the window.

"That's when I panicked. He was coming in the only door to the lab. I thought about trying to get out one of the front windows, but I figured he'd hear me and run back outside just as I got there. I decided I'd have a better chance if I turned out the light and hid in the shelves in the back."

"Do you know who it was? Did you see the guy's face?"

"No." She frowned, almost as if she were angry at herself. "All I could see was a man's hand. Long-sleeved denim shirt. Surgical gloves."

"Excuse me?" It was one of the EMTs. Miranda and I both looked at him, startled. I'd been so caught up in the story I'd forgotten there were other people in the room. "How do you know it was a man's hand, if it was gloved?"

Miranda looked exasperated. "I've only measured a zillion male and female hands over the past four years," she said. A zillion was an exaggeration, but only a slight one. "I can tell the difference at fifty yards." That, I felt sure, was not an exaggeration.

I pointed to the smear of blood on the door. "That's not yours, is it?"

"No," she said, with obvious satisfaction. "That's his."

"Good. The crime lab shouldn't have any trouble getting DNA out of that."

"I'll claim credit for getting the sample," she said.

I looked at her quizzically.

"When I jumped up to turn out the light, I grabbed a femur that was lying on the table. Just as he got the dead bolt open, I gave him a good whack on the arm. Must have forced his arm down onto the broken glass." Her coolness astonished me. "If his humerus isn't fractured, he's at least got one hell of a bruise."

"Probably two," I corrected. "One where you whacked him and one where his arm hit the door." She grinned, and I marveled at her bravery.

"But that didn't scare him off?"

"I wish. By then he was yanking the door open. I flipped off the light switch and ran toward the back of the lab."

My heart was pounding. "God," I said, "I know it turns out okay, and I'm still scared to death."

"If you're not peeing your pants, you're not as scared as I was," she said. She pointed down at the blue sheet covering her, and I saw a damp stain at the center. "Last time I peed my pants was in first grade," she said, "on the swings after school one day. My mom was late picking me up, and I was too shy to go inside and ask Mrs. Downey if I could use the bathroom. I couldn't think what to do, so I just sat there, swinging back and forth, dribbling arcs of pee on the bare dirt of the playground."

The image of six-year-old Miranda peeing on the swing set broke the spell of fear, and I reached out and squeezed her shoulder. "So tell me the rest."

"I climbed on top of one of the shelves—that one right there," she said, pointing to a rack halfway toward the back of the lab. "I figured that in the dark he might not find me up there. I could hear him going up and down the rows, stopping to listen for my breathing. Finally he walked toward the door, and I thought he was leaving. But then the lights came on."

"Damn," I said.

"I knew he'd see me with the lights on, so I decided to try climbing out that little window up there."

"You're brilliant," I said. I'd completely forgotten about the windows. Set high into the side and back walls of the bone lab were a few small windows, each measuring about two feet high by three feet wide. They led not to the outside of the stadium but to its deepest labyrinthine recesses—the catacombs at the very base of the stands.

"It's true what they say about fear and adrenaline," she said. "It took the strength of ten graduate assistants to slide that window open through forty years of gunk." She flexed a muscle, and both the EMTs laughed. "Anyway, when I dropped down the other side my foot caught something, and I rolled my ankle pretty hard. I figured I was in real trouble at that point, but then I heard the sirens coming, and I heard him running out of the lab and up the stairwell. And here I am, and here are all of you. And jeepers, Auntie Em, there's no place like home."

I didn't know whether to laugh or cry, so I did a little of both. "Thank God you're okay," I said. "Let's get you to the ER and get that ankle X-rayed."

"Good grief, I don't need an X-ray," she scoffed. "You think I don't know if my ankle is broken?"

"She's only measured a zillion ankles," said the head EMT, earning a laugh from her.

Miranda used her right foot to kick the sheet off her left leg. The EMTs already had the ankle immobilized in a strap-on boot; cold packs surrounded her foot and lower leg. "If you can just pull a string or two," she said, "and get me in to see one of the football team's physical therapists tomorrow, I'll be fine in a couple of days."

"I think I can arrange that," I said, and turned to the EMTs. "Can you let her go now, or do you have to take her to the hospital since you're already here?"

"I'd advise an X-ray," said the lead EMT, "but no, we're not going to force her to get treatment against her will, if she's competent to refuse it."

"She's one of the most competent people I know," I said.

He shrugged and went out to the ambulance, returning with a long form, in triplicate, requiring multiple signatures. She handed the forms back, and he glanced over them.

"This 974 phone number here," he said. "Is that . . . ?"

"That's the number here in the lab," she said. She hopped down from the gurney onto her good leg, then hobbled over to the desk and sat on the edge, tapping the phone with a finger.

"You want to put your other number—home or cell number—here beside it? Just in case?"

"Just in case *what*—my foot falls off when I get home?"

He turned bright red, then mumbled, "I guess maybe this one's enough." He gave her a few unnecessary instructions on caring for a sprain, wished her a speedy recovery, and then retreated, trailing his gurney, his colleague, and his shredded dignity behind him.

"'Just in case' he wanted to ask you out," I said once he was gone. "You sure shut him down fast."

"Yeah," she said. "Kind of a shame—he was cute. But that was a test, and he flunked. If he doesn't have the moxie to answer that in front of an audience, he doesn't have enough moxie to deal with me."

"You could be right," I said. "Hey, you ever tried speed dating?"

She snorted. "Naw. Waste of time. I just fast-forward straight to speed rejection."

I laughed. "If you ever get tired of anthropology, I think you should write a relationship self-help book. *Smart Women, Foolish Men* or some such."

The campus police officers were standing around aimlessly, so I hoped maybe we could call it a night. "You guys gonna call a KPD forensic team to come get a swab of that?"

"They're already on the way," he said. "Should be here in a couple of minutes."

"Do you need me to stay around and lock up once they're done?"

"No, sir," he said. "We've got keys, so we can lock up. We can also call the physical plant people, get them to replace the glass in the morning."

"I'd appreciate that," I said. "Can you ask them if they've got wire-reinforced security glass, or bulletproof glass, to make sure this kind of thing can't happen again?"

He nodded, and then I saw him looking at the bank of big windows across the front of the lab.

"I should probably give them a call, too," I said. "Talk to them about some bars for those front windows."

"I'd say that's a good idea," he said.

I looked at Miranda, realized what a close call she'd had. "Wish I'd thought of that sooner," I said.

"You can't think of everything," Miranda said. "If he hadn't gotten in, he might have just been waiting for me outside. Point is, I'm fine."

"That's part of the point," I said. "Another important part is to *keep* you fine."

I offered Miranda my guest room for the night, partly because I was worried about her safety and partly because I feared she'd have trouble getting around with a badly sprained ankle.

"Not a chance," she said.

"Why not?" I said. "I've got no designs on you."

"I know," she said, "and I couldn't take the disappointment." Then she turned serious. "Actually, I figure you're the next item on this guy's to-do list. He was probably looking for you when he came down here in the first place. I was just the consolation prize."

A thought struck me suddenly. "I don't think so," I said. "I suspect you're his new favorite." When I quoted the line from the card on the flowers, the color drained from her face. Then she shook her head fiercely.

"No," she said. "I'm not going to think that way. I don't want to spend every moment looking over my shoulder, expecting some pervert or creep to be there."

"Then don't," I said. "But at least keep some pepper spray handy."

"I have some in the nightstand."

I drove Miranda home and helped her up the stairs and into her house. "I've never seen your house before," I said. "It's charming."

"You've never seen the *inside*," she said pointedly. She saw the look of shame on my face, and she laid a hand on my arm. "It's okay," she said, and those two simple words of understanding and forgiveness were among the most profound and generous things anyone had ever said to me. I wrapped my arms around Miranda and gave her a bear hug, probably as tight as the one the UT police officer had given me outside the bone lab. After a moment she tapped me on the back, so I let go.

"I might need to go to the ER now," she said. "I think you just fractured half my ribs."

"God, you're something," I said. "What would I do without you?"

"You'd find somebody else," she said. "The world's full of brave, brilliant women. Hell, graduate school's full of brave, brilliant women."

"I don't think there's another one like you out there," I said. "Good night, Miranda."

"Night, Dr. B."

She closed her door. I waited at the bottom of the steps until I heard the dead bolt snick shut, and then I went only as far as my truck. I reclined the seat a few inches, rolled down the windows so I could hear, and passed the night in an uneasy vigil outside her house.

CHAPTER 22

AIM FOR THE HEAD, I REMINDED MYSELF AS I LINED up the sights. *The center of the head—the surest kill.* The gun felt solid in my hand, more solid than I felt within myself. As I took aim at the shadowy figure, I hoped I could borrow a bit of steadiness from the heavy weapon in my right hand. Sweat trickled down my forehead, pooling in my eyes and clouding my view, and I squinted to squeeze it out. *Focus. Center of the head. Don't rush your shot.* My finger tightened against the trigger. Could I really shoot Garland Hamilton? *Don't forget what he tried to do to you*, I told myself, yet still I hesitated. *Don't forget what he did to Jess, and what he might have done to Miranda.* It was Hamilton, I felt sure, who'd attacked Miranda—the police had interviewed both Latham and Garcia, and had found their arms uninjured—so that left Hamilton the likely source of the assault and of the flowers that had preceded it. That did it. I pictured Jess's body tied obscenely to another corpse, and Miranda laid out on the gurney, and the gun jumped in my hand as I yanked the trigger. "Die, you son of a bitch," I hissed, "die." I fired again and again, until the gun had nothing left to fire. My arm dropped to my side. I was trembling, I realized, and tears were streaming down my face.

"Press," said a voice behind me. "*Press.* If you jerk the trigger, you jerk the gun. And if you jerk the gun, you miss the target. And if you miss the target, *you* end up getting shot."

I turned. Steve Morgan and a TBI firearms instructor—John Wilson—stood together just behind my lane of the KPD firing range. True to his word, Morgan had gotten a permit for me to carry a weapon, and he'd even loaned me one of his own spares, a nine-millimeter Smith & Wesson. The permit apparently hadn't been too difficult to arrange, since I already carried a TBI badge as the bureau's forensic-anthropology consultant. The bigger hurdle, it appeared, would be qualifying with the gun. To qualify, I'd have to shoot with an accuracy of 70 percent—that is, 70 percent of my shots had to strike the kill zone, the smaller shaded areas within the upper chest and head of the target, a thuglike male outline whose right hand pointed a pistol directly at me.

Morgan, Wilson, and I walked the thirty feet to the target to see what damage I'd done. It wasn't much. I'd yanked off eight shots. The paper had just three holes in it, and two of those lay outside the lines of the body: Only one of my eight shots would actually have hit Garland Hamilton if this had really been him. That one shot, though, pierced the shaded area of the head, just left of the target's midline, in what would have been the region of the right nostril.

Morgan pointed to it. "Doc," he said encouragingly, "if that was your first shot, he'd be a dead man."

"Actually, that *was* his first shot," said Wilson. "His barrel crept up a little higher after every shot, which is why these two other hits are above the head. Those last five shots probably landed somewhere up in Kentucky."

"Well, here's hoping Garland Hamilton was walking around in southern Kentucky just now," I said.

"If you can just remember to press the trigger instead of yanking it and remember to keep the sights lined up, you'll nail this by the end of the day."

I had my doubts, but Wilson was right. After unloading that first, emotional magazine, I managed to separate myself from the issues of life and death and vengeance and instead to immerse myself in the physics of shooting a gun and acquiring a feel—a muscle memory, Wilson called it—for the precise amount of force needed to trip the trigger, and the slight lowering of the barrel required to realign the sights after each jump of the barrel. Over the course of three sweat-soaked hours, I fired nearly three hundred rounds. My forearm and shoulder ached from holding the two-pound weapon aloft at arm's length, but I qualified.

If I were taking aim at Garland Hamilton, would I be able to hang on to my newly acquired muscle memory—remain calm and focused as I pressed precisely and grouped my shots into his head? I didn't know that. I also didn't know whether to hope I'd get the chance to find out—or to pray I didn't.

CHAPTER 23

BURT DEVRIESS HAD BEEN RIGHT. HIS PHONE HAD started ringing the day the crematorium scandal first aired on CNN, and it had scarcely stopped. Some of the calls came from people who wondered what was really in that fancy urn or that plain box they'd gotten back from the crematorium. Others came from reporters who sought (and got) punchy quotes—some of them from Nephew Burt, grieving over the indignity done to Aunt Jean, some from Counselor DeVriess, crusading for justice, or at least for millions in restitution.

It didn't seem to matter—to Burt, to prospective clients, or to legions of reporters—that he'd never before practiced anything but criminal defense. Nor did it actually matter to the Tennessee Bar Association. "Tennessee does not certify attorneys in specific areas of the law," read the disclaimers on countless television commercials and phone-book ads. "The law is the law," Burt had thundered when one reporter asked about the sudden, sharp switchback in his career path. Somehow that slick bit of fancy footwork got transformed into the story's headline and then into the slogan of Burt's campaign to bring the funeral industry to its knees. The truth was, if Burt had chosen to hang out his shingle in a small town somewhere in the hills—Jonesport, for instance—he'd have been forced to piece together a living out of whatever cases walked through his door, be they criminal defense, civil suits, wills and estates, prenups, or divorces. It was only because he'd been so spectacularly successful that Grease had gotten pigeonholed as a defense attorney. Burt was wearing, I supposed, a version of golden handcuffs. No reason he shouldn't trade them for a platinum pair, if he wanted to; Burt's greatest talent, in fact, was generating large amounts of news coverage and revenue. A big class-action contingency suit, particularly one as juicy as this, would generate copious quantities of coverage. And the revenue stream might well rival the Tennessee River at flood stage—and keep flowing strong for years to come.

It wasn't long, I noticed, before the rising tide started lifting my own academic boat. I had gotten involved with the crematorium mess when Burt had sent me the urn that should have contained Aunt Jean's knees but didn't. We now knew there were hundreds more Aunt Jeans and Uncle Bobs and Mamas and Daddies out there—hundreds more bogus sets of cremains sitting on mantels, and possibly thousands of additional, legitimate urns that people suddenly suspected, and would continue to suspect, until someone proved the contents to be authentic.

That someone, at least for Burt's new clients, turned out to be me. Chloe began sending me packages almost daily; one day, in fact, I got three packages. The outer containers ranged from plain cardboard boxes to intricately carved wooden or brass chests, but the contents seldom varied, at least when the cremains hailed from Georgia. The twist-tied plastic bags from Trinity Crematorium nearly always contained the same mix of powder, sand, and pebbles I had found in Aunt Jean's supposed cremains—a mixture, it turned out, remarkably similar in composition to Quikrete concrete mix. The day I got the three packages, I called Burt's office to tease Chloe.

"Too bad I can't keep this material," I said. "I've been thinking about pouring a patio in the backyard, and you've sent me enough Quikrete this week to pave half an acre."

Mine was not the only professional boat bobbing on the tide; my colleagues in Chemistry and Geology and even Forestry were helping analyze the mixtures from Georgia. Burt's class-action suit was headed for trial, and he'd named a long list of defendants. First on the list, of course, came the crematorium and its owners. But I'd seen where the Littlejohns lived, and they didn't look rich. The real prize, the mother lode Burt planned to mine for millions, was the list of funeral homes that had done business with Trinity. The funeral homes carried liability insurance, and the coverage typically ran to a million dollars or more per case. On paper, at least, that added up to a jackpot of more than $300 million. If Burt's class-action suit could land the entire sum, his 30-percent contingency would be worth $90 million. The insurance companies were starting to sweat, and they'd already sent a few settlement feelers in Burt's direction. Their initial offers were low, and Burt had rejected them swiftly, indignantly, and quotably—at a press conference that made page one of every newspaper in the Southeast, as well as several national network newscasts. "We seek the full measure of justice for these families who have suffered so much," said Burt, in a voice that would have

done a Baptist preacher proud. "We will not rest until their pain
has been heard, their wounds have been healed, and their wrongs
have been set right." He'd paused to let the words sink in, and
the television camera zoomed in for a close-up. When it did, I'd
have sworn I saw a solitary tear trickle down his cheek, right on
cue. God, the man was amazing.

On the heels of that press conference, the consortium of insurance companies added another zero to the string of digits they
were offering Burt to settle. He rejected that offer as well and
readied for trial. He planned to call me to testify that the cremains I'd examined were not purely human bone, and I was ably
qualified to do that. What I was not qualified to do, under the
constraints of what was known in legal circles as the "Daubert
rule," was to testify about the actual composition of the bogus
cremains. I could testify that the mixture appeared to contain
sand, cement powder, and pebbles, but it would take Daubert-
qualified experts—Ph.D.-packing geologists and chemists—to
verify that the sand was indeed sand, the cement was bona fide
cement, and the pebbles really were pebbles. Funding this small
army of experts would whittle down Burt's big bonanza, but not
by much. In the first ten days after Burt started reeling in clients, I examined twenty-three sets of cremains. Of the twenty-
three, the ten oldest cases were legitimate—for a while, up until
a year or two earlier, the crematorium seemed to have done a
decent job—but thirteen were problematic, containing the same
odd mixture of human bone, animal bone, and Quikrete. Most
of them weighed about half what they should have, judging by
my regular trips out to East Tennessee Cremation, where Helen
Taylor had graciously allowed me to come weigh cremains on a
regular basis—using the new postal scale that had mysteriously

appeared on my desk one day after my third unauthorized use of Peggy's scale.

I invoiced Burt $6,900 for the twenty-three examinations. Burt notified the insurance companies he'd added another $13 million in liability claims for the thirteen bogus cremains, plus half a million apiece for the ten legitimate cremains—compensation for the pain and suffering incurred by families whose faith had been shattered by the revelations about the crematorium's shocking practices.

My conversations with Burt were frequent, brisk, and focused, as the class-action suit gained clients and gathered momentum. Then one Thursday he called, and I noticed as soon as he spoke that he sounded upset and hesitant. "I was calling to ask a favor," he said.

Normally I'd have replied with a joke, but something in his tone told me now was not the time for humor. "Something wrong, Burt?"

"The GBI just released my Aunt Jean's body," he said. "She's at the funeral home in Polk County now, the place that handled the funeral two months ago. I've arranged to have her cremated up here in Alcoa tomorrow, at your friend Helen's place."

"She'll do an excellent job," I assured him.

"That's good to know," he said. "I want it done right this time." He hesitated. "Would you be willing to come, Doc? I want to be absolutely certain there's no mistake about which body they've sent."

"I can't imagine that the GBI would mistakenly release the wrong body," I said. "They're going to be bending over backward to get everything right."

He didn't say anything for a moment, and the next words

sounded difficult for him. "I'm not just asking you as a scientist," he said. "I'm asking you as a friend."

"I'll be there, Burt."

At four o'clock Friday afternoon, a gleaming black hearse with a Polk County tag pulled up outside East Tennessee Cremation. Burt and I were already there waiting, chatting with Helen Taylor, who'd called to give us a heads-up an hour before the hearse was due to arrive.

The driver who emerged from the hearse wore a black suit and a nervous expression. The nervousness escalated to terror when Burt introduced himself and me. I shook the man's hand; Burt, conspicuously, did not.

In the back of the hearse was an elegant wooden coffin, which appeared to be crafted from solid mahogany. It looked less like a coffin than like fine furniture, and it surprised me to see what an opulent coffin was about to be put to the torch. Helen Taylor rolled a gurney toward the back of the hearse, and as she passed me, she cut her eyes toward the coffin and silently mouthed the words, "Ten thousand dollars." Part of me wanted to ask Burt, *Are you sure about this?* But the wasteful extravagance of incinerating a fancy coffin was none of my business. Besides, I supposed, burning an expensive coffin was no more of a waste than burying it. The fanciness was meant for the survivors, not for the deceased.

Then a more pragmatic consideration occurred to me. Burt probably had this rural Polk County funeral home on the hook for a million dollars, I realized—maybe more, if he and his Uncle Edgar testified convincingly about their pain and suffering. I thought back to my conversation with Norm Witherspoon, the Knoxville funeral director who'd resisted the cost-cutting over-tures of Trinity's cheaper services. Along about now, Norm had to be thanking his lucky stars that he'd never switched his business. And I felt sure the Polk County funeral home, like all the others in Burt's crosshairs, rued the day they'd started sending bodies to north Georgia.

The sweating, nervous mortician in the black suit was not, I realized, some flunky. He was probably the owner or the manager of the funeral home, here to make sure that nothing, absolutely nothing, went wrong this time around with this particular cremation. And if offering up a ten-thousand-dollar coffin as a gesture of atonement—a burnt offering, of sorts—could appease a ferocious lawyer, it would be money well spent.

The funeral director and Helen grasped the carved handles of the coffin and pulled. The wood slid effortlessly on the rollers built into the bed of the hearse. Those rollers had probably gotten a fresh misting of WD-40 just before the coffin had been loaded, and the hearse looked freshly waxed. We followed Helen as she wheeled the coffin into the building, and she closed the overhead door.

"All right," said Burt, "open it." His voice carried a combination of anger and sadness I'd not heard in him before. I'd heard dramatic indignation from him, of course, in court, but never personal fury and never such pain.

The man hesitated. "It's not going to be . . . She's not . . . It's been a while," the mortician stammered.

"Open it," said Burt, more softly but more menacingly.

The man looked at me in silent appeal.

"We need to see," I said. "We need to be completely sure there's no mistake this time."

His face turned pale, but he nodded. He fished a small crank from somewhere underneath the coffin, inserted it into a hole down near the foot, and began to turn.

Almost as if by magic, the lid levitated an inch or so. When it did, the strong and unmistakable smell of decomposition roiled out of the interior. Burt flinched, and his face tightened into a mask, but he reached out, grasped the polished wood, and lifted the lid. Inside was Aunt Jean, still in the stained blue dress. Her hair was cleaner than when I'd seen her in the refrigerated trailer, and somebody had made a valiant effort to curl and brush it. The effect was bizarre but poignant, coiffed hair fringing a nearly bare skull. The few remaining tatters of skin served mainly to underscore how much bone was showing through: the zygomatic arches, the gaping teeth, the pointed chin, the sharp-edged eye orbits. When the light from the overhead fluorescents hit the face, a few maggots scurried for cover, and the funeral director turned a whiter shade of pale.

"We did our best to clean her up," he said. "I'm so sorry about that."

Burt didn't respond, so I kept quiet, too.

Burt leaned down and studied the teeth, just as I had, down at the makeshift morgue a few days before. "I'd know that smile anywhere," he said, "even without the face around it. Damn, Doc. She died two months ago, and I made my peace with it then. But seeing her like this, it's as if she just died all over again, only worse. The indignity, you know?" He pulled out a handkerchief and wiped his eyes. This time Burt wasn't playing for the cameras.

"I know, Burt. I'm sorry," I said.

"Mr. DeVriess," began the mortician, "on behalf of all of us at Eternal Rest Mortuary, I'd just like to express our deepest—"

"Shut up," snapped Burt. "Don't you say one single sanctimonious word to me."

The man's jaw sagged, then clenched tight.

Burt pointed at the lustrous lid. "Now close it up."

The man scurried to crank the lid shut, and Burt nodded to Helen. "Whenever you're ready," he said.

She pressed a button, and the furnace door opened. She slid the coffin in, closed the door, and touched the button labeled Afterburner, then Pre-Ignition. I heard the whoosh of flame, and in a matter of moments the hand-rubbed finish of the mahogany ignited and Aunt Jean began to burn.

CHAPTER 24

ON THE WAY BACK FROM THE CREMATORIUM, I STOPPED at a Hardee's for a bacon cheeseburger. I was just about to pull up to the drive-through speaker when I remembered what Helen had said about the crematorium's ashy dust—"it gets every-where"—and I flashed back to the small cloud that had erupted from the processor when she'd ground the bones that day. *Let's wash our hands,* I thought. Maybe it was just my imagination, but the water that swirled down the drain did seem a tad murkier than usual.

I ordered the burger and a sweet tea, and while I waited for the sandwich, I went to the drink counter to get my tea. There's no consensus in the South about the ideal sugar-to-tea ratio in sweet tea, and over the years I've found that the ratio can vary wildly, depending on who's doing the mixing. I dispensed a small sample into the bottom of the cup, so I could see where on the scale this batch happened to fall. The tea was so thick and syrupy I could almost have eaten it with a fork. There had to be at least a five-pound bag of sugar in the five-gallon urn. *One pound per gallon,* I thought. *It's easy to remember, and there is a certain symmetry to the formula.* To lower the risk of a sugar coma, I looked for lemon—one lemon per cup would probably be about right—but there was none. The next-best thing, I decided, would be to cut the tea with lemonade from the soda fountain. I filled the cup halfway with tea, then began adding lemonade, pausing to re-sample every few spurts. By the time I'd gotten to a fifty-fifty blend, I'd reined in the sweetness, but the tea flavor was now pretty dilute. *Life is a series of compromises,* I reminded myself.

As I snapped a lid onto the cup, I heard what I took to be low, sustained laughter behind me. I turned with a smile, looking to see who was laughing, and why. It took me a moment to realize that I'd been 180 degrees wrong about the sound. A young woman in a Hardee's uniform was bent over one end of the cash-register counter, her face in her hands, sobbing steadily. She looked young—a girl, really, no more than twenty—and plump, and when she raised her face for a moment, something in it made me wonder if she might be mildly retarded.

I looked at the man behind the cash register, expecting to see him rush to offer aid or comfort. Instead he leaned toward the next customer in line and said, "Would you like to try a patty-melt combo today?" The customer—a man in a black suit and a white shirt, a red tie cinched tight at his throat—studied the menu board intently, then ordered a chicken fillet sandwich with large fries. It was as if the weeping woman at his elbow simply weren't there. Another employee, a middle-aged woman, glanced at the girl, then looked away. As she turned back to the milk-shake machine, the woman avoided my questioning gaze.

It was none of my business, I realized. Perhaps the girl's co-workers had a good reason for ignoring her distress—maybe instead of stepping outside for a smoke when her break time rolled around, she hunched over the counter and sobbed twice a day. But somehow I doubted that, and I felt an answering sadness welling up within me. Moving slowly to her, I laid a hand on her shoulder. "Is there anything I can do to help you?"

After a moment she raised her head and looked at me, her face blotchy and her eyes swollen and bleak. "No," she whispered, then dropped her face into her hands again and resumed sobbing.

"I'm sorry," I said.

"Bacon cheeseburger to go," announced the man at the register. I lifted my hand from the girl's shoulder, picked up the bag, and returned to my truck, wondering why this world contained so much pain. Wondering why some people's share of the pain seemed so much greater than others'. Wishing some of the surplus sweetness in that urn of tea could somehow spill over into that poor girl's life.

CHAPTER 25

DARREN CASH APPEARED AT MY OFFICE DOOR MONDAY morning. A long, thin tube of rolled-up paper—a blueprint, I was guessing—was tucked under one arm. I said hello, then nodded at the tube. "Whatcha got?"

"I was hoping you'd ask." He slid a rubber band down off one end and flattened a property-tax plat map on my desk.

"Fascinating," I said.

"Actually, it is. This is Middlebrook Pike here," he said, tracing a line that curved from near downtown out to the west and then south. "Here's the Lathams' farm."

I studied the boundaries on the plat map. "How big is it—a hundred acres?"

"Almost," he said. "Eighty."

"That's a mighty big parcel so close to downtown Knoxville," I said. "I'm surprised it hasn't been carved up into subdivisions and shopping centers by now."

"Mrs. Latham was quite attached to it. She grew up on that farm; it'd been in her family over a century. Notice anything unusual about the plat map?"

I studied it. "Looks like somebody set a cup of coffee down on it," I said, pointing to a circular brown stain in one corner.

He laughed. "True, but not quite what I was after. If you were a developer, is there anything particular about that piece of property that would catch your eye?"

"Besides there being a lot of it?" He nodded, so I studied the map more closely. "Well, it's got great frontage along Middlebrook Pike."

"Keep going," he said.

"It also backs up to the 640 bypass," I said.

"Anything else?"

"And the railroad cuts through one corner. So potentially it's easy to reach by road or by rail."

"And if you were going to do something with that property, what would you do?"

"I'd expand the Body Farm," I said. "We're running out of space for all the donated bodies we're getting these days."

Cash laughed.

"If the neighbors wouldn't let me do that, maybe I'd put in a fancy office park. Or a mix of office buildings, high-end retail shops, and fancy condos."

"You missed your calling," he said. "That's exactly the master plan the developer had in mind for it."

"What developer?"

"The developer Stuart Latham was talking to behind his wife's back. You got any guess what that land would be worth?"

I thought for a moment. "Oh, I'd say at least several million."

"More like twenty-five," he said, and I whistled. "Land in that area's going for three hundred thousand an acre, and that's a unique parcel. Of course, it's worth twenty-five mil only if somebody's willing to sell it."

"Mrs. Latham wasn't willing to sell?"

"Bingo," he said.

"Was *Mr.* Latham willing to sell?"

"Mr. Latham was *eager* to sell," he said. "I guess he'd gotten tired of renting cars. He approached a developer—same folks who built the big Turkey Creek development—about three months ago. Stuart was a man with a plan."

"But the farm wasn't Stuart's to sell—it was his wife's family's, right?"

"Right."

I thought back to an earlier conversation. "You said Mrs. Latham didn't have a life-insurance policy, but did she have a will?"

"She had a will."

"Was he the heir?"

"He was."

"Ah. Motive," I said.

"Motive," he said. He waited half a beat, then added, "We're going to the grand jury for the indictment tomorrow. Stay tuned."

CHAPTER 26

I WAS PICKING AT A HEALTHY CHOICE ENTRÉE—A TRAY
of bland lasagna I'd overcooked in the microwave—when the
phone rang. I jumped, which was my standard response whenever a phone rang or a door slammed these days, then reached
for the cordless on the kitchen table. "Garland Hamilton's hiding
out up here in Cooke County," Jim O'Conner's voice said, and
instantly I was on full alert. "He rented a cabin up on Fish Creek.
It's on a private gravel road all by itself, way off the highway."

Part of me leapt to embrace the news. I desperately wanted
Hamilton to be found, and Cooke County made sense: If I were
a fugitive on the run, Cooke County—with its hills and hollows
and frontier mentality—might well be my hideout of choice. Still,
I was afraid to get my hopes up. "How do you know it's him?"

"Two days after Hamilton escaped, this guy called a realty
company in Jonesport that rents out vacation cabins. Asked if
they had something really private, way off the beaten track."

"Hell, Jim, if I were renting a cabin in the mountains, I'd ask for something like that, too."

"He paid cash for the first week."

"So?"

"Two days ago he paid for another week. He used a credit card this time." I felt the hairs on my neck and arms stand up. "It's Hamilton. Or else a guy who fits his description and stole his credit card. The TBI got a call from the bank, and Steve Morgan looked into it. Morgan's convinced it's him."

"He had to know that the credit card was being watched," I argued. "Why would he risk using it?"

"I asked Morgan the same thing," said O'Conner. "We went round and round about it, but Steve finally convinced me. First, Hamilton's probably out of cash by now. Second, this cabin-rental outfit is way back in the Dark Ages, technologically speaking—they use those old-fashioned mechanical gizmos to take an imprint of the card. Send it to MasterCard by carrier pigeon. Besides, who else could it be? Who else is going to be using Hamilton's card and wearing Hamilton's face?"

My hands were shaking. So were my knees.

"Bill? You okay?"

"Just a little jittery," I said. "Now what?" I checked the wall clock; it read eight-fifteen, and the light outside was getting watery.

"We've called in the heavy artillery. A SWAT team is moving into position after dark, and they'll go in at sunup."

"What if he spots them and makes a break for it?"

"The SWAT-team commander? He was in the Army Rangers with me. For practice he used to sneak up on the guys in the squad. You'd know he was coming after you, but you wouldn't know when—not till you felt the flat of his knife at your throat. If his guys are half as good as he is, even the owls and the coyotes won't see 'em coming."

"But you'll wait till morning?"

"Safer that way. Besides the SWAT team, we'll have helicopters, K-9s, state troopers, TBI agents, and every Cooke County coon hunter I can deputize between now and then. We'll come down on him like the wrath of God."

I felt my throat tightening, my heart pounding, and my breath coming in quick gulps. "You're sure you'll get him, Jim?"

"I don't see how anybody but the devil himself could wriggle out of this noose."

A shiver ran through me. "Damn, Jim, I wish you hadn't said that."

"Don't worry. We'll get him."

"Be careful. Call me when you've got him."

It took everything I had not to jump into the truck and head for Cooke County as soon as I hung up, but I knew I'd only be in the way and might even jeopardize the operation. So I paced around the kitchen awhile, stirring a fork through the congealed lasagna every few laps of the table and the island. Then I went outside and paced Sequoyah Hills awhile, winding my way down the mazy streets toward the river. Darkness was falling now, but the park along the riverfront remained lively. A young couple, their eyes better adjusted to the twilight than mine, tossed a Frisbee back and forth. A pack of dogs—friendlier than the ones that had chased Art and me out of the Georgia woods—raced and roughhoused across the field, occasionally colliding in a five-dog pileup of tumbling fur. A runner jogged past, lifting a hand in silent greeting, like some athletic priest conferring a sweaty blessing on me. "Peace," the gesture seemed to say, but peace was nowhere within reach for me.

By the time I'd walked a mile along the river, it was too dark to see my feet, so when I got to the parking lot by the Indian mound, I followed the gravel up to Cherokee Boulevard. A cinder path ran down the center of the boulevard's median; mileposts ticked off every quarter mile from the lower end of the street, down by the river, to the stoplight up at Kingston Pike. Just beyond the 1.5-mile mark, the median widened to accommodate a large fountain ringed by grass and a traffic circle. Normally the fountain shot a plume twenty feet into the air, but the drought and water rationing had dried it up, and tonight the fountain's built-in lights illuminated stained concrete and empty air. Beyond the fountain the boulevard curved away from the river, winding over one low ridge and then up a second to the intersection with Kingston Pike. Old-fashioned streetlamps along the median lighted the cinder path, and I kept walking, past palatial houses whose pediments and even surrounding trees were lit like Hollywood sets.

When I reached Kingston Pike, I turned and retraced my steps, all the way back to the far end of the boulevard, 2.6 miles away. I repeated the circuit twice more—I covered fifteen miles without getting a step closer to peace. But although peace eluded me, fatigue did not. I staggered into my house at midnight, fell onto the bed, and drifted into a fitful sleep, haunted by dreams of Jess's corpse and Garland Hamilton's sneering face.

The phone woke me.

"Bill, it's Jim O'Conner."

I shook myself awake. "What's up? Have you got him?" I glanced at the window and saw that it was still dark outside.

The digital clock on the nightstand read 4:59. An uneasy feeling grabbed hold of my stomach. "Jim? Is everything okay?"

There was a pause, and the uneasy feeling turned into a knot. "I . . . I think so, but we're not sure yet. All hell broke loose up here about an hour ago."

"What? Tell me."

"There was a big explosion and a fire. Cabin's destroyed and the mountain's on fire. I think Hamilton's dead."

"But you don't know?"

"We can't get in there to check for a body yet, but I don't see how anybody could have survived. Couple of the SWAT guys got knocked flat, and they were fifty yards away."

"Come on, Jim, what would cause a log cabin in the mountains to explode, just as an army of lawmen is about to arrest the guy inside? That can't be a coincidence."

"Hang on, hang on." In the background I heard a crackling voice on a radio, and then I heard O'Conner saying, "You're sure? Hundred-percent sure?" Then he was talking to me again, his voice racing. "Waylon says he just spotted a human skull. Burned, but definitely a skull, and definitely human." My emotions felt like they were on some sort of theme-park thrill ride, tumbling headlong up and down and around, faster than I could give names or even meaning to.

After a while I noticed the voice in my ear. "Doc? Are you there?"

"Yeah," I managed to say. "I'm here. Give me just a minute." I focused on breathing—slow, deep, steady breathing. The ride slowed, and I felt my adrenaline subside. I also felt my conscious, curious mind start to assert itself. "We'll need to make a positive identification to be sure it's him," I said. "You want me to come up with a team and do that?"

"Well . . ." O'Conner paused again, this time for longer than before. His voice sounded measured and careful now. "If you're up to that and feel like you can step back from your personal involvement enough to focus clearly, sure, come on up. But if that's asking too much, say so and I'll request some assistance through the TBI or the FBI or the medical examiner's office over in Memphis. There's a forensic anthropologist over there that you trained, isn't there?"

"There is, but I'll be fine." I thought of a fire scene I'd worked in West Tennessee a few years before. "Listen, Jim, if you've got firefighters there, ask 'em to take it easy with the hoses," I said. "Burned bones are very fragile, and the pressure from a fire hose can scatter them all over the place or smash them to bits. Wet ash tends to set up pretty hard, too—like concrete, once it dries. Do what you need to do to keep things safe, but the less water gets to those bones, the better."

He excused himself, and I heard him relaying that message into a radio.

"Don't worry about me, Jim. Once I'm there and looking at bones, it'll be like any other case."

He didn't challenge me, but I could tell he wasn't entirely convinced. Finally he said, "Okay, come on up. Just remember, there's no shame in asking for help."

"Okay, deal," I said. "Listen, leave the bones right where they are. Don't disturb the scene unless somebody's safety is in jeopardy."

"We won't touch a thing," O'Conner said. Then he gave me directions to Fish Creek and signed off. As soon as he did, I dialed Miranda's pager and punched in my home number. It seemed like hours before my phone rang, although the digital clock on the nightstand claimed that only a minute had passed.

"Hey," said Miranda sleepily, "you okay?" A lot of people seemed to be asking me that question lately.

"I'm okay. Garland Hamilton might be dead. They tracked him to a cabin in Cooke County, and just before they swooped in to arrest him, the cabin blew up and burned down. They say they've found an incinerated skull."

"Holy hand grenade, Batman," she said. "You think he knew the jig was up? Decided to go out in a blaze of glory?"

"I wish. But that doesn't seem like his style. He was always so smug and superior, you know?"

She considered this. "That's true," she said. "Even when he was wrong, he was sure he was right. Hard to picture him making the ultimate admission of failure. But maybe it wasn't suicide. Maybe it was an accident."

"What kind of accident causes a huge explosion?"

"I don't know," she said. "Maybe he was trying to rig some sort of booby trap, and it got away from him."

"Possible, I guess. Let's get up there and see what we see. Do you want me to pick you up at your house?"

"No, that's okay—it's out of your way. Just meet me on campus. I'll park down by the bone lab and hope we get back before I get ticketed or towed."

"Okay. Half an hour?"

"Half an hour."

Thirty minutes later I turned down the narrow asphalt ramp that led to the base of the stadium. As I rounded one of the pillars holding up the south end-zone stands, I saw the brake lights of a VW Jetta wink out, the dome light switch on, and the door open. Miranda was already clad in a biohazard suit, and the glare of my headlights on the white Tyvek nearly blinded me. I cut the headlights, eased up beside the Jetta by the glow of my parking lights, and opened the passenger door.

"Anybody else going?"

"Nobody from the department." Normally I took three graduate students into the field with me—one to recover bones, one to record everything we found, and one to shoot photographs—but I didn't want a whole crew this time. "I'm a little nervous about this," I said. "I didn't want to take any of the other students."

"Oh, I see," Miranda said. "Just take the expendable one. Nice."

"No," I said, "the indispensable one. I've dragged Art out of a deep sleep, too. He's not as swift on the osteology as a grad student, but he's faster with a gun if need be."

"Isn't that whole mountainside going to be crawling with cops?"

"Probably. But I'll feel better knowing one of them's Art."

I threaded the truck back up to Stadium Drive, then along Neyland Drive toward downtown and KPD headquarters. The big downtown bridges loomed above us—the Henley Street Bridge with its graceful arches, then the sharp triangular trusses of the Gay Street Bridge. The night was warm and still, and the river was smooth except for gentle swirls and eddies created by currents unspooling over ledges and hollows and other secret shapes deep beneath the surface. The dark, flat water caught the harsh streetlights on the bridges, melted and smeared it into pools and streaks of gold and orange, like fireworks in slow motion. I slowed to take it in, and Miranda said softly, "Mmm, it is beautiful, isn't it? Strange that such beauty and such evil can exist side by side in this world, isn't it?" I didn't answer. But it didn't matter, because she didn't really expect me to.

Passing under the Gay Street Bridge, we curved away from the river and away from the beauty, winding up a concrete gully of a ramp to Hill Avenue and KPD headquarters. The acre of asphalt out front did nothing to soften the glare of the sodium-vapor lights standing sentinel; if anything, the asphalt seemed tuned somehow to reflect and amplify the harshness of the orange lights. Art's Crown Victoria was idling in the least bright corner of the lot, which is to say the only corner that didn't make me long for my sunglasses. As he got out of the car, I saw that he was wearing a nine-millimeter pistol at his waist—and I suspected he had more firepower strapped to one ankle, or even to both.

Art squeezed into the cab beside Miranda, and we sped east on I-40 toward Cooke County.

O'Conner had told me to follow River Road for three miles after getting off I-40, then look to the right and follow the flames. He hadn't been exaggerating; I could see the glow on the horizon even before we got off the interstate, the flames curling up the hillside and disappearing into roiling smoke, like a scene out of Dante's *Inferno*. I half expected to see demons and damned souls writhing amid the flames. The gravel road snaking upward into the fire zone was blocked by a Cooke County Sheriff's vehicle, a black-and-white Jeep Cherokee that I remembered getting carsick in once, during a case a year or so before. The vehicle's light bar was strobing, and the blue lights shot solid-looking beams into the pooling smoke.

I cut my headlights, pulled to a stop alongside the SUV, and got out. As I approached, the driver's window slid down. "Hello," I said into the dark interior, "I'm Dr. Bill Brockton. Sheriff O'Conner asked me—"

I was interrupted by what sounded like rolling thunder or the growl of a bear. "Hey there, Doc," rumbled a deep voice from inside the vehicle. "Jim sent me down here to meet y'all."

"Waylon!" In spite of my anxiety, I felt myself smile.

A massive, shaggy head loomed out of the window toward me, the coarse beard split by a crooked grin. "I heard a little something about what-all you been rasslin' with, so I didn't take it personal. 'Sides, we ain't exactly been beatin' a path to your doorstep neither. I reckon maybe we'll forgive you." He eyed my truck, then trained a blinding spotlight from the SUV through the passenger window. "Is that Art and Miss Miranda in there? Howdy!" he bellowed. "Good to see y'all!" Inside the truck, Art and Miranda shielded their eyes with one hand and waved the other in the general direction of Waylon and his searchlight.

Waylon—I'd never heard a last name for him—was a mountain man in every sense of the term. A hulking, homespun fellow who had heedlessly put me in harm's way and also selflessly saved my hide during a series of Cooke County adventures, Waylon had recently traded an outlaw's life for a lawman's uniform. "How you like being on this side of the law, Waylon?"

He chuckled. "Hmm. Verdict on that ain't in yet. Me and Jim's had our work cut out for us, that's for damn sure. Some of my own kinfolks ain't on speakin' terms with me no more. But mostly it feels like we're doin' some good. Clearing out some of the nastiest vermin, leastwise. I tell you, though, Doc, I sure do miss them cockfights since we shut down the pit." He frowned about the loss of what had been Cooke County's favorite spectator sport, but then the ragged smile returned, even broader, and I thought I saw a few flecks of chewing tobacco wedged between blue-lit teeth. "Hey, I delivered a baby last week, Doc, in the backseat of this-here Jeep. Lady called in a panic, said her husband weren't home and the baby was a-comin'. Her and me was haulin' ass for town with the siren on when she started hollerin' that she couldn't wait no more—she got to push *right now*. So I pulled off on the shoulder, and she popped a little baby boy right out in my hands. Named the little feller Waylon. That made me right proud."

"That makes me proud, too, Waylon. You keep up the good work. Say, you think maybe we can get up this road without melting the tires or blowing up the gas tank?"

"Oh, sure, Doc—didn't mean to keep you here jawin'. You'll be all right up there. Ever'thin's kindly burned itself out right around the cabin. What used to be the cabin anyways. Fire's still climbin' the ridge behind it, but it'll stop when it gets to the bluffs up top. Go on up—I'll radio Jim you're here."

I thanked Waylon, got back into the truck, put it in gear, and began idling up the gravel. The road meandered through what looked, in the headlights, to be stands of tulip poplars and hemlocks; twice it forded a small stream, making me glad I was driving a truck instead of some low-slung sports car. Finally, after a mile that seemed like several, we emerged into a clearing. In the glare of headlights, work lights, and the red and blue strobes of a dozen fire trucks and police cars, the smoke that still hung in the air looked thick as water. The ruins of the cabin still smoldered, and as I got out of the truck, I felt a blast of heat radiating from the splintered and charred debris. A burned vehicle was parked in front of the burned structure, a thread of smoke still curling up from it to join the larger pall of smoke hanging over the whole area.

Jim O'Conner's short, wiry frame emerged from a cluster of deputies and firefighters to greet us. He looked tired, worried, and chagrined. "What a mess," he said, shaking my hand. "So much for my optimistic prediction about how easy it would be."

"Any idea what set things off?"

O'Conner shook his head. "As best we can tell, the explosion came first, then the fire. The blast blew off part of the roof—you can see some pieces of burned trusses and joists over there," he said, pointing to an area halfway between the cabin and some smoldering tree trunks. "But the fire started right away, and it built fast." O'Conner checked his watch, then checked the sky. "Should be sunup pretty soon now," he said. "You want to go ahead and get started or wait for daylight?"

I looked up and thought I saw a hint of paleness. "Might as well wait," I said. "It's gonna be hard to see the bones in broad daylight, let alone in the dark. If Hamilton's in there, he's not gonna get any deader if we wait an hour." I was recycling my jokes, I realized as I said it, but it was new to O'Conner, and the sheriff laughed—a touch ruefully, I thought, but at least he laughed.

The cabin was big, or had been, before its decimation—more like a log home than a weekend getaway. O'Conner said it had two stories aboveground, plus a basement dug into the ground. Now all that remained standing were the basement's concrete-block walls and most of the stone chimney, whose massive fireplaces could probably have roasted a whole pig on each of the house's three levels.

O'Conner pointed toward the basement fireplace with the beam of a four-cell flashlight. "Over there, about six feet straight out from the hearth, is where Waylon saw a skull." I looked, and I saw broken pottery and what appeared to be a pair of charred tree branches, but the more I studied their odd symmetry, the more unlike branches they appeared—and the more like burned antlers from some hunting trophy that had hung over the mantel. Then—tucked down amid the antlers—I glimpsed a familiar rounded shape, with two dark ovals tunneling into it. A skull, unmistakably human. "Miranda?" She turned from her own survey of the floor and looked at me, as did Art. "Over there, under those antlers." Her gaze tracked mine.

"Wow," she said. "That's not something you see every day. Like an interspecies hunting trophy."

The blaze had completely consumed the staircases inside the house; to get to the basement floor, we'd need to clamber down a ladder. I asked for the ladder to be lowered into a corner near the fireplace, which was centered at one end of the building.

While waiting for full daylight, we unloaded the truck, suited up in disposable Tyvek coveralls, and staged our gear at the top of the ladder—trowels, rakes, shovels, wire screens, and paper evidence bags. Once we were ready and the light was bright, I nodded to O'Conner, and we began. One of the begrimed firemen descended first, then steadied the ladder for Miranda, Art, O'Conner, and me.

As soon as I got down, I noticed oddly bright bits of color amid the gray and black world of ashes and embers at my feet. Crouching, I sifted through the ash to extract one of the bits—a thin, ragged thread of metal, reddish orange in color, about six inches long. It had drooped up and down to follow the slight contours of the debris beneath it, but viewed from above, it ran in a straight line. Instinctively I looked up, though there was nothing to see now except the pale morning sky in place of the joists that had burned and the copper wiring that had melted and dripped.

"Any idea what the melting point of copper is?" O'Conner's question echoed my own thoughts.

"I was just trying to remember," I said. "Pretty hot. Somewhere around a thousand degrees, I think."

The firefighter who had come down to hold the ladder for us spoke up. "I think it's a lot more than that. Hell, lead melts at something like six hunnerd, and copper's a lot tougher than lead."

"Oh, sorry, I was talking Celsius," I said. "A thousand Celsius would be, let's see, close to two thousand Fahrenheit."

The firefighter nodded. "Sounds more like it. Only other time I seen melted wiring was in a paint-store fire. Way all them solvents went up—lacquer thinner, turpentine, acetone, oil-base paints, what have you—you'd've thought it was the world's biggest case of arson. Weren't, though. Just a accident."

"So what's the typical temperature when a wooden building burns down?"

"Eight hundred, maybe a thousand Fahrenheit," he said. "More if they's plenty of fuel and a good oxygen supply. You get a stack effect going—say, one of them old three- or four-story Victorians—you can get up to fifteen hunnerd or two thousand. Log house like this, though, would normally burn slower than a stick-built house—just like logs in a campfire burn slower than twigs. But this thing burned like it was made outta cardboard. Had to've been a shitload of accelerant in here."

I laughed. "'Shitload'—is that a technical, arson-investigation term?"

He grinned sheepishly. "Yessir."

A pair of deputies leaned over the edge of the basement and relayed our tools down to us. The concrete floor slab was coated in a layer of wet ash, but the stone hearth, which stood about eighteen inches above the floor, was barely damp. Sliding my feet along the floor so as not to risk stepping on any bones, I turned the hearth into a makeshift lab table, laying out the equipment. The wire screens, of the same sort used by archaeologists, were framed of one-by-four-inch lumber, with the screen nailed to the bottom of the frame. When we were sifting dirt at a dig, the wooden frame helped keep the dirt from sliding off the sides. Here, since the bones were likely to be damp, I laid the screens upside down on the hearth, so the wire mesh would be elevated by several inches, allowing the skeletal material to dry.

"Okay," I said, "since we've got a skull just a few feet away, let's start searching here from the hearth forward. Hands and knees, about two feet apart." I gave everybody a trowel and an artist's paintbrush, and gave a quick demonstration in how to use them to tease out and clean small bones. "Art, you and Jim start at the corners of the hearth; Miranda and I will take the centerline. We'll work from this end to the middle of the house, then work back along the edges. That way we're starting where we know there's at least some material. Take your time; look at everything or feel everything, all the way down to the concrete. Get back in touch with your inner toddler, the one who loved to dig in the mud. If you're not sure what something is, ask Miranda or me."

I dropped to my hands and knees, and the rest of them followed suit. The concrete slab had been transformed, quite literally, into an immense ashtray, containing seven layers of burned debris: the basement's contents, the main floor's joists and flooring, the main floor's furnishings, the second floor's joists and flooring, that floor's furnishings, the second floor's ceiling joists, and remnants from the roof trusses and roof. The explosion had blown much of the roof skyward, and the blaze had carried some of the interior aloft as a plume of burning embers. That made the debris layer thinner than it might have been. Still, the going was slow, and I suspected we'd be lucky to finish the search by sundown.

I had a head start, literally, with the skull, but Miranda, two feet to my right, started finding material within minutes. "Finger bones," she said, flicking the tip of her trowel lightly into the damp ash. "Left hand. Wrist. Metal wristwatch." She sounded clinical and detached, but I knew her well enough to hear the excitement underneath.

"Here's a radius and ulna," she said a moment later.

"Slow down," I teased her. "You're making the rest of us look like slackers." At this point we weren't trying to recover and bag anything; we'd start by brushing off the top layers of debris and simply exposing the bones where they lay. "Eyeglasses," I said. They looked familiar—they looked like the wire-rimmed reading glasses I'd seen on Garland Hamilton—but I reminded myself that wire-rimmed reading glasses were common.

Miranda's paintbrush flicked rapidly. "A humerus. The arm is flexed in the pugilistic posture."

O'Conner, working his way along the wall on Miranda's other side, looked puzzled at that. "Pugilistic? Isn't that an oldfangled word for boxing? The gentlemanly art of fisticuffs?"

"Bingo," I said.

He looked even more puzzled.

"When a body's exposed to a fire," I explained, "the muscles shrink as they start to dry out."

"You mean as they cook?"

"You could put it that way. And the flexors—in your arm, the muscles you use to clench your fist and curl it toward you—are stronger than the extensors. So the flexors overpower the extensors, and the fingers and arms curl up. The legs flex slightly, too."

"So a body burned in a fire assumes a boxer's stance?" O'Conner clenched his fists and held them up near his shoulders, posing his body as he posed the question.

"Exactly. Unless there's some reason it can't."

"Such as?"

"If the arms and legs are tied, for instance. I worked a case once where a burned body was found in a bedroom. The guy was a heavy smoker, and they figured he fell asleep smoking in bed. But the arms were extended, and they were behind the back. I knew that wasn't right, so I used a magnifying glass and a two-millimeter screen to comb through the ashes of the mattress. Found a few burned fibers the TBI identified as rope. Turns out he was murdered by his business partner, who had a million-dollar insurance policy on him."

"Amazing," said O'Conner, "that you were able to figure it out from the position of the arms."

"Just a matter of paying attention to little details, noticing when something's not right," I said.

As I said it, I started to notice that something was definitely wrong here. Miranda's swift efforts had now exposed virtually the entire arm, and I'd worked my way down the neck to the clavicles and the top of the rib cage. The bones we'd exposed so far were burned to a uniformly grayish white color, which meant they were calcined: reduced to their bare, brittle mineral matrix.

One good squeeze with my hands could probably crush the skull to pieces. Both the calcined bone and the melted wiring suggested that this fire had burned hotter than a cremation furnace. Hot enough to cause green bone to warp and splinter. But I didn't see signs of warping and splintering.

"Damn," I said, staring at a pelvis I'd just found. The pelvis was draped with the metal teeth of a steel zipper—and was neatly crosshatched with fractures. "This isn't a burned body. This is a burned skeleton." The search crew froze, and I felt everyone's eyes riveted on me. "This was dry bone before the fire."

I looked around at the search crew and the firefighters. Miranda and Art were nodding in understanding, but the rest looked confused. O'Conner voiced the question for everyone. "How is that possible?"

"It's possible if Garland Hamilton put it here."

I could see O'Conner struggling to process the information—struggling to accept its implications.

"Sheriff," I said, "this isn't Garland Hamilton."

There was a long silence while that sank in. Then I heard a quick gasp. I looked around just in time to see Miranda lift a blackened object from the floor. "Well, if that's not Hamilton," she said, "maybe this is."

In her outstretched hand, she cradled the shattered cranial vault of a second skull.

CHAPTER 27

IN THE LAST RAYS OF DAYLIGHT, WE STOOD IN A circle—Miranda, Art, Jim O'Conner, Waylon, and I—staring down at the two body bags spread on the ground beside my truck. On them, arranged in anatomical order, were the skeletons of two white males.

Something about the first skeleton—the one I was sure had been clean, dry bone even before the fire—seemed oddly familiar to me. I swept my eyes over it from head to foot, then back up again. And then my eyes returned to the chest—the right side of the rib cage. "Son of a bitch," I said softly. "Miranda, take a good look at the right ribs."

She looked, and her eyes widened. "Son of a bitch," she echoed. "I never thought I'd see Billy Ray Ledbetter again."

"Who is Billy Ray Ledbetter," said the sheriff, "and what makes you think this is him?"

"Billy Ray was a guy whose autopsy Garland Hamilton

screwed up," I said. "He got stomped in a bar fight, then died a couple weeks later from internal bleeding—a punctured lung. His busted ribs were partially healed when he died."

"And *this* one," said Miranda, plucking the seventh rib from the arrangement, "was missing a sliver about an inch long, right about *here*." With the tip of her trowel, she traced a long notch in the bone.

"How on earth," persisted O'Conner, "did Billy Ray happen to end up here? Bar fights and burning basements—I'm thinking he had some bad karma."

"All roads lead to Cooke County," I said. "You remember when Leena's skeleton was stolen?"

He nodded, looking hopelessly confused.

"A second skeleton was stolen at the same time—this one. Garland Hamilton stole them. He probably took Leena's just to muddy the water; this was the one he was desperate to lay his hands on, because this was the case he'd botched so badly."

The first skeleton we'd recovered, Ledbetter's skeleton, intrigued me, but it was the second skeleton that mesmerized me. Unlike Ledbetter's, these bones appeared to come from a man who was alive and well until the moment he wasn't—the moment he was blasted and then burned beyond a crisp. Like the first skeleton, this one was calcined, so I doubted that any DNA remained in the bones. But the fractures had the splintered, spiraling appearance characteristic of green bone subjected to intense heat. Mingled with the bones of the feet and ankles were two dozen eyelets from a pair of boots, each eyelet stamped Herman Survivors. Scattered amid the bones of the pelvis were the melted rivets and charred zipper of a pair of Levi's, along with coins, keys, and the buckle and metal tip from a military-style belt of canvas webbing, now minus the canvas. "Here's a historical footnote I bet y'all didn't know," I said, holding up the metal waistband button stamped with the jeans company's name. "For the first sixty or eighty years, Levi's had reinforcing rivets in the crotch, too. But sometime in the 1940s, the company's president was sitting too close to a campfire and got burned by the crotch rivets."

Miranda laughed. "Second-degree hot pants—I love it." Waylon's bushy eyebrows shot up at her comment, but he was smart enough to keep his mouth shut.

Several feet from the shattered second skull, we'd found the frames of a pair of eyeglasses. The frames were twisted and the lenses missing, but the glasses looked identical to the pair we'd found beside the first skull. They also looked identical to the pair I'd seen Garland Hamilton perch on his nose to inspect stab wounds and review autopsy notes. The moment I had realized that the first set of bones couldn't possibly be Garland Hamilton's, I'd felt my blood pressure skyrocket, but as the second skeleton and its accompanying artifacts had come to light, my pulse slowed and my blood pressure settled back to within shouting distance of normal.

We'd also found the twisted remnants of a Coleman gasoline lantern and a five-gallon gas can, which helped explain the intense heat of the fire. On the face of it, at least, the second set of remains appeared to be Hamilton's. The positioning of the bones, and the trauma they had sustained, hinted at what might have happened in that fiery explosion. The skeleton was in a supine position—faceup—as if the body had fallen over backward. The bones of the face were essentially gone, as were both hands. A pair of thin wires ran beneath the other debris, stretching from the vicinity of the body to a lump of molten lead several feet away. These wires—their insulation burned away but the copper intact—had lain directly on the basement slab, where the temperature stayed slightly below the metal's melting point.

"Here's what I think happened," I said to the group. "Garland Hamilton decides to fake his death, using this skeleton, but as a medical examiner he knows he's got to cover his tracks pretty thoroughly. He decides to use dynamite to produce more trauma in the bones—probably to destroy the teeth, so we can't compare them to his dental records. But somehow he screws up when he's inserting the blasting caps, and that battery over there"—I gestured at the blob of lead—"sets off the caps while he's holding the dynamite in his hands."

"And kablooey?" said Art.

"Kablooey," I said, smiling at the reference. Either nobody else realized Art was quoting Barney Fife or nobody else found Andy Griffith's bumbling sidekick as amusing as Art and I did.

"Works for me," said Miranda. "I can just picture Garland looking all clever and smug with a stick of dynamite in his hands, imagining how he's going to outwit everyone. Just before shorting out the wires."

"And kablooey," Art deadpanned again.

"It's just a theory at this point," I said. "We've got to get a positive ID before we can be sure."

"How you gonna do that?" Waylon asked. "Fucker's all burnt up and blowed up."

O'Conner laughed. "Waylon's got a point there. Can you get DNA out of this?"

I shook my head dubiously. "Don't know. We'll try, of course, but the heat may have destroyed it. I'm hoping we can match the dental records." I picked up the remnants of the mandible and studied them closely. The lower jaw had been shattered by the blast, and most of the teeth were missing. The upper jaw was in equally bad shape, not surprisingly, since the face—the cheekbones, the nasal bone, the fragile bones of the eye orbits—had been virtually obliterated by the explosion. All told, what was left of the upper and lower jaws contained just five teeth. But two of those five had fillings, so I was optimistic I had enough to compare with Hamilton's dental records.

"Doc?" O'Conner looked thoughtful. "This might be a dumb question, but I'm gonna ask it anyhow."

"No such thing as a dumb question, Jim. I tell my students that almost every class."

"Okay. So let's assume you're right," he said, "and Hamilton was using a skeleton as a stand-in for himself."

I nodded.

"How come the bones were in the pugilistic posture? If there's no muscle attached to the bone, there's nothing to flex the arms and legs, is there?"

I pondered O'Conner's question for a moment, and I realized I was puzzled. Not by the question itself, but by the realization that I had already asked and answered that same question in my own mind hours before, without even consciously noticing it. "God is in the details," I said, more to myself than to O'Conner. "Or the devil. He'd have known to arrange it that way."

"How can you be so sure?" O'Conner asked.

Miranda spoke up before I had the chance. "I know! I know!" she exclaimed, sounding more like a third grader than a Ph.D. student. "Because he and Dr. B. worked together on that burn case, the one where the guy was torched in his bed with his hands tied behind him."

"That's it," I said. "I knew he'd know, but I didn't remember *how* he'd know."

Art raised his hands in mock surrender. "Okay, I give up," he said. "You two are like twins, with some secret language all your own. I know I should've understood that, but I forgot to remember it."

"No, I get it," the sheriff said with a laugh. "If he's smart enough to dress the bones in clothes and to stage that Coleman lantern and the gas can, he's smart enough to make it look like the arms and legs are flexed."

We spent the final half hour of daylight bagging up the bones and artifacts, long after the SWAT team and the firefighters departed. The bones had dried quickly in the heat of the day, once we'd fished them out of the soggy ashes, brushed them off, and laid them on the wire screens. The soggy ashes coating the basement floor were beginning to bake dry, too, forming a crust nearly as hard as concrete, so I was glad we'd gotten an early start, gotten the skeletal material out before everything set up around it. We gave the bones another gentle scrubbing with soft-bristled brushes, then carefully laid them in brown paper evidence bags. One set of bags contained the dry-bone skeleton I knew was a decoy. The other held the green-bone skeleton I fervently hoped was Garland Hamilton's.

CHAPTER 28

MIRANDA AND I WERE DOWN IN THE BONE LAB—OUR home away from home—huddled over the jigsaw puzzle that had once been a human skull. The cranial vault had been crushed by falling boards as floor joists and rafters had burned through and collapsed into the basement. The two sets of remains didn't appear to be commingled; luckily for us, the force of the blast had flung the bodies apart rather than together, and since we'd already identified the first skeleton as Billy Ray Ledbetter's, we were free to concentrate on the second one. But reassembling the second skull was proving to be a herculean task.

We had poured a couple of inches of sand into the bottom of two cake pans. The sand was soft, so it cushioned the fragile skull fragments. It was easy to shape, too, into a depression that matched the curvature of a skull. As we found and fitted together additional cranial fragments, we'd trace a thin line of Duco cement on one edge, press the piece into place, and then nestle it into the sand and look for another match while the glue dried for a minute. It wasn't as fancy as the high-tech wonder gadgets on television, but it worked. Still, reassembling the skulls out of a heap of tiny shards—none much bigger than my thumbnail— was tedious at best, and I knew there'd come a point at which we simply ground to a halt, unable to find any distinctive edges to match in the tiny bits of bone.

I heard a rap on the steel door. It swung outward, and Steve Morgan walked in. Morgan and I had spoken earlier in the day, as he was headed over to see Garland Hamilton's dentist and get me Hamilton's dental records. I was surprised to notice that he was empty-handed.

"Problem with the dentist?" I asked.

"You might say that," he said. "He died last week. Heart attack."

I remembered reading a short item in the newspaper, but I hadn't paid it much attention at the time. "That was Hamilton's dentist? Dr. Vetter, or some such?"

Morgan nodded glumly.

"How old was the guy?"

"Sixty."

"Any history of heart disease?"

"You'd have made a good physician," Morgan said. "Or a good police interrogator. Vetter had a pacemaker put in a couple of years ago."

"I thought the whole idea of the pacemaker was to prevent a heart attack."

"Me, too," he said, "so I called and asked Dr. Garcia that same question. Garcia told me that if your heart stops, the pacemaker will jump-start it. But if your coronary arteries clog up, a pacemaker won't save you. It's like getting a new battery for your car—if the fuel line clogs, the battery's no help."

"Did Dr. Vetter have partners?"

Morgan shook his head. "Solo practice," he said. "A hygienist and a receptionist, that was it."

"Couldn't one of those get the records for you?"

"Not there to get," he said. "They couldn't find the file."

"Hel-*lo*," said Miranda, looking up from her sandbox, "how convenient is *that*? The dentist codes just before you come calling, and the crucial records vanish into the ether?"

I didn't like the sound of that much myself. "Did Garcia do an autopsy?"

"No," said Morgan. "The widow objected. She said he wouldn't eat right and he wouldn't exercise. She tried telling him he was headed for a heart attack, but he wouldn't listen. Sounds like she thinks he got what he had coming to him."

"Sounds like maybe she's at the 'anger' stage of the grieving process," I said.

"Sounds like maybe he died in the arms of a girlfriend," said Miranda. "Isn't that what tends to send you old codgers over the edge, myocardially speaking? That would explain the heart attack and the widow's anger."

"Hey, he wasn't old," I squawked. "Sixty is the new fifty-nine."

"He didn't die in the heat of passion," said Morgan. "Not unless the hygienist was under the desk while he was dictating records. The receptionist found him slumped over his desk, microphone in his hand."

"But he wasn't slumped over Garland Hamilton's chart?"

Morgan shook his head again.

"And Hamilton's dental records are nowhere to be found?"

"Nowhere."

"Damn," I said. "That's going to make it hard to match these teeth. Can you check for other medical records? Any healed fractures we should be looking for? Any cranial X-rays that might show us some teeth?"

"I already left a message for Mrs. Vetter," said Morgan, "asking for a list of his doctors. I'll try her again later this afternoon. Sorry for the delay."

I sighed. "Well, it's not like we're sitting here twiddling our thumbs. We'll be at this for a while yet. As you can see, we've got about a thousand more pieces to glue back together."

"Aha!" Miranda exclaimed. With a pair of tweezers, she reached down and plucked a small fragment of bone from the unmatched pieces. The piece was shaped like the continent of Australia, as were three or four hundred other pieces, as best I could tell. But she tucked it into an Australia-shaped gap in the forehead of the second skull, and it seemed to fit.

"Only nine hundred ninety-nine more pieces," I said to Morgan. "Better get moving, Steve. Time's a-wastin'."

THE PHONE in the bone lab rang just after Morgan left. It was Darren Cash's boss, District Attorney Robert Roper. "We're holding a press conference this afternoon at four, but I wanted you to hear this from me first," he said. "Stuart Latham just pled guilty to murder."

"First degree?"

"No, second," he said. "He wanted involuntary manslaughter, but we wouldn't settle for that."

"What's his story? His new one, I mean."

"He claims they were arguing about selling the farm. They'd both had a lot to drink, and things got out of hand. He hit her, and she fell backward and cracked her head on the kitchen floor. He thought she'd passed out—at least that's what he claims—and he carried her to the bed. When he woke up the next morning, she was dead. He swears he never meant to kill her, but once he realized she was dead, he panicked."

"Sure," I said. "And two weeks ago, he swore he'd kissed her good-bye the morning he caught that plane to Vegas, too. If it was an accident, why'd he plead to second-degree murder, then?"

"Because we had him by the short hairs. It's possible—barely possible—he's telling the truth. But even if he didn't mean to kill her, we could probably convince a jury he did. Besides, even with his new story, we had him nailed on evidence tampering, obstruction of justice, and desecration of a corpse. That last one alone could get him twenty years."

He didn't have to remind me of the penalty for mutilating a body—the state legislature had passed that law early in my career, after I'd detailed the way a killer had hacked his victim to pieces, then fed the remains to his Doberman.

"What made Latham start to crack," Robert continued, "was when Darren told him how he did it—how he put the ice under the car and how many hours that gave him to get to Vegas. Darren showed him pictures of those two little burned circles you found in the grass near the barn."

Actually, I'd found only one of the two, but I didn't want to interrupt Roper to correct him.

"Then I took over," the D.A. went on, "pointing out how those research experiments would be the nail in his coffin on the issue of premeditation." Roper chuckled. "Hell, I'd no sooner said the words 'death penalty' than he started crying and begging to plead out."

"So how long will Latham serve?"

"If the judge approves the deal, he'll get a ten-year sentence. Could be out in five."

"Five years—that's not much for killing your wife and burning her body," I said.

"No, it's not," he agreed. "But it's a lot more than zero. And then there's the fine."

"What fine?"

"His twenty-five-million dollars that just went up in smoke."

CHAPTER 29

I REACHED ART JUST AS HE WAS FINISHING LUNCH, judging by the smacking sounds on the other end of the line. "If you needed a body," I said, "where would you get one?"

"Gee, let me think," he answered. "Who do I know that has a body or two lying around?"

"Okay, smart aleck. If you needed a body and you couldn't get it from the Body Farm, where would you get it?"

"Down in Georgia. They're stacked up like cordwood down there."

"Too late," I said. "The GBI had those under lock and key by the time Garland Hamilton escaped."

"In that case," he mused, "maybe I'd try a funeral home. Buy a fresh body off an unscrupulous undertaker."

"How would he explain the empty coffin to the grieving family at the viewing or the service?"

He thought for a moment. "Maybe he wouldn't have to. Wait

till after the viewing, then swap the body for two or three concrete blocks, so the pallbearers don't get suspicious."

"Why wouldn't this undertaker report you to the cops?"

"Because he's unscrupulous?"

"So unscrupulous he's going to help a notorious killer who's just escaped? That seems mighty risky," I said.

"Okay, I give up," he said. "You're fishing for an answer that I'm not coming up with. What is it you're after?"

I told him the idea that had occurred to me, the way I might try to procure a stand-in if I were trying to fake my death.

"That could work," he said finally.

"Could you check missing-persons reports, see if there's anything on file?"

"Sure," he said. "Oh, and Bill?"

"Yeah?"

"Remind me never to turn my back on you in a dark alley."

I laughed as he hung up.

A half hour later, he called me back. "Only one new report in the past two weeks," he said. "Teenage girl—a runaway. You sure those burned bits of skull are male?"

"The pelvic bones are in pretty good shape," I said, "so it's definitely male. And we've got two fully erupted third molars in what's left of the mandible and maxilla, so he was at least eighteen. Harder to estimate the age because of the condition of the bones, but I'm thinking I see some signs of osteoarthritis on the vertebrae, which suggests he was middle-aged."

"That could fit with your theory," he said, "though it sure doesn't prove it. I called Evers and ran it past him. The good news, sort of, is that he said it's possible."

"The bad news?"

"He said it sounds like the ultimate wild-goose chase. Even if somebody saw something, they're not likely to tell the cops."

"Well, damn." I was saying that a lot lately, I noticed. I thanked Art and hung up. But I wasn't ready to let go of the idea. I dug out the phone book and looked for a number.

"Public Defender's Office," said the woman who answered the phone.

"Is Roger Nooe in?" His name, despite the double *o*, rhymed with "Chloe," not "kablooey," I realized while I was on hold. The thought of Chloe and her speed dating made me smile, and I wondered if she'd met any good prospects.

Roger had taught for years in the UT College of Social Work; he'd retired several years before, but when he did, he took a job in social services at the Public Defender's Office. The PD's clients were the polar opposite of the well-heeled criminals represented by Burt DeVriess: Roger's work put him in daily touch with people who were poor, unemployed, and often impaired by alcohol, drugs, or mental disorders—the kind of people who were falling through the widening gaps in America's safety net by the millions in recent years. The challenges facing Roger and his colleagues seemed grim and insurmountable to me, but grimness is in the eye of the beholder; over the years—always to my surprise—I'd spoken with many people who regarded my own work as grim, too. I'd seen Roger a few times since he'd joined the PD's office, and he'd seemed energized by the chance to develop programs and services to keep low-income defendants—and their families—from spiraling downward through poverty, crime, and imprisonment.

We played catch-up for a few minutes, as longtime colleagues and friends do when it's been a year or so between conversations.

We traded progress reports on our grown children and speculated about UT's prospects in the upcoming football season—iffy, we agreed, given how many of the team's key players had graduated the prior spring. Roger didn't mention Jess's murder or Garland Hamilton's escape, and I appreciated that, even though I was about to bring up the subject myself. By letting me steer the conversation, he allowed me to frame things forensically rather than personally, and that made it easier for me. "Roger, you know more about street people and homelessness in Knoxville than anybody else in town," I began.

"I wouldn't go that far," he said, "but I can probably bore you with statistics for a few hours." Roger was being characteristically modest, I knew—at the request of the city mayor and the county mayor, he'd led a ten-year study of homelessness, and his group had gone on to develop an ambitious plan to tackle the roots of the problem.

"If I needed a body," I said, "would it be fairly easy to kill a homeless person and get away with it?"

He didn't say anything at first; when he did speak, he sounded taken aback—shocked, even—by the callousness of the idea or the bluntness of the question. "Let me think about that for a minute," he finally said.

"Here's why I'm asking," I said. "I've got two burned skeletons down in the osteology lab under the stadium. We know who Skeleton Number One was—a guy named Billy Ray Ledbetter. Skeleton Number Two might be Garland Hamilton's." If Roger was puzzled by what I was saying, he didn't let on, so I assumed he'd been reading the newspapers. I described what we'd found in the basement of the cabin in Cooke County—one skeleton that appeared to have been defleshed before the fire and a second set of bones, clearly from a fresh body. "We're thinking—and I'm very much hoping," I admitted—"that Hamilton died while trying to fake his death with Billy Ray's skeleton. But we're having trouble making a positive identification. But maybe Skeleton Number Two isn't Hamilton either—maybe it's a double fake. You follow?"

"Just barely," he said. "We social-work types aren't as devious as you forensic types. We tend to worry about how to save people, not kill 'em."

"This isn't actually how I normally think either," I said. "I'm just trying to think like Hamilton, which isn't easy, since he's either psychotic or pure evil. But I'm hoping you can tell me whether a homeless person might be a fairly easy target, if Hamilton were looking for someone to abduct and kill as a stand-in."

"Tell you what," he said. "If you've got an hour or two, we could do some field research. I'll drive you around a little, you can take a look through the eyes of a potential killer, and then decide for yourself."

"Sounds great. When?"

"You free late this afternoon, early this evening? There's something going on tonight you might find interesting, if you don't already have dinner plans."

"My dinner plans revolved around the carousel in the microwave," I said. "I had a hot date with Healthy Choice."

He laughed. "Well, I don't promise anything that fancy, but I can offer you a meal along with whatever data you can get."

"Roger, you've made me an offer I can't refuse," I said. "Where should I meet you, and what time?"

"Do you know where our offices are?"

"You're on Liberty Street, aren't you?"

"We are," he said. "Considering how often our clients end up behind bars, that seems either wildly optimistic or cruelly ironic. But the street name was here before we were. You want to come by around four?"

A few hours later, I bumped across the railroad tracks between Kingston Pike and Sutherland Avenue, took a left at the concrete plant, and headed west along Sutherland, past the playing fields and group homes of the John Tarleton Home for Children, and then turned right up Liberty Street. The Public Defender's Office was in a modern building of red brick and green glass. Roger opened the front door to let me in. "The receptionist has gone for the day," he said. "Have you ever been in our new building?" I said I hadn't, and he invited me in for a quick look around, starting with the lobby and reception area, a high, semicircular glass atrium. The space looked stylish and cheerful—not the dreary, dilapidated quarters I'd have expected the public defender to be relegated to. At the back of the building was a gymnasium, which doubled as a meeting room where clients and families could participate in support groups and connect with social-service agencies. The building—like Roger—seemed to reflect hope, energy, and considerable thought.

Leading me out the door and across the parking lot, Roger offered to do the driving. Since I had no idea where we'd be going, that sounded like a good idea. He had a Honda SUV, and it wasn't long before we went off-road. Behind a freestanding, glass-fronted building with a sign that said LaborReady, he pulled onto a graveled area that bordered the railroad tracks and Third Creek. A footpath led into the trees and bushes lining the creek, and I saw shirts and pants hanging from the limbs—nature's clotheslines. LaborReady, Roger explained, was a place where employers could hire day workers—and a place where homeless or transient people could get a job. "Is it a nonprofit agency," I asked, "or a business?"

"Very much for profit," he said. "At the end of the day, the employer pays LaborReady about twelve dollars an hour for the person's work; then LaborReady pays the worker minimum wage. So they're taking a fifty-percent commission." It wasn't exactly altruism, but it also wasn't that different from the way UT paid me and other professors out of student fees, after subtracting a larcenous overhead tax. As we backed into the street and then headed for downtown, Roger pointed to the railroad tracks just behind the business. "For the homeless, the railroad tracks are a pretty good way to get from one place to another," he said. "They're straight and flat; they often follow creeks, so there's a source of water; and there are plenty of places where people can set up camps." I glanced down the tracks, and sure enough, a wide swath of trees and bushes bordered the creek and right-of-way—and the rails ran directly to downtown, a broad, bumpy freeway for people bumping through life on foot.

As Roger threaded the Honda downtown through intersections and around corners, I was struck by how much longer and less efficient our route was than the railroad tracks. We could almost have walked the mile in the ten minutes it took to traverse it by car. We passed the gutted shell of an old warehouse along Jackson Avenue, which had been destroyed a year or two before in a huge, spectacular fire. Prior to the fire the building had occasionally been inhabited by squatters, who would settle in for a few weeks or months, before being rousted—also for a few weeks or months—by the police, acting on the pleas of downtown merchants. Just up the block, near the corner of Jackson and Gay—

Knoxville's main street—Roger stopped in front of a storefront called the Volunteer Ministry Center. Peering inside, I glimpsed a couple of scruffy men and a young woman working at a computer. "This is the dayroom," Roger said. "People who need a meal or someplace to just spend the day can hang out here. Or they can sign up for a program that helps them deal with drug or alcohol dependency."

"Not many people in there," I said. "Looks pretty small."

"There's a lot more to it than what you can see through the window," he said. "They have a big dining room in back and a huge basement and courtyard down below. There might be fifty or a hundred people in there you can't see from here."

The young woman glanced up from her computer and studied the SUV stopped in front of the dayroom. She looked at me, then over at Roger, and her face broke into a smile of recognition. Even through the soot on the glass, I saw a pair of world-class dimples in her cheeks. She waved, then pushed back from the desk and came outside, leaning down to speak to Roger through my open window. She wore an ID badge with her picture, her name, and the letters VMC.

"Bill, this is Lisa; she runs the dayroom. Lisa, this is Dr. Bill Brockton, a forensic anthropologist from UT. He's trying to identify a murder victim." She reached through the window to shake my hand and flashed me the dimples on high beam. I nearly forgot the question I'd wanted to ask her.

"If one of these people went missing," I finally said, gesturing toward the dayroom, "how likely is it they'd be missed?"

She didn't have to think long. "You know that old saying about a tree falling in the forest—if nobody's there to hear it, does it still make a sound? Most of these people don't have anybody there to hear them if they fall. It's when they're *not* missing—when they're out walking the streets, or sleeping under a bridge, or asking for money—that folks notice them. If some scruffy guy stops wandering past your downtown business or condo, you're probably just grateful he's moved on." I nodded; she was probably expressing the sentiments of ninety-nine out of a hundred people. A car behind us honked, so we waved good-bye. She smiled one last time as she waved, and I guessed that her smile would be the brightest thing most people in the day-room would see today. I found myself wanting to hang out in the dayroom awhile, just for the sake of that smile. But Roger was already pulling away from the curb.

He made a quick right at the corner of Jackson and Gay, taking us through a block of upscale lofts and condos tucked into high-ceilinged brick warehouses and retail stores dating from the early 1900s. Some of these stylish urban residences sold for half a million dollars or more, and I couldn't help commenting on their ironic proximity to the dayroom and its homeless clientele.

"That's not all," said Roger, pointing to the building right on the corner. "Volunteer Ministry Center has sixteen apartments in this building"—transitional housing, he said, for people trying to get back on their feet. The rest of the block revolved around fancy condos, galleries, design firms, and a trendy sushi restaurant. I was guessing that the clientele for the businesses came from the lofts and condos, not the dayroom or the transitional housing. "As you can see, there are two very different worlds here," he said, "and those worlds collide just about every day. The police get a lot of complaints from the merchants and residents in this block. Sometimes they're legitimate—cars getting broken into, drunks wanting to use the bathroom or the telephone. But sometimes it's just harassment—the haves wanting the have-nots chased away."

"Chased to where?"

"That's the problem," he said. "It can turn into a shell game. They get forced out of downtown, so they head up Broadway, toward the Kroger and the pawn shops. Or way west, to the truck stops on Lovell Road. Or they just hang out in the bushes or under bridges. Here, I'll show you." He made two more rights, turning north on Broadway. As we passed beneath the eight-lane viaduct that carried I-40 past downtown and my eyes adjusted to the shade, I saw twenty or thirty people in the gloom—some standing in clusters on the sidewalk, some sitting on a low wall that bordered it, others stretched out on the barren ground farther back. Some had backpacks or duffel bags or trash bags filled with possessions; others had just the dingy clothes they wore. A few stared at us as we idled past; some ignored us, intent on conversations with other people or with voices in their heads; others slept or stared off into space. "The businesses down here *really* hate this," he said, nodding at a paint store and a company that sold industrial pumps. "Except for that convenience market"—he pointed at a small store I'd never noticed, its plate glass gridded with stout steel bars—"which sells a lot of beer."

Emerging from the shadow of the viaduct, we came to the missions. The Salvation Army, on the west side of Broadway, ran a large thrift store fronting Broadway—a store where many of my graduate students over the years had bought cheap clothing, worn furniture, or battered kitchen gadgets. Behind the thrift store were other buildings—offices and a modern dormitory-style building. Strictly speaking, the Salvation Army wasn't sheltering street people or transients, Roger said. Like Volunteer Ministry Center, the Salvation Army provided transitional housing, for families in crisis and for people enrolled in Operation Bootstrap, a six-month program designed to treat drug or alcohol problems and find people jobs. "In general, the Bootstrap people aren't the ones you see roaming around or hanging out during the day," said Roger. "They're inside, or off taking a class or working a job."

Across the street, facing the Salvation Army, was Knox Area Rescue Ministries, which Roger referred to by the acronym, KARM. It was one letter shy of "karma," I noticed. KARM had renovated an old church, converting the education building into an overnight shelter, Lazarus House, with more than 250 beds. "The shelter doesn't open until suppertime," he said, "so a lot of those people under the viaduct are waiting for that. The police come through every couple of hours and chase folks away, but five minutes later they start congregating again."

Roger headed north another few blocks on Broadway, then angled left onto Central, another artery radiating out of downtown. Like Broadway, Central had largely gone to seed, at least in this section, though its downtown stretch had gotten gentrified over the past couple of decades, the century-old brick buildings transformed into a two-block cluster of restaurants, bars, and boutiques called the Old City. The northern boundary of the Old City was a clear and rough-hewn one: a bumpy two-track railroad crossing, just before the White Lily flour mill and the Greyhound bus depot, another Knoxville crossroads for the downwardly mobile.

Roger turned left off of Central, taking us around the back side of the national cemetery—a neatly mowed veterans' burial ground, its hundreds of graves marked by precise rows of identical white tombstones: the soldiers uniformly outfitted and holding perfect formation, even in death. Just behind the cemetery, after crossing another set of railroad tracks, Roger turned off-road again, jouncing onto a wide gravel service road that ran alongside the tracks. On the left, the tracks bordered a row of industrial-looking buildings that I guessed to be machine shops. On the right, out my window, was a wall of greenery. He stopped the Honda and led me into the trees along a broad, well-worn path. The patch of woods was surprisingly large—it sprawled for fifty yards or so to the banks of First Creek. Along the path, we passed shirts and pants hanging from branches, piles of bedding nestled in small clearings, heaps of trash and garments everywhere. "Until a few days ago, this was a pretty big camp," Roger said. "Probably two dozen people in here. The railroad had some big metal culverts stacked along the edge of the trees back there, and there were people sleeping in the culverts, so the railroad called the police and asked them to clear the whole area."

"How do they do that? A bunch of cops come in and arrest people, or drive through with the loudspeaker on, telling them to get moving, or what?"

"It's not quite that harsh," he said. "The police tell the missions and the social-service agencies they're about to shut down a camp, so then the social workers come out and warn people, tell them if they've got stuff they don't want to lose, they should pack up and leave beforehand. The railroad's already hauled the culverts to somewhere else, and the city will probably send a crew to clear out everything else here in a few days or weeks or months. Meanwhile, the people find some other place to camp."

"The shell game?"

"The shell game."

We walked back to the Honda and bounced along the gravel,

back toward town. Up ahead, I could see the rear of the Salvation Army complex approaching, and the looming concrete supports and decking of the I-40 viaduct. We'd come almost full circle, although we were off-road still, a hundred yards west of Broadway, approaching a large graveled area beneath the interstate. Earlier I'd been surprised at how many people were gathered under the viaduct where it crossed Broadway; now I was astonished at the bustling scene taking shape. It was almost as if I'd wandered down a staircase and found myself in the service tunnels hidden beneath Disney World—a realm I'd barely known existed, yet one alive with people and activity.

Dozens of cars and trucks were pulled off to one side of the graveled area beneath the viaduct, which measured roughly the size of a football field. Near the parked vehicles sat a steel storage unit, of the heavy, corrugated type carried by container ships. The yellow container was labeled Lost Sheep Ministries, though if I'd been naming the program, I'd have called it "Worker Bee Ministries" or "Well-Oiled-Machine Ministries," because I'd never seen such efficiency. A steady stream of workers, mostly fresh-faced teenagers and young adults, ferried folding chairs and tables from the container's interior and set them up, row on row, facing a portable lectern or pulpit. A bank of high-intensity lights—the sort used by highway construction crews at night—switched on, banishing the gloom beneath the viaduct. As Roger and I watched, the space beneath the rumbling viaduct became an impromptu assembly hall, filled with dozens of tables and hundreds of chairs. Several tables were set up end to end farther back from the pulpit, and a separate squad of workers began loading these with restaurant-style steam tables, hundreds of soft drinks, stacks of sandwiches and potato chips.

"This is amazing," I said to Roger. "If the U.S. military moved with this much speed and focus, we'd have been in and out of Iraq in one week."

He nodded.

I caught a whiff of beef stew wafting from the steam table, and it smelled better than any of the convenience foods I'd microwaved for myself this week. A ragtag band of humanity converged on the food tables from every direction—scores of people, then hundreds, emerging from the bushes and railroad tracks and sidewalks and streets—and began queuing up neatly for food. One of the first in line was a young woman with a pair of children, a boy and a girl who seemed to be about the ages of my grandsons. The mother and children appeared clean and healthy, but they had a wary, weary look in their eyes, even the kids, and that grieved me—to see them beaten down so early in life. Behind them in line was a man who moved with uneven, shuffling steps; his head and right arm twitched periodically as he mumbled, steadily and incoherently, to himself or to some unseen companion.

A public-address system crackled to life, and I heard a woman introduce herself over the noise of the traffic overhead as Maxine Raines, the founder of Lost Sheep Ministries. She quoted a passage from the Bible—"Trust in the Lord with all thy heart; and lean not unto thine own understanding; in all thy ways acknowledge him, and he shall direct thy paths"—and then proceeded to expound on it. Maxine herself had been homeless once, Roger told me. Her brief sermon made it clear she believed that her divinely guided path had led to precisely this place, precisely this program of providing food and clothing under the interstate. Not everyone shared Maxine's vision, according to Roger—some social workers saw Lost Sheep and other mission-type programs as "enablers," crutches that made it easier for people to avoid getting jobs and becoming self-supporting. But what jobs, I wondered, could some of these lost and broken souls do?

Maxine handed over the microphone to a young man who—by his own account—had been one of Knoxville's biggest drug dealers before finding God and cleaning up his life. He was followed by a singer—a pretty young woman with long brown hair, an acoustic guitar, and the sweet, simple voice of a folksinger. *"When the music fades,"* she sang, *"I simply come longing to bring something that's of worth, that will bless your heart."* I wasn't sure how many people were following the lyrics—most seemed more intent on what awaited them at the food tables or the tables of men's and women's clothing and over-the-counter medications—but perhaps the words weren't the most important part of the message. I remembered the inscription on Jess's plaque at the Body Farm—work is love made visible—and I admired the compassion of this army of volunteers, more than a hundred strong, even if they were treating symptoms rather than curing the root causes of homelessness.

Almost as swiftly as it had begun, the service—and the services—came to an end. Even as the final stragglers received their rations of stew and shoes and aspirin, the furniture brigade began folding and storing the chairs and tables. The plates of food had been picked clean by the five hundred people who had converged on them, and the throng dispersed toward the shelters and the bridges and the creek-side camps where they would lay their heads on this particular night. One of the last to wander off, I noticed, was the twitching, mumbling man I'd seen near the head of the food line. As he shuffled toward the trees flanking the railroad tracks, a man fell in beside him and took his arm, stopping him for a brief conversation at the edge of the darkness.

It was one of the Lost Sheep volunteers, I realized, probably concerned for the man's well-being. But it could just as easily have been Garland Hamilton waylaying him—offering money to a down-at-the-heels alcoholic, who might literally die for a drink.

THE SURREAL scene beneath I-40 was still vivid in my mind the next morning as I studied skull fragments in the bone lab. When the phone rang, I ignored it, intent on the oval of pieced-together temporal bone cradled in one hand and the jagged shard clasped in a pair of tweezers. After half a dozen rings, the phone fell silent, then began clamoring again. Glancing at the display, I saw that it was Peggy, the one caller I couldn't ignore. I sighed, laying the larger segment in the sand of the cake pan and the single piece back in the tray with countless other bits.

"Hello, Peggy," I grumbled.

"Are we a tad grumpy this morning?"

"We are," I said. "Sorry."

"There's a Lisa Wells on line one for you," said Peggy.

"Wells?" That name didn't ring any bells. "Could you take a message? I've got my hands full at the moment."

A moment later the phone jangled again; Peggy again. I cursed under my breath as I reached for it. "Now what?"

"I'm sorry, Dr. B., but Ms. Wells says it's important. She says she might know a homeless man you're looking for."

"Oh, put her on," I said. A moment later the quiet background sounds of Peggy's office were replaced by a cacophony of street noise in my left ear—cars whizzing past, wheels thumping into potholes, a jackhammer off in the telephonic distance somewhere. "Hello," I said, "is this Lisa with the dimples?"

"Excuse me?" I wasn't sure whether she was taken aback or simply hadn't heard me over the noise.

"Hello, this is Dr. Brockton," I said, a bit louder and more formally. "It sounds busy there at the dayroom."

"I stepped outside to call," she said. "There's not a lot of privacy inside. Dr. Brockton, I've been thinking a lot about what you asked me yesterday."

"Thinking is good," I said.

"I'm in an awkward position," she said. "I have to protect the confidentiality of our clients, but you've got me worried about one. A regular, a man named Freddie. He's been here nearly every day for the past six months, but I haven't seen him in over a week now." She hesitated. "He does drink, but he'd been doing better lately. When he stopped showing up, I worried he'd gone on a binge. Now I'm afraid it's something worse."

"Can you describe Freddie for me—white, black, short, tall, young, old?"

"White," she said. "Middle-aged—forty-five going on sixty. Homeless people tend to age fast—life on the street takes a toll. Probably about five-ten, fairly thin. A hundred fifty pounds, maybe."

"Remember anything about his teeth?"

"You mean, did he have some?"

I laughed. "Well, that would be a start."

She laughed, too. "Some of them don't," she said. "Beyond that, no, I don't remember anything about his teeth."

"Then I don't suppose you'd know where we might get hold of his dental records?"

"Dental records? No," she said. "The people we work with are barely hanging on, Dr. Brockton. We've got a dentist who volunteers one day a month, to provide very basic care, but dental records? Not on the radar screen of our clients."

"That's what I figured," I said, "but I had to ask. It'd be a lot easier to identify this burned skeleton if we had dental X-rays."

"X-rays?" Even over the street noise, I heard something in her voice shift. "Do they have to be dental?"

"Dental's usually best. An arm or leg X-ray might work, if it showed something we could compare to—a healed fracture or an orthopedic plate or some such."

"How about a head?"

"A head?"

"An X-ray of the head. The skull?"

I heard something in my own voice shift. "Do you *have* an X-ray of Freddie's skull?"

"I don't, but UT Hospital might. Not long after he started coming around here, he slipped in the lunchroom and hit his head hard—knocked him out cold. We called an ambulance, and they took him to the ER at UT."

I got Freddie's last name from Lisa, then phoned the Radiology Department.

"Hi, this is Dr. Brockton," I said to Theresa, the Radiology receptionist. "A guy from one of the homeless missions might have come through the ER for a cranial X-ray about four months ago. Name was Freddie Darnell, D-A-R-N-E-L-L. We're trying to ID a murder victim, and we think there's a chance it's Darnell. Would you be willing to check and see if you've got a record for him? We can get a court order if you need us to."

"Hang on just a second, Dr. Brockton," she said. She put me

on hold. A minute passed, then three, then five. I was watching the bars on my cell phone, which I'd forgotten to charge overnight. Now I was down to one battery bar, and I worried the phone might die before she came back.

"I couldn't find anything filed under Darnell," she said. My heart sank. "But we did have a guy named Parnell, with a *P*," she said. "Could that be it? Maybe somebody at the mission got it wrong—or maybe the ER intake clerk misunderstood."

My pulse started to race. "First name Freddie—Fred or Frederick, maybe? White male, forty-five, give or take a few years?"

She hesitated. "I don't suppose you have a HIPAA release from him, do you?"

"I don't," I said, "and I'm afraid he's too dead to sign one for me. Would you need a subpoena to let me look at his X-rays?"

"Hang on one more minute, Doc."

I hung on. My cell phone's low-battery indicator started to beep—draining the battery all the faster.

Finally she came back on the line. "This is such a coincidence, Dr. B.," she said. "Dr. Shepherd was just saying that he needs to consult with you about that very case."

I laughed. "Theresa, you're the best. Can I come over in about ten minutes?"

"I've already pulled the file," she said. "I'll tell Dr. Shepherd you're coming to speak with him."

Fifteen minutes later Ben Shepherd switched on a light box and clipped a cranial X-ray onto the glass. Dr. Sherpherd and I had worked together on several cases, and it was Ben who'd gotten me a portable X-ray machine to use down at the loading dock, so that when decomposing bodies needed to be X-rayed, we didn't have to haul them inside and stink up his department.

I gave a slide lecture every year for the Radiology staff and residents, showing shattered skulls and dismembered bodies. "I like a good gunshot wound," he'd said to me once. "The beveling of the entry and exit wounds. The lead wipe around the edges. The lead spatter inside the cranium. It's so much more interesting than a skateboarder's broken arm."

Ben studied Parnell's cranial X-ray. "Hmmm," he said. "Not much to see. His chart says he had a mild concussion, but of course that doesn't show up in an X-ray."

I studied the ghostly image. The teeth weren't the reason for the X-ray, so the image wasn't oriented to capture much dental detail. And the skull showed no sign of healed fractures we could try to match to the burned cranium. But there was one hope, I realized, studying the frontal view of the cranium. Just above the brow ridge, in the center of the forehead, a wavy boundary between dark and light traced a delicate scalloped pattern, almost like the lobes of a ginkgo leaf, within the skull. That scalloped line was the upper edge of the frontal sinus, a cavity in the middle of the skull's three layers of bone. Every person's frontal sinus was unique, and was therefore a possible means of positive identification—in theory, at least, although the theory hadn't been applied or tested nearly as exhaustively as identification through fingerprints, dentition, or DNA. I pointed to Parnell's frontal sinus and traced the edge with the tip of a pen. "If we get lucky piecing this skull back together," I said, "we might be able to match that, or exclude a match."

"Whenever you get enough to compare," he said, "bring it over and we'll shoot an X-ray."

"Actually," I said, "I don't think we even need to shoot an X-ray. When the cranium burned, the inner layer of bone peeled loose, so the frontal sinus is actually exposed. If we had a copy of the X-ray, we could compare the bone directly with the image."

"Tell you what," he said. "I think I just got paged. I'll be gone a few minutes. If you're not here when I get back, I'll figure Theresa's come in and reshelved that chart." He gave me a wink, shook my hand, and wished me good luck.

CHAPTER 30

I TUGGED OPEN THE DOOR OF THE OSTEOLOGY LAB
and walked in waving the manila envelope of X-rays as if it were
the winning ticket in the $50 million Powerball game.

Miranda sat with her back to the door, bent over one of the
lab tables, peering through a magnifying lamp. She looked almost like a statue, and in fact I couldn't remember seeing her in
any other position but this—staring through the lens, tweezers in
one hand, a chip of cranium in the other—in the eight days since
the Cooke County fire. It was as if she'd always been sitting here
and always would be, forever reassembling the fragments of what
we hoped was the skull of Garland Hamilton.

Miranda heard the crinkling of paper and X-ray film and
glanced around. I waited expectantly. She raised her eyebrows. I
jiggled the envelope.

Finally she said dryly, "Okay, the suspense is killing me. What's
in the envelope?"

"I could tell you were dying to know," I said. "Cranial X-rays of a homeless guy."

"And you have those because . . . ?"

"Because he might be a missing person. Because I don't trust Garland Hamilton, alive or dead. Because I worry that what you're piecing together might not be Hamilton's skull."

"You think it might be this guy instead?"

"I hope not," I said, "but it can't hurt to compare. How much frontal sinus you pieced together so far?"

"This much," she said, holding up a bony mosaic the size of a postage stamp. "Probably not enough to compare yet. But there's a light box over there in that corner, if you want to plug it in."

The light box was actually a slide sorter. Before I started using a digital camera, I shot 35-millimeter slides of every case I worked. By now I had tens of thousands of slides, so even though photography was fast going digital, I'd always need slide sorters and carousel trays. I'd taken a couple of stabs at converting my slides to digital images and plugging them into PowerPoint presentations, but the image files were so big they tended to crash the computer or fill up the hard drive. If I converted all my slides to digital images, I'd need a hard drive the size of Neyland Stadium to store them all.

I retrieved the slide sorter from the corner, set it on the desk, and knelt down to find a plug in the power strip. There wasn't a vacant outlet, so I grabbed hold of a white plug. Just as I was pulling it free, I heard Miranda say, "Don't unplug the white—" Then I heard her say, "Oooohhh . . . ."

"What's wrong?"

"That was the computer," she said. "I had a file open I hadn't saved yet. Oh, well—it was only my dissertation proposal. I'm sure I can reconstruct it in, say, three months."

Knowing Miranda's thoroughness, I felt sure she saved her work every three minutes.

"Anything worth doing is worth doing over," I teased.

"Thanks," she said. "One pearl of wisdom like that makes the long hours and the low pay seem worthwhile."

Straightening up, I dusted my hands on my pants and switched on the light box. The fluorescent tubes flickered briefly, then glowed steadily through the milky glass. I laid down the X-ray of Freddie Parnell's skull, centering the scallops of the frontal sinus over the brightest light.

"What do you think? Look familiar?"

"Sure thing," she said. "That's Billy Bob What's-His-Name, well-known frontal sinus–about–town."

"I just thought maybe since you've been spending so much time with those cranial fragments, some of those curves would register with you."

"I'm trying to match fracture lines," she said, "so I haven't really been worrying about the sinus itself. Besides," she added, "I'm still missing a lot of the upper edge. I doubt that we've got enough yet for a match or an exclusion."

She held out the postage-stamp-size mosaic, then plucked a second scrap of bone from the sandbox and aligned an edge with the bigger piece. The edges fit fairly well but not perfectly, and I knew that Miranda had spent days gauging such minutiae.

She flipped the pieces over so we could see where the inner layer of bone had peeled away, revealing the sinus cavity. Along one portion of each piece that she held, I saw a faint line where the sinus cavity ended.

"We've got some edge line here and here"—she pointed—"but there's not much, and it's not particularly distinctive. You want to flip the X-ray over, since we're looking from the back side?"

I flipped it, and she shifted and rotated the pieces of bone above the X-ray, seeking some elusive alignment.

"Hard to say." I frowned.

"Very hard," she agreed. "How reliable did you say frontal-sinus comparison is?"

"Very," I said. "No two are the same."

"You're sure?"

"I think I'm sure."

"Who's researched it?"

"Doug Ubelaker, up at the Smithsonian, did an article on this about ten years ago. He concluded it was a good basis for identification or exclusion."

"How many sinuses did he look at? And how'd he quantify the match?"

"He looked at a few dozen," I said. "I don't know that he quantified it on any numerical scale. I think he drew on his experience and judgment to determine whether or not things matched."

"Hmm," she said. "Sounds like the way they compared fingerprints about a hundred years ago."

"You got a better idea?" I was feeling a little defensive, though I wasn't sure why.

"No," she said, but then, after a pause, "Well, maybe. I mean, the edge of the sinus traces a curving line, right?"

"Right."

"So if you can define those curves mathematically—the curve shown in Parnell's X-ray here and the curve of Humpty Dumpty here, once we get him back together again—you should be able to graph how closely those equations match."

I was having trouble following her, but she seemed to be warming to the idea.

"Actually," she said, "that might be a pretty nifty dissertation topic. I'm in the market, since you just erased my proposal."

"I did not," I said. "Besides, I have a draft of your proposal. You're going to refine age estimates using the pubic symphysis."

"I thought I was," she said. "But the more I think about it, the less excited I get. The idea of squinting at four or five hundred pubic bones for a year seems like a very tedious project."

"Gee, not like squinting at graphs and statistics for a year," I said.

"But it would be *original* graphs and statistics," she said. "The pubic symphysis has already been studied up one side and down the other, so anything I did would be so derivative. This could be new territory. It could help us with exactly the problem we've got right here: Is this Freddie Parnell's burned skull or isn't it? We don't have the mathematical tools to measure that right now. My experience and my judgment—that's what I'm supposed to rely on, in the absence of statistical tools, right?—my experience and my judgment say this ain't Freddie." Her voice was rising, and I heard her frustration rising, too. "But my experience and my judgment also say we don't have near enough of this damn puzzle done yet to say that with any damn confidence."

With that, she laid the two pieces of bone in the sand, stood up, and walked out of the bone lab.

As the door banged shut behind her, I realized that she'd been pushed—by me, by eight days of squinting at skull fragments, and by her terrifying assault—to the breaking point.

I also realized she was right about the frontal sinus. It would indeed be a good dissertation topic. And this particular scrap of reconstructed sinus wasn't nearly enough to tell us whether Garland Hamilton was safely dead or dangerously alive.

CHAPTER 31

EVER SINCE BURT DEVRIESS HAD FILED HIS CLASS-action lawsuit against Trinity Crematorium in Georgia, he'd been sending me a steady stream of cremains to analyze. I'd also been making frequent trips to Alcoa with my postage scale to weigh the cremains from Helen Taylor's furnaces.

By now I was nearing thirty cases from Trinity, and they showed interesting similarities and fascinating differences. One consistent trend was the weight of the cremains: Those from Georgia tended to weigh three or four pounds, which was less than two-thirds the weight of those from Tennessee.

The cremains from Georgia usually contained a mixture of human bone and animal bone, as well as a bewildering array of extraneous contaminants: bits of charred wood, zippers, nails and screws, and heaping helpings of Quikrete concrete mix, which accounted for the powder, the sand, and the pebbles. Most puzzling of all, the Georgia cremains contained small, fluffy spheres

of fabric—I took to calling them "fuzzballs"—whose only pur-
pose, as best I could tell, was to puff up the cremains and keep
them from looking so skimpy.

Early in Burt's suit, I'd gone to Chattanooga to give a deposi-
tion. I was cross-examined by a legion of lawyers, representing
not just Trinity but a consortium of funeral homes that were being sued by DeVriess for defrauding their customers. The lawyers
made several scornful attempts to show that it was impossible
to tell the difference between burned human bone and burned
animal bone. I'd brought numerous slides, though, and the questioning gave me a chance to present a lecture on the distinctive
differences between human bone and animal bone.

One thing working in my favor was the fact that the fragments of actual bone that came back from Georgia hadn't
been as finely ground as the cremated bones that came out of
Helen Taylor's processor. Either Trinity didn't have a processor
or, like the cremation furnace, it sat untouched and gathering
dust. Trinity did, however, have a wood chipper parked behind
one of the sheds—and right beside a commercial-size barbecue
smoker. The two pieces of equipment, operating separately or in
tandem, conjured up images that boggled the mind—and turned
the stomach.

Burt had waged an aggressive campaign to keep the case before
the media, and it had worked. More and more clients signed on,
and the magnitude of his damages claim kept multiplying. Within three weeks, thirty plaintiffs had joined the class, and Burt was
seeking a million dollars for each plaintiff. If every remaining
wronged family signed on, it was possible the claim could grow
to $900 million.

One scorching afternoon during the dog days of August,

the UPS man brought me a flat cardboard envelope instead of the cremation containers I'd come to expect from him. Tucked into the cardboard was an envelope embossed with the name of Burt's firm, and tucked inside the envelope was a check for fifty thousand dollars—drawn not on the firm's account but on Burt's personal one. I dialed his office and got Chloe.

"Hi, Chloe. Is the champion of the underdog in at the moment?"

"I'm not sure about the champion of the underdog," she said, "but Mr. DeVriess is in. Would you like to speak with him?"

"Sure, he'll do in a pinch," I said. I heard the click of the transfer.

"Hello, Doc," said Burt.

"Hello, Burt," I said, "I got your check. What's the occasion? That's about ten times what I invoiced you."

"I'm returning the retainer you paid me last spring," he said.

"Why? You earned it," I said. "You helped clear my name and keep me out of prison. It was worth every penny, and I owe you a debt of gratitude for that. Always will."

"I owe you one, too," he said. "You found my Aunt Jean for me. You also landed me the case of my career."

"So you're feeling confident about it?"

"You might say that, Doc. I've just accepted a settlement offer for thirty million dollars."

I whistled. "That's great, Burt," I said. "That's over a million dollars a family. Even after you skim off your rapacious commission, that's still seven hundred thousand a family."

"Well, it won't end up quite that good," he said. "That thirty million has to cover every claim that comes forward during the next twelve months. It'll dilute everybody's share considerably if another fifty or a hundred people come forward. Still," he said, "it should give every family at least several hundred thousand dollars."

And it would give Burt a cool $9 million. I glanced again at the check in my hand, and suddenly $50,000 didn't seem like quite so much anymore. Still, it was the most anybody had ever handed me.

CHAPTER 32

THE HEAT HAD BEEN BUILDING FOR DAYS: NINETY-five degrees, ninety-seven, ninety-nine. Every morning the sun swam up through the haze like a blood orange, and it set the same way, ragged and shimmering. The cicadas buzzed angrily from midmorning till night, and the hotter it got, the louder they buzzed. Or maybe it was the opposite: The louder they buzzed, the hotter it got, all that rubbing of legs or vibrating of membranes generating massive doses of heat. Looking up into one particularly noisy tree in my yard, I half expected to see hundreds of cicadas burst into flame.

The towers of downtown Knoxville were invisible from more than a mile or two away; driving upriver along Neyland toward the UT campus and downtown was like an act of creation, with buildings gradually materializing out of the murk, though they never seemed to make it all the way to crisp, sharp-edged solidity. Walking was like swimming through Jell-O.

Every patch of ground that wasn't watered was cracking open from the heat and the drought. Cornstalks were withering in the fields; the pastures at the UT cattle farm, across the river from Sequoyah Hills, had gone from emerald green to desert brown. The Holsteins that normally dotted the hillside pasture seemed to have given up on the grass altogether, huddling miserably in the shallows on the inside of the river's big bend.

A flock of Canada geese had given up migrating to take up permanent residence in a small, grass-ringed pond beside the UT Hospital's parking garage; I passed them every day on my way to the Body Farm. The flock, which had doubtless congratulated itself on its wisdom and good fortune in laying claim to such a choice pond, had gradually taken on a look of despair and betrayal as the pond shriveled, shrinking to a puddle, then a mud flat, and finally a circular patch of red-clay desert—a mocking reversal of the oasis it had once been. I stopped one day on the shoulder of the road and got out to take a closer look. The cracked earth—saucer-size slabs of curling clay, divided by dark, deep fissures between—looked like a nightmarish, 3-D version of a flayed giraffe skin. Peering down into the fissures, I flashed back to a childhood fear that had haunted me one hot, dry summer half a century before: What if the devil managed to escape from hell and break free through the cracks in the ground? What if he emerged just as I happened by, my tender young soul ripe for the picking? Suddenly it hit me: It wasn't just a childish fear. Garland Hamilton was roaming free on the face of the earth this hellish summer. I shivered in spite of the heat and fled to seek refuge and distraction amid the corpses at the research facility.

But even there, even after death, the bodies seemed to be suffering from the heat. Dark, greasy stains—volatile fatty acids leaching out of tissue as it liquefied—pooled around the bodies, just as the sweat pooled and soaked my shirt. One body, which Miranda and I had laid in the sun at the edge of the clearing just two days before, had actually burst like a balloon, the gases in its abdomen building up so fast that the skin could no longer contain the pressure. What had been a man's belly was now a gaping crater, fringed by ragged entrails. I stared. In all these years of research experiments, I'd never seen a body pop. Scientifically, it was fascinating; emotionally, it was disturbing, one more omen hinting that we were gripped by a torrid plague of biblical proportions. I took a few photographs to document the event—without them I wasn't sure anyone would believe my description—and then fled for the shaded, air-conditioned corridors beneath Neyland Stadium.

I had been wishing for a serious rain, to clear the air and cool the blasted earth. By midafternoon, thunder was vibrating the stadium's grimy windows and mammoth girders. But by evening, when I drove home, the air was still steamy and the ground was still parched, and I decided it was just heat lightning toying with my hopes.

I was wrong. By the time I microwaved a can of soup for dinner, the branches of the big oaks in the front yard were whipping around like palm trees in a hurricane. The sky turned purple, then black, in a matter of minutes. A flash of lightning lit the world, followed by the tearing crack of thunder, and sheets of rain—torrential, horizontal rain—lashed the west-facing windows of my house.

Often I liked to sit out on my screened-in back porch during thunderstorms; in this case, though, when I stepped out the door, a soaking mist—rain shredded but not stopped by the wire mesh—drenched me from face to foot and sent me scurrying in-side for protection and dry clothes.

One of my favorite features of the house was the bank of win-dows lining the west wall of the living room. Most summer eve-nings the living room stayed bright enough to read in until after eight. Tonight, seven o'clock was dark as midnight—blackness punctuated by blinding flashes of lightning, which lit the room like a flash gun, searing a negative afterimage onto my retinas. Reflexively, ever since childhood, I'd been in the habit of count-ing the seconds between the lightning's flash and the thunder's boom: "one Mississippi, two Mississippi, three Mississippi . . ." If I got to "five Mississippi" before the thunder rolled over me, I knew the lightning was a mile away. Within minutes after this evening's storm broke, I found myself lucky to get through "one Mississippi"; sometimes I didn't make it even through the "one."

Then came a flash so bright, accompanied by a boom so loud, that I was sure the house itself had been hit dead on. When my vision returned, I saw a brief shower of sparks from a utility pole out by the street, and I knew that part of the boom was the sound of the electrical transformer on the pole exploding. I glanced at the face of my DVD player for confirmation and saw that the numerals had gone dark. I figured it might be a while before the power came back on, so I felt my way to the kitchen, opened the drawer beside the refrigerator, and fished around until I felt the box of wooden matches. I could have gone to the bedroom and retrieved the flashlight from the nightstand instead, but the idea of the flashlight beam, harsh and impersonal, made me choose the matches. They were the old-fashioned strike-anywhere kind—the kind you can strike on a stone fireplace, or a zipper, or even with your thumbnail if you're daring and dexterous. I'd always preferred them to the kind you have to strike on the box—I liked getting to choose where to strike them, maybe, or liked the look of the red match heads tipped with white—but it was getting harder and harder to find this sort these days. The grocery store had stopped carrying them; the only place I knew where to buy them anymore was Parker Brothers, an old-style hardware store run by old-fashioned guys—guys like me, I supposed. Funny, I thought, people think nothing of careening through freeway traffic at ninety miles an hour, weaving in and out with a foot of clearance between their bumper and the next car's. But God forbid we should do something as risky as strike a wooden match on a fireplace brick.

I felt my way into the living room, where an oil lamp—its glass chimney and base grimy to the touch—occupied a dusty spot on the mantel. Lifting the chimney free of the metal clips that held it in place, I set it on the mantel beside the base, then slid open the matchbox and removed one of the square wooden matches. I pressed the tip lightly against the surface of a brick above the mantel, then dragged the match upward. As it scratched across the rough surface, it gave off a small shower of sparks, then bloomed into a dazzling flower of yellow and blue. Once the flame shrank to a small teardrop of yellow, I touched it to the lamp's wick, which took the flame and amplified it.

I tucked the box of matches into my pocket and buttoned the flap closed, then wiggled the lamp's chimney back into position and lifted the lamp from the mantel by the narrow glass neck. Holding it aloft before me, like the Statue of Liberty—the Statue of Electrical Outage, actually, or the Statue of Paranoia—I made my way back to the kitchen and set the lamp on the table. The kitchen had always felt safer, somehow, or more comforting than any other room in the house, but tonight even the kitchen seemed perilous.

Leaves clawed and slapped at the windows like hands—like Garland Hamilton's hands, slapping me in the face, again and again. Another flash split the darkness, and for a blinding moment I thought I saw a man silhouetted against the lashing rain and shuddering hedge. Then the night went black again, and the afterimage on my retina reversed to a negative: The dark figure looming against the brilliant background lingered as a ghostly shape in white on a field of black, the edges fringed by the bleached-bone fingers of tree branches. When the afterimage faded and my eyes returned to normal, all I could see was my own image reflected in the kitchen window, the oil lamp beneath and to one side of me, casting ominous shadows in the hollows of my eye sockets. I did not look like someone I'd want to meet in a dark alley.

I sat down at the table, close to the lamp, and tilted and angled my head to dispel the shadows around my eyes. Finally satisfied that the sinister expression was gone, I turned my gaze to the lamp itself. Its cotton wick nestled just below a slit in a small metal dome; a small hexagonal knob extended from the dome on a spindly shaft, and by twisting the knob I could roll the wick up or down with gears that were hidden within the dome. Twisting the wick slowly down, I watched it gradually disappear, like sand edging downward into the neck of an hourglass as time begins to run out. As the wick's edge threatened to vanish through the small metal sleeve between the reservoir of oil and the glass chimney, the flame shrank to a pale blue flicker along the charred edge of woven cotton. I twisted the knob in the other direction, and the wick slowly rose, the flame blooming bright yellow again, its edge as sharp and solid as the edge of a full moon. *How is it, I wondered, that something as nebulous as burning oil can look so solid? Why isn't it ragged and flickering, like the flames of a fireplace or campfire? Why is there no fuzzy transition from glow to not-glow? And why can't my own life feel so well defined, so neatly edged, anymore?*

I lifted the oil lamp by its narrow neck, where the metal collar and wick mechanism screwed onto the glass base. Halfway up the base, at its widest part, oil sloshed within the clear container. The wick—a flat ribbon of woven white cotton—undulated within the liquid, like a tapeworm preserved in alcohol. The lamp's neck felt small and vulnerable in my grasp, and I forced myself to ease the tension in my grip, lest it snap in my hand, sending the glass base and its flammable contents crashing onto the kitchen's tile floor. I made my way through the house by lamplight, like some restless ghost from a campfire story, checking each outside door to be sure it was dead-bolted. Then I went into my bedroom, locked the door, and sat in my bed, my back against the headboard. I set the oil lamp on the nightstand beside me, scooting its useless electric companion to the far edge to make room. Then I slid open the nightstand drawer and took out the handgun Steve Morgan had loaned me. I studied it—the tiny blue-black pyramids machined into the grip, the matter-of-fact words and numbers etched into the barrel, the small, precise button of the safety, which I clicked back and forth, off and on, in a hypnotic pattern that was nearly as regular as the ticking of a clock.

I told time that way until a pale gray light seeped through the window, gradually erasing the reflection of the lamp's glow, replacing it with the shapes of raindrops and bits of shredded leaves on the outside of the panes.

CHAPTER 33

THE ANTHROPOLOGY DEPARTMENT WAS LOCKED AND dark when I arrived—not surprising at eight o'clock on a summer Sunday morning. Without bothering to shower or even change my rumpled clothes, I had eased my truck down the narrow service drive that ringed the base of the stadium, parking at the foot of the stairs beside the bone lab. Once inside, I flipped on the fluorescent lights overhead, then impulsively flipped them off again. Enough light filtered between the stadium's girders and through the grimy windows to guide me across the lab, and for what I needed to do, semidarkness was better than the glare of the fluorescents.

The slide sorter was still plugged in, and the cranial X-ray of Freddie Parnell still lay atop the frosted glass. I switched on the light, and the homeless man's ghostly skull lit up. I studied the overall contours awhile, then focused on the scalloped edges of the frontal sinus. The contours resembled a coastline, but it was an unknown country I was trying to steer toward. Retrieving the tray of cranial fragments from the Cooke County fire scene, I sighed in despair. It wasn't a matter of simple navigation; what I had to do—what Miranda had been struggling for days to do— was reassemble a second map, the map of tiny, charred bits we'd plucked from the smoldering ruins of the cabin. If we couldn't piece together more of that second map, we'd never be able to tell whether its landmarks matched Parnell's or not.

I flipped the X-ray, so I was looking at the frontal sinus from the back—from the inside of Parnell's skull, in effect—and then laid the two fragments Miranda had painstakingly reassembled just below the image of the sinus, with their curved inner surfaces facing up. Framed by the openings of the stadium's steelwork, the daylight was spilling through the windows at a low angle, an angle that highlighted the contours of the cavities in the blackened bone. Staring first at one fragment, then at the other, I rotated and angled the bits in almost microscopically small shifts, my eyes darting from the bone to the X-ray and back again with each subtle movement. You'd think it would be easy to tell if a half-inch stretch of bone corresponded to some portion of a two-inch image, but it was maddening. Instead of a coastal map, I decided, what I was working with was a thousand-piece jigsaw puzzle depicting an overcast sky. I was trying to match one tiny detail to the image on the cover of the puzzle box—that's what the X-ray was like—without actually knowing that this puzzle had indeed come out of that box.

After half an hour of this, my eyes were playing tricks on me. I didn't think the fragments matched the X-ray, but then again, I didn't want them to match. I wanted this to be the skull of Garland Hamilton, not some down-on-his-luck derelict. In any other forensic case, I'd have been able to compare the sinuses with sci-entific rigor and objectivity—I wouldn't have anything personal invested in whether the comparison yielded a positive identifica-tion, a positive exclusion, or insufficient information to support either conclusion. Go with the facts, speak the truth, and let the chips fall where they may—that had always been one of my guid-ing principles. But never before had the chips come solely from the pockets of my own life. What's more, the facts here were proving mighty hard to pin down.

Still holding both skull fragments, I reached up to rub my eyes with the back of one hand. That's when I saw it: a sliver of light glinting through one of the seams where Miranda had pieced to-gether the larger of the two fragments. I angled the piece this way and that, studying the slight gap. Then I laid down the other piece so I could examine this one more closely. Swiveling around to the lab table behind me, I switched on the magnifying lamp and held the piece under the lens. The bone practically glowed beneath the built-in fluorescent light that encircled the lens. Magnified five times, the glue joints appeared wavy and jagged, almost like the sutures that form naturally in the skull as its individual plates knit together during childhood. The innermost of the skull's three lay-ers of bone, the diploe, had peeled away, exposing the boundary where the sinus cavity stopped and the spongy inner layer of bone began. If not for the peeling, Miranda and I would be forced to X-ray the reconstructed pieces to see the sinus boundary, rather than being able to see the cavity take shape as we worked.

Even under the magnifying glass, it was difficult to find the gap where I'd seen the light shining through. Twice I had to twist the head of the lamp upside down, shining it up toward my face, in order to send light through the tiny opening again; the second time I did this, I took a pencil and drew faint arrows on both the inner and outer surfaces of the bone so I could find the spot again easily. Having marked the location, I held the bone beneath the magnifier once more and leaned in for a close look. From the outside, the fit looked fine: From one piece to the next, the edges of bone transitioned almost perfectly across the glue joint. But from the inside—a spot that would have lain just beneath the left eyebrow—something didn't exactly match up.

Rebuilding a shattered skull is a lot like rebuilding a Ming dynasty vase you've hurled into the fireplace in a fit of rage. The first few pieces fit together perfectly, zigs and zags and undulations mating exactly—partly because you've started with the biggest, easiest pieces, but also because it's too soon for imperfection and distortion to rear their cumulative, misshapen heads. Gradually, though, minor imperfections start to compound, and the jig is up. Even if you tell yourself you can live with the cracks showing—they add a certain character and drama to the vase, after all, like tattoos and scars on skin—you know that the cemented shards will never again possess those elegant Ming lines. A missing crumb here or there distorts the fit by a thousandth of a degree; the china glue, though it be thin as water and only a few molecules thick, enlarges a reconstructed triangle just enough to keep it from nestling into its triangular niche. The edges and angles gradually cease to mate, forcing you into approximations and compromises—just as in the rest of life.

The piece of frontal bone I held in my hand had been patched together from seven irregular fragments, none as large as the nail of my little finger; glued together, the seven pieces were about the size of the fat end of a Grade-A Large egg. The chunk of bone fit within the palm of my hand—with an inch of palm showing all around it. Even so, even as small as it was, the multitude of irregular seams and angles and edges had begun to rebel against being forced back together. As I zeroed in on the edges marked by my penciled arrow, I could see that the fracture lines on one edge didn't correspond exactly to those of the adjoining edge. What's more, now that I was examining the fit with a dubious eye, I gradually became aware of a slight difference in the hue of the char on the bone's outer surface. The difference was slight—so slight it tended to vanish if I looked at it directly, the way a faint star vanishes if you look at it directly—but whenever I glanced at it slantwise, rather than dead on, there it was, an elusive and skittish truth, crouching in the forensic underbrush: Miranda had glued the wrong piece here. I batted the magnifying lamp away; it spun around in a half circle on the end of its spring-loaded arm, then stopped and swayed in place. "Damn," I said angrily, then "damn" again, this time softly and sadly. The angry damn was for the wasted time and misdirected effort, butting our heads against the wrong wall, in our efforts to compare a faulty reconstruction with an X-ray. The sad damn was for Miranda, who would doubtless be devastated to learn of her mistake.

I thought on that for a while. Did she actually need to learn of her mistake? Did she need to learn *from* her mistake? The teacher in me was inclined to think she did; otherwise she might make it again someday, in a case where there was no mentor looking over her shoulder to catch it and correct it. But another voice in me suggested that maybe I should cut her some slack, just this once—that I pushed too hard, expected too much, and held her to impossible standards; that the world wouldn't end, and Miranda's abilities wouldn't self-destruct, if I didn't point out this one small, understandable error. My inner teacher was winding up for a self-righteous retort—something to the effect that it would be condescending to protect Miranda from knowing she'd made a mistake—when my eye was caught by a glimmer in the tray of cranial fragments. The cascade of light from the magnifying lamp was now pooling in the tray of cranial fragments, and the lamp's slight sway was causing a piece of bone to appear to move back and forth across the lens, growing and shrinking as it passed through the central field of view. It was almost as if the piece were breathing, expanding and contracting, coming to life. As I watched it, I realized that it looked familiar, in a backward sort of way, and then I realized why: Its jagged edge was the mirror image of one of the pieces in the reconstructed fragment. If I moistened the glue with just enough acetone—enough to detach Miranda's mistake but not so much that all the pieces fell apart—I could substitute the piece that was dancing under the magnifying glass right now.

Ten minutes later the line of Duco cement was still damp where I'd plugged in the new piece of the puzzle. I left it drying on the light box—alongside the X-ray I'd just compared it to—and locked up the lab, springing into my truck. Threading out from beneath the stadium, I emerged into what I was surprised to find had become late-afternoon sunlight. I'd had my head buried in bone fragments for more than eight hours.

Hurrying west along Neyland Drive, I veered onto the north-bound ramp of Alcoa Highway, the quickest way to I-40 east. As I merged onto the interstate, I checked the sun's height in the rear-view mirror. I estimated I had three hours of daylight left, maybe just two in the mountains. The drive would take one of those hours. I hoped the other would be enough time to find whatever it was that lay waiting for me in Cooke County.

CHAPTER 34

THE TRUCK'S REAR TIRES ISSUED A SERIES OF STEADY screams as I careened around the curves of River Road. It was a good thing the day's sun had already dried the pavement; otherwise I'd already be wrapped around one of the sycamores edging the riverbank.

The yellow line in the pavement fishtailed back and forth beneath the truck as I took every curve down the center or the inside—"straightening the curves," southerners called it, and when I realized I was doing it, I laughed. I'd made my first foray into Cooke County less than a year before, and on that trip, on this very stretch of road, I had been a white-knuckled, dizzy-headed, carsick passenger. Now I was driving every bit as recklessly as that deputy sheriff had driven. *Things change,* I thought.

But not all things change, I realized. I felt a wave of nausea rising fast, and the beginnings of dizziness that warned me I was on the verge of triggering a bout of Ménière's. *Not now,* I prayed, *please not now.* Sweat suddenly drenched my head, and my mouth flooded with saliva. I slowed the truck, turned the air-conditioning up to hurricane force, and started sucking in cold air for all I was worth.

Back when I was a kid in grade school, my teachers and I had learned—learned the hard, messy, humiliating way—that when I started to sweat and salivate like this, I had about thirty seconds before my breakfast or lunch came churning up. I had always hated the sense of impending doom—the sweat and saliva never lied—but I did feel grudging appreciation for the early-warning system. Not everyone had it, I noticed, and those who didn't sometimes suffered even more humiliation than I. There are few experiences more degrading for an eight-year-old than spending half a day at school in clothes that reek of vomit. Wetting or soiling your britches was about the only thing worse than throwing up on yourself. Any one of the three could haunt you for the rest of the school year—as if the faint aroma of your accident still clung to your hair and clothing, weeks or even months later.

Careening along this snaking backcountry road, I wasn't worried about shaming myself in front of a bunch of third-graders. But I had no desire to throw up in my truck. I scanned the road for a bit of shoulder, someplace to pull off safely, but the pavement was notched into a narrow ledge. Five feet to the right was solid mountainside; five feet to the left, rocky riverbank. I was caught, as the old saying goes, between a rock and a hard place.

My thirty seconds were ticking down fast. Finally, in a right-hand curve, I let the truck drift all the way into the left lane, the outside of the curve, where I hoped it would be more visible. I hit the brakes, hung two wheels off the pavement as far as I dared, and turned on my emergency flashers. I flung open my door and leaned out just as the heaves began.

I hadn't eaten anything since a hurried bowl of cereal nine hours earlier, so there wasn't much coming up—just a little gastric juice, sharp and acrid in my mouth and nostrils. But the force of the dry heaves squeezed tears from my eyes. When the convulsive heaves stopped, I took in a few deep breaths and then was hit by a second round. As I hung out the door of the truck, I heard brakes squeal behind me. I expected to feel a vehicle slam into mine, but the impact never came, and with another, different squealing of tires—sudden acceleration—the unseen vehicle sped on.

Feeling wrung out but also relieved—it had always puzzled me, how much better I tended to feel after throwing up, especially when there was nothing in my stomach causing me distress—I sat up, drew in a few more breaths, and wiped my mouth with my handkerchief. I took mental inventory and was relieved to find that the sense of impending vertigo had largely faded. A bottle of water, half full, lay on the passenger seat beside me, and I took a small, grateful sip to rinse my mouth. Then I put the truck in gear, eased the left wheels back onto the pavement, and continued along River Road, this time at my typically prudent pace.

A few sedate miles farther, I came to the gravel drive marked Almost Heaven and took a right. Crime-scene tape was still tied to a tree on one side of the driveway, but rather than stretching across the entrance, the tape lay wadded at the base of the tree, splattered with mud from last night's downpour.

As I splashed up the gravel through a succession of puddles, I noticed that someone else had done the same. Jim O'Conner, I guessed, or maybe an insurance adjuster handling the damage claim for the cabin-rental company. When I reached the clearing, I saw a pickup parked near the crater that had once been the cabin. I called out—"Hello? Hello?"—but got no answer. The clearing was still ringed with blackened tree trunks and vegetation, but already the ravaged look of the place was beginning to soften, thanks to a carpet of new vegetation. Cleared ground with a view of the sky was a rarity in the mountains, and these optimistic, opportunistic botanical pioneers had wasted no time laying claim to this choice patch of sunlit real estate, a sudden and unexpected windfall.

I walked slowly to the edge of the crater and peered down. By now half the basement was in shadow, and I knew I didn't have much time—thirty minutes or so—before it would get too dark to work. I wasn't sure what I was seeking here, but I knew there must be something: something small and subtle that we'd overlooked as we focused on the excitement of plucking not one but two incinerated skeletons from the debris.

The day of the search and recovery, we'd had more than a dozen law-enforcement officers and firefighters on hand to assist. We'd also had a ladder planted firmly on the basement's concrete slab. If I'd planned ahead, I'd have brought a stepladder from home, but I hadn't planned ahead; I'd leapt up impulsively from the table in the bone lab the moment I solved the puzzle of the frontal sinus. Equipment needs had been the furthest thing from my mind.

The basement slab lay about ten feet below the top of the cinder-block wall on which I stood. It wouldn't be hard to hang from the wall and drop down into the basement. It was getting back out again that I was concerned about. A drop of several feet was easy; an upward leap of several feet was a whole 'nother matter. I could have done it back in my teens, when I was playing high-school basketball, but my knees and thighs and calves were no longer what they'd been thirty-five years before. I'd need to find or engineer a more reliable way out.

I scanned the floor for any tall objects I might stand on—an empty oil drum would do very nicely, I thought, or even a metal folding chair. Unfortunately, whoever had originally furnished the house seemed to have thought that a wooden cabin deserved wooden furnishings, for there was very little in the basement's debris field that wasn't some variation on the theme of charred cellulose. If I piled enough debris in a corner, I could probably jump up and grab the top of the wall, but I wasn't entirely sure I had the upper-body strength it would take to hoist myself up. As I frowned at one of the corners, my gaze strayed to the massive stone fireplace and chimney, built into the one end wall that was not entirely below grade. Was the stonework rough enough to allow me to climb the rocks? And if so, was my balance good enough to allow me to walk the top of the cinder blocks to the nearest corner, where I could step safely back onto solid ground? As I studied the chimney and the wall, I realized there was an easier way out. On either side of the massive fireplace—set into the four-foot-wide section of cinder blocks flanking the stonework—was a small window opening. The lower sills were about chest-high, and the openings in the block measured a couple of feet square. The windows themselves had been blown out by the explosion, and the wooden frames had burned as flames roared out the openings. I'd get a pretty good coating of soot if I wriggled out through one of them, but soot was a lot less objectionable than substances I encountered on a daily basis in my line of work.

I sat down atop the wall, my feet dangling down into the basement. Twisting my body toward the corner, I leaned across and put my right hand on the end wall, keeping my left hand on the long side wall where I sat. I twisted my hips next, swinging my right leg toward the inner face of the end wall, lifting my butt off the blocks so I could turn and lower my body down into the corner. My toes scrabbled on the blocks, and I felt myself begin to fall, but then my right foot caught the windowsill and I regained my balance. Shifting both hands now to the wall above the window opening, I centered my feet on the sill, then reached down with one hand and gripped the top of the opening. Letting go of the top of the wall, I made a graceless transition from standing in the opening to squatting in the opening, then jumping down onto the concrete floor. If Olympic judges had been scoring my dismount on a scale of 1 to 10, my scores would probably have ranged from 0.1 (from the hostile French judge) to 2.1 (from the friendly U.S. judge). Still, I was down in one piece, and I was confident I could get up and out the window opening.

But now that I was here, what was I looking for? I still didn't know. I scanned the debris, halfway hoping to spot a bright red evidence flag, maybe one labeled Look Here for Important Clue, but nothing so helpful met my inquiring gaze. In the absence of a miracle, I'd need to resort to old-fashioned work—a swift but systematic search. I decided to start by reexamining the area where we'd found the skeletons, then spiral outward toward the basement walls.

The search didn't take long. Tucked into the angle at the base of the long wall, I found a second pair of thin, unmelted copper wires leading from the melted car battery—the battery that had set off the dynamite jammed between Freddie Parnell's teeth. This pair of wires had been concealed by a line of bricks strung along the wall. I gave the wires a tug, and they slid out from beneath the bricks. As I continued to tug, the wires led me toward the corner of the basement; by the time I got there, I'd already figured out where they went next: out the small window. Hamilton had staged the Ledbetter skeleton, the homeless man's body, the dynamite, and the accelerant, then crawled out the window and triggered the destruction from outside. It would have been easy, I guessed, to slip away in the pandemonium created by the blast and the blaze.

I was startled by the toot of a car's horn, then the slam of a door and the cadence of footsteps.

"Let me guess," I heard Miranda's voice saying above me. "It's not him. The second skeleton's not Hamilton, is it?"

"No," I said. "But why do you need to guess? You saw it for yourself, didn't you? I left the sinus right there by the light box."

Now it was Miranda who sounded puzzled. "By what light box? In the osteo lab? I haven't been on campus at all today."

"Then how'd you know it's not Hamilton? I thought about calling you once I found the missing piece of frontal sinus, but I just jumped in the truck and headed out here instead."

Suddenly I felt a wave of dizziness, like the Ménière's was about to kick in again.

"What are you doing here, then? How'd you know I was here?" I demanded.

"I got your message."

"What message?"

"The text message on my pager. 'M—Meet me at Cooke County fire scene ASAP. Urgent. BB.'"

"That message came from my cell phone?"

"Yes. Wait. I don't know. It said 'private number.' I figured you'd just changed your settings."

"I've never sent a text message in my life," I said. "I don't even know how." Alarms were shrieking in my head, and either Miranda saw the fear in my eyes or she'd figured something out on her own. "I think we should get out of here."

Miranda held up a hand, then froze, and then spun to face something behind her. I heard the beginnings of a gasp, and then the gasp turned into a grunt, and suddenly Miranda was falling, tumbling backward into empty space, her arms and legs wind-milling as she fell. If this had been a scene in a movie, that's when everything would have happened in slow motion; I'd have lunged and somehow managed to catch her, or at least managed to break her fall. But this was not a movie, and I stood rooted to the spot, not even comprehending the fact of her fall until the moment she thudded to the floor on her back and her head snapped down onto the concrete with a sickening crack. Her body convulsed once, then lay still. I felt horror rising in my throat, and suddenly I was retching again, retching and crawling through the wreckage of the basement to where she lay.

I felt for a pulse in her wrist. When I couldn't find it, a blind panic began racing through my veins and nerves—a primitive, wild-animal sort of panic, the kind that short-circuits all semblance of thought, all powers of language. I forced myself to slow the rapid, racking breaths that were pouring oxygen and adrenaline onto the blaze of my fear. I laid a hand on Miranda's neck, guiding my fingertips to the left side of her throat, to the hollow between her windpipe and the muscles at the side of the neck—the valley where her carotid artery lay. I stilled the pounding of my own heart enough to feel the faint flutter beneath my praying fingertips. She was alive. I felt a shudder of relief run through my frame, heard a gasp or sob of some sort coming from my chest, and then shuddered again as the words floated down from above. "I hope the fall didn't kill her," said a familiar voice mildly. "I have a much better death in mind." I looked up to see Garland Hamilton standing at the top of the wall, sneering down at Miranda and me.

CHAPTER 35

"YOU PIECE OF HUMAN SHIT," GROWLED A VOICE THAT resembled my own. "You twisted son of a bitch."

Hamilton laughed. "Actually," he said, "I don't think my mother had much to do with this. I think most of the credit goes to you, Bill."

"Bullshit," I said without turning around. "You're insane or you're evil. Or both."

"But why, Bill, and since when? I was a model of decency and stability until a year ago. Until you ruined me."

Now I turned to face him—above me, silhouetted against the fading daylight—though I remained kneeling beside Miranda. "I pointed out a mistake you made in an autopsy, Garland. A mistake that would have cost an innocent man his life. It was a bad mistake, but it didn't have to ruin you. You chose the path of ruin."

"The path of ruin? The *path* of *ruin*?" He sneered it, coating the words with the slime of mockery. "Christ, it's tough to pick just one thing," he said, "but I think it's the simplistic Brockton sanctimoniousness I'll miss least of all."

He bent down briefly, and when he straightened, he was holding a large container: a five-gallon gas can. He shook it, and light sparkled through a broken stream of liquid the color of tea. Then I felt the sting of the gasoline on my skin and in my nostrils.

"Fitting, don't you think? Instead of me burned to death here, it's going to be you and Little Miss Lovely."

"No!" I jumped to my feet and lunged toward the corner of the basement. Leaping up as I ran, I planted a foot on the wall and transferred my forward momentum into vertical motion. I managed to grab both walls at the top and scrabbled at the concrete with my toes as I pulled with my arms.

Something swatted me down like a giant's fist. I collapsed into the corner, bewildered at first. Then I felt a searing pain in my chest and realized I'd heard a loud pop. It gradually dawned on me that I'd been shot.

Bracing myself against the corner of the wall, I struggled back to my feet and staggered toward him, holding up both hands. "Don't kill Miranda," I begged. "She doesn't deserve to die. She never did anything to you."

"You still don't get it," he said. "I'm not killing her because she deserves it. I'm killing her to make you suffer. Just like I killed Jess to make you suffer." He pointed at me and I saw a flash, and then my left leg collapsed. I tumbled to the floor beside Miranda, lying on my left side, my back to Hamilton. My field of vision began to shrink—as if I were peering through the wrong end of a telescope or a pair of binoculars—and I knew I was on the verge of losing consciousness. I felt more gasoline splashing me. *Just let go,* I thought. *It won't hurt as much that way.* I focused on the blackness around the edges of my vision and I tried to embrace it, or let it embrace me, before the flames could.

But something wouldn't let me let go, and through the pain and despair I realized that the something was Miranda. She was the only thing I could still see through the small tunnel of light, but she stayed there, stubborn as ever, refusing to fade to blackness. If I gave in now, I realized—if I took the easy, unconscious way out—I was giving up Miranda, too. I'd be giving her to Hamilton, who had already gotten Jess. *I'll be damned,* I thought, *if I let you take Miranda, too.* Jess had been my lover, sweetly but briefly; Miranda had been my assistant, my colleague, and my protégée for years. *Protégée,* I thought: from the French word for "protect."

Through the pain in my chest and my leg, I felt a surge of protectiveness and rage and hatred. It was small and tentative at first, but it caught and grew, like a fire whose heat draws in oxygen to feed its growth. For reasons I didn't understand, I felt myself clutching at my chest, tugging at my shirt, fumbling with the flap of the pocket. Then I felt my fingers close tightly around something, and I realized what I held in my grip: Maybe it would be death, or maybe it would be deliverance, but it sure as hell would not be giving in. Miranda and I might be doomed—clearly we were—but I would not surrender her willingly.

I dragged my clenched fist across the concrete floor, then flung my arm into the air and opened my hand wide, as if waving goodbye to this world and all I'd held most dear within it. The fistful of kitchen matches I'd found in my pocket—the ones I stuffed there during the night's storm—scratched and sparked, then burst into flame as I hurled them skyward. I looked up in time to see fire racing up the stream of gasoline that Garland Hamilton was pouring down on us. Hamilton recoiled reflexively from the fire, and when he did, the jerk of the five-gallon can drenched him in a shower of gasoline. Flames and smoke engulfed him instantly. He screamed and flailed atop the wall, a human ball of flame, and then I saw a tongue of fire licking toward me as well. I shielded my face with my arm and rolled atop Miranda to shield her. Casting a final glance up through the inferno, or through a dying dream of it, I thought I saw Garland Hamilton's body take flight and arc through the darkening sky above me. It blazed like a human meteor, or some fire-demon released from hell. Then—only then—the constricting tunnel of vision and consciousness collapsed on me at last, and I sank into blackness and oblivion.

CHAPTER 36

THE FACES WERE BLURRY, HALOED IN HAZE. I BLINKED and squinted. They remained hazy, but I recognized some familiar features. Jeff's high, broad forehead. Art's dwindling hairline and growing paunch. Jim O'Conner's bantam-rooster stance and Waylon's immense presence. Edelberto Garcia's dark, quiet elegance.

"Are you the five people I meet in heaven?" The words came out in a dry croak, as if a raven had spoken them. Then I recognized a sixth person standing behind Art. "I guess not," I rasped, "since I see Grease there in the back." The faces smiled fuzzily, and I heard a sound that reminded me of laughter.

Someone was missing—I closed my own eyes to think who it was, and when I managed to get them open again, everyone but Jeff was gone, and he was sleeping in a recliner beside the bed. Sleeping seemed like a good idea, so I closed my eyes again.

■　■　■

WHEN I AWOKE, daylight was streaming in through a set of miniblinds, and a nurse was jabbing rusty daggers into my hip, judging by the feel of things. "*Ow!*" I said. "If that's not prohibited by the Geneva Convention, it ought to be."

"You think it hurts now," she said, "wait till the pain meds wear off."

"This is the feel-good version?"

"'Fraid so. Hip replacement's a bitch."

"Somebody replaced my hip?"

"Seemed like the thing to do," she said, "since somebody shot the old one to smithereens. You're lucky they were able to save your leg." She paused. "Actually, with that hole in your chest, you're lucky they were able to save your life. A couple more minutes and you'd have bled out." She lifted a clipboard from the foot of the bed and checked the chart. "You were five pints low when you got here," she said.

"That's pretty far down on the dipstick," I said. "How'd I get here? And where *is* 'here' anyhow?"

She smiled. "UT Hospital, Dr. Brockton," she said. "You could look out the window and see the Body Farm if you weren't strapped to the bed."

I glanced down. My arms were suspended by a complicated system of wires and pulleys, and instead of hands, I saw a pair of white paws floating several inches above the sheet. "What day is it? How long have I been here? What's wrong with my hands?"

"Wednesday. You came in on LifeStar three days ago. You've got second- and third-degree burns on your hands and arms, but you'll be fine. 'The Forensic Phoenix,' the *News Sentinel*'s calling you. Your lawyer friend just donated a million dollars to UT in your honor, and you not even dead. You've been quite the story."

"You want to tell it?"

"You ready to hear it?"

"Depends," I said. "Is it a happy ending or a sad ending?"

"For you, fairly happy, considering. But not for everybody. Hold on. I'm not the one should be telling you."

She hung the clipboard back on the foot of the bed and whisked out the door. Jim O'Conner came in, looking like he hadn't changed his uniform in a week.

"Morning, Doc," he said. "Mighty good to see you. How you feeling?"

"Not bad, I guess, considering somebody chopped out my left hip and drilled a hole through my chest."

"You should see the other guy," he said.

The other guy. "Hamilton?" He nodded. "I think I did," I said. "Or maybe I just dreamed I did. He was on fire, and he flew across the sky like a comet." I laughed a little at the absurdity, and it hurt a lot, so I quit. "Some dream, huh?"

"Pretty close to right, actually. I got there just in time to see him catch fire." O'Conner's face was grim. "He went sailing over your head because I shot him. With a twelve-gauge. Pretty close range." He looked away, then back at me. "He wouldn't have survived those burns," he said. "I didn't really need to shoot him."

"I think you did," I said. "If you hadn't, he might have fallen on Miranda and me. Hell, he might even have jumped on us, flames and all, to finish us off."

He gave a slow nod, and something in his face eased. "You feel like telling me what happened before I got there?"

I told him the story as best I remembered it. I started with the moment in the bone lab when I matched the burned frontal sinus with Parnell's X-ray—the moment I realized that Hamilton had murdered the homeless man to fake his own death while *pretending* to fake his own death with Billy Ray Ledbetter's skeleton. I finished with the moment Hamilton was dousing us with gasoline, the moment I fished the matches from my pocket and struck them on the basement floor.

O'Conner shook his head. "Amazing," he said. "A guy with kitchen matches outguns a guy with a .357."

"I like to think of it as virtue triumphing over evil," I said, and he smiled. "What brought you and your shotgun there in the nick of time?"

"Miranda," he said. "She phoned from her car on the way there. Said something was happening up at the fire scene, she didn't know what, but she was worried."

Miranda. She hadn't been in the room the first time I'd awakened, I realized, and her absence was ominous. I remembered how hard her head had struck the concrete and how faint her pulse had been, even before the world erupted in flame "Jim, tell me about Miranda," I said. "I'm afraid to ask, but I need to know."

"What do you need to know?"

The voice came from the doorway, and I thought my heart would burst at the sound of it. Miranda! Her head was clouded in bandages, but her eyes shone clear as the morning.

"Miranda," I breathed. "Jesus, I thought you were dead. The way your head hit that slab . . ."

"I'm pretty hardheaded," she said. "You know that."

Jim O'Conner reached out, gave my knee a squeeze, and left the room.

I studied Miranda's head, turbaned in gauze. She lifted a hand and touched the gauze gently, posing like a model in an old-fashioned hair-spray ad. "Like it?" I wiggled a thumb horizontally, halfway between thumbs-up and thumbs-down. "I have a brand-new cranial suture under here," she said, "so they've duct-taped me back together for now. But once the bone knits and the hair grows, I'm good as new."

"That's pretty damn good," I said. The white gauze glowed in the early light, and she could almost have passed for a medieval saint, the ones with the dinner plates painted behind their heads. "I thought I'd lost you, Miranda," I said. "I was so afraid I'd lost you."

"But you didn't lose me," she said, "you saved me. Against all odds, you saved me."

THE SKULL

BONES OF

PARTS OF

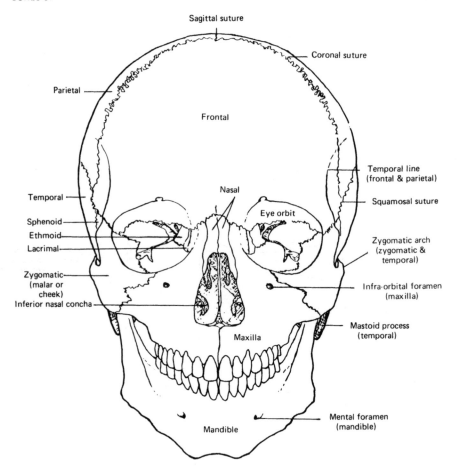

Sagittal suture

Coronal suture

Parietal

Frontal

Temporal line
(frontal & parietal)

Nasal

Eye orbit

Squamosal suture

Temporal

Sphenoid

Ethmoid

Lacrimal

Zygomatic arch
(zygomatic &
temporal)

Zygomatic
(malar or
cheek)

Infra-orbital foramen
(maxilla)

Inferior nasal concha

Maxilla

Mastoid process
(temporal)

Mandible

Mental foramen
(mandible)

THE SKULL

BONES OF

PARTS OF

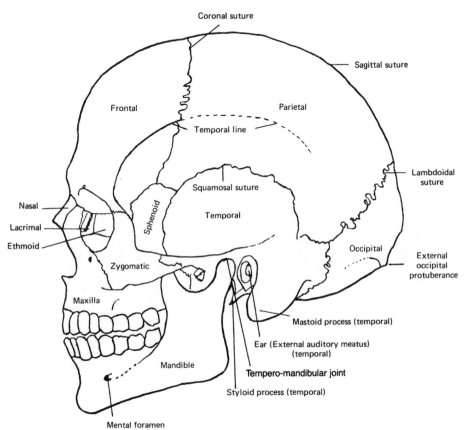

Coronal suture

Sagittal suture

Frontal

Parietal

Temporal line

Lambdoidal
suture

Nasal

Squamosal suture

Lacrimal

Sphenoid

Temporal

Ethmoid

Occipital

External
occipital
protuberance

Zygomatic

Maxilla

Mastoid process (temporal)

Ear (External auditory meatus)
(temporal)

Mandible

Tempero-mandibular joint

Styloid process (temporal)

Mental foramen

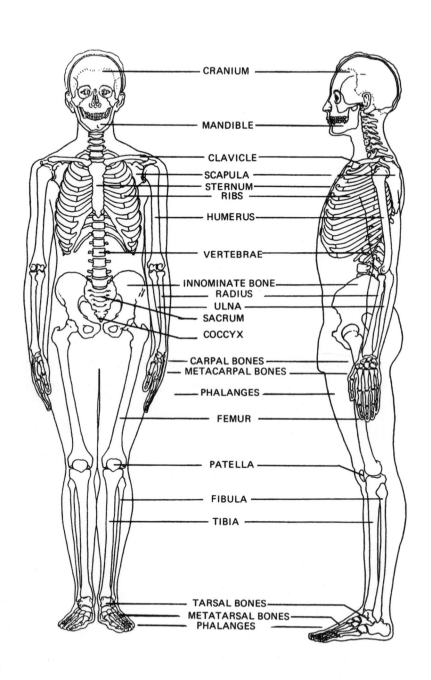

CRANIUM

MANDIBLE

CLAVICLE
SCAPULA
STERNUM
RIBS

HUMERUS

VERTEBRAE

INNOMINATE BONE
RADIUS
ULNA
SACRUM
COCCYX

CARPAL BONES
METACARPAL BONES

PHALANGES

FEMUR

PATELLA

FIBULA

TIBIA

TARSAL BONES
METATARSAL BONES
PHALANGES

ACKNOWLEDGMENTS

It's always a pleasure to thank people who have been kind enough to help us. It's a long list, and even at that, we've probably left some folks out. If you're one of those, we do apologize!

We're grateful to several other forensic anthropologists—all products of the UT Anthropology Department's graduate program—whose research we've drawn on in this book: Joanne Devlin, Steve Symes, and Elaine Pope have done fascinating experiments to explore how cars burn and how fire affects flesh and bone. Angi Christensen—now serving as the FBI's staff forensic anthropologist—has extensively studied the use of frontal sinuses in human identification (for her Ph.D. dissertation) and not-so-spontaneous human combustion (for her M.S. thesis). Rick Snow, the staff forensic anthropologist for the Georgia Bureau of Investigation, knows firsthand—thanks to the Noble, Georgia, crematorium scandal—what it takes to identify hundreds of uncremated bodies.

Dave Icove, a superb arson investigator and whip-smart engineer, increased our understanding of fires, and of people who set them. Roger Nooe, a retired UT professor of social work (who now works for the Knox County public defender's office), provided a remarkable look at the world of the homeless in Knoxville, as did Maxine Raines of Lost Sheep Ministry and Lisa Wells and Donna Rosa of Volunteer Rescue Ministry. Roger, Lisa, and Maxine also bravely allowed us to use their real names in the book.

Helen Taylor—the real-life Helen—welcomed us into East Tennessee Cremation Services, showing us what an impeccably run crematorium is like.

Art Bohanan continues to allow us to fictionalize him, and continues to be a close friend, as well as a remarkable source of information about fingerprints, other trace evidence, police work, and life in general.

Karen Kluge—the hostess with the mostest—provided a quiet and elegant writing refuge, without which this book could not have been completed on time (or almost on time, anyway).

Heather McPeters, a fast and brilliant reader, praised the good parts of the first draft and helped make the not-as-good parts better. So did our copy editor, Maureen Sugden, who went above and beyond the call of duty.

We are deeply thankful for the faith and encouragement of our editor, Sarah Durand, and our publisher, Lisa Gallagher, who have made us feel so welcome at William Morrow. Sarah's able assistant, Emily Krump, keeps the wheels turning smoothly a surprising amount of the time, and always leaps in to help when we need something unexpectedly and quickly. We're also thankful for the fine work of the Morrow art and production staff— especially our production editor, Andrea Molitor—for turning our

ACKNOWLEDGMENTS

It's always a pleasure to thank people who have been kind enough to help us. It's a long list, and even at that, we've probably left some folks out. If you're one of those, we do apologize!

We're grateful to several other forensic anthropologists—all products of the UT Anthropology Department's graduate program—whose research we've drawn on in this book: Joanne Devlin, Steve Symes, and Elaine Pope have done fascinating experiments to explore how cars burn and how fire affects flesh and bone. Angi Christensen—now serving as the FBI's staff forensic anthropologist—has extensively studied the use of frontal sinuses in human identification (for her Ph.D. dissertation) and not-so-spontaneous human combustion (for her M.S. thesis). Rick Snow, the staff forensic anthropologist for the Georgia Bureau of Investigation, knows firsthand—thanks to the Noble, Georgia, crematorium scandal—what it takes to identify hundreds of uncremated bodies.

Dave Icove, a superb arson investigator and whip-smart engineer, increased our understanding of fires, and of people who set them. Roger Nooe, a retired UT professor of social work (who now works for the Knox County public defender's office), provided a remarkable look at the world of the homeless in Knoxville, as did Maxine Raines of Lost Sheep Ministry and Lisa Wells and Donna Rosa of Volunteer Rescue Ministry. Roger, Lisa, and Maxine also bravely allowed us to use their real names in the book.

Helen Taylor—the real-life Helen—welcomed us into East Tennessee Cremation Services, showing us what an impeccably run crematorium is like.

Art Bohanan continues to allow us to fictionalize him, and continues to be a close friend, as well as a remarkable source of information about fingerprints, other trace evidence, police work, and life in general.

Karen Kluge—the hostess with the mostest—provided a quiet and elegant writing refuge, without which this book could not have been completed on time (or almost on time, anyway).

Heather McPeters, a fast and brilliant reader, praised the good parts of the first draft and helped make the not-as-good parts better. So did our copy editor, Maureen Sugden, who went above and beyond the call of duty.

We are deeply thankful for the faith and encouragement of our editor, Sarah Durand, and our publisher, Lisa Gallagher, who have made us feel so welcome at William Morrow. Sarah's able assistant, Emily Krump, keeps the wheels turning smoothly a surprising amount of the time, and always leaps in to help when we need something unexpectedly and quickly. We're also thankful for the fine work of the Morrow art and production staff—especially our production editor, Andrea Molitor—for turning our

ACKNOWLEDGMENTS

It's always a pleasure to thank people who have been kind enough to help us. It's a long list, and even at that, we've probably left some folks out. If you're one of those, we do apologize!

We're grateful to several other forensic anthropologists—all products of the UT Anthropology Department's graduate program—whose research we've drawn on in this book: Joanne Devlin, Steve Symes, and Elaine Pope have done fascinating experiments to explore how cars burn and how fire affects flesh and bone. Angi Christensen—now serving as the FBI's staff forensic anthropologist—has extensively studied the use of frontal sinuses in human identification (for her Ph.D. dissertation) and not-so-spontaneous human combustion (for her M.S. thesis). Rick Snow, the staff forensic anthropologist for the Georgia Bureau of Investigation, knows firsthand—thanks to the Noble, Georgia, crematorium scandal—what it takes to identify hundreds of uncremated bodies.

Dave Icove, a superb arson investigator and whip-smart engineer, increased our understanding of fires, and of people who set them. Roger Nooe, a retired UT professor of social work (who now works for the Knox County public defender's office), provided a remarkable look at the world of the homeless in Knoxville, as did Maxine Raines of Lost Sheep Ministry and Lisa Wells and Donna Rosa of Volunteer Rescue Ministry. Roger, Lisa, and Maxine also bravely allowed us to use their real names in the book.

Helen Taylor—the real-life Helen—welcomed us into East Tennessee Cremation Services, showing us what an impeccably run crematorium is like.

Art Bohanan continues to allow us to fictionalize him, and continues to be a close friend, as well as a remarkable source of information about fingerprints, other trace evidence, police work, and life in general.

Karen Kluge—the hostess with the mostest—provided a quiet and elegant writing refuge, without which this book could not have been completed on time (or almost on time, anyway).

Heather McPeters, a fast and brilliant reader, praised the good parts of the first draft and helped make the not-as-good parts better. So did our copy editor, Maureen Sugden, who went above and beyond the call of duty.

We are deeply thankful for the faith and encouragement of our editor, Sarah Durand, and our publisher, Lisa Gallagher, who have made us feel so welcome at William Morrow. Sarah's able assistant, Emily Krump, keeps the wheels turning smoothly a surprising amount of the time, and always leaps in to help when we need something unexpectedly and quickly. We're also thankful for the fine work of the Morrow art and production staff—especially our production editor, Andrea Molitor—for turning our bare-bones typescript into beautiful books, sometimes on very tight schedules!

The work doesn't end when a book is published. At Morrow, no one knows that better than our publicist, the tireless Buzzy Porter. Buzzy and Ben Bruton have performed Herculean labors to publicize our books, and we'll be very grateful—just as soon as we recover from the book tour! The sales and marketing staff at Morrow have also done a wonderful job building demand for our books. So have freelance videomeister Buck Kahler and Web designer Jack Hardcastle, the creative minds behind Jefferson Bass.com.

Susan and Jim Seals and Mary Jo Tarvin have volunteered many hours of their time to help make our book signings run like clockwork. Their graciousness, thoughtfulness, and generosity are remarkable. Similarly, Donna Griffin—the Anthropology Department's secretary—is helpful in more ways, on more occasions, than we can even begin to keep track of.

Our agent, Giles Anderson, never ceases to amaze us; we appreciate the fine job he's done of keeping us off the streets and gainfully employed these past several years.

Last, but far from least, we're especially grateful to the many booksellers and readers who have embraced us, our books, and our characters so warmly. Many thanks, y'all.

—Jon Jefferson and Dr. Bill Bass: Jefferson Bass